The old house waited, dark and foreboding

The clock in the dash showed eleven-fifteen. He hadn't realized it was so late. Still, he jerked the car to a stop, got out and bounded up the steps. Feeling dizzy, he pounded on the front door.

Focusing, Nate saw that Amber stood in the doorframe. She was dressed in creamy silk pajamas. Her hair was disheveled and her face clean of makeup. She looked sexy. She seemed surprised. She was irritated as hell.

Something told Nate his behavior wasn't making sense, that he might be scaring Amber. But it was too late to turn back.

"I want to see Kim," he blurted out. "I want to see my daughter."

ABOUT THE AUTHOR

The countryside surrounding Anne Laurence's home
city of St. Louis, Missouri, is the setting for this popular author's second Superromance novel. Fans of
Anne Laurence will be delighted to learn that she has
also written a third Superromance novel, which will
be published early in 1994. She is the mother of three
children.

Books by Anne Laurence

HARLEQUIN SUPERROMANCE
394—ALWAYS SAY YES

Remember When

Anne
Laurence

Harlequin Books

TORONTO • NEW YORK • LONDON
AMSTERDAM • PARIS • SYDNEY • HAMBURG
STOCKHOLM • ATHENS • TOKYO • MILAN
MADRID • WARSAW • BUDAPEST • AUCKLAND

Published March 1993

ISBN 0-373-70539-5

REMEMBER WHEN

For Larry
And for Reid, John and Pete
Heroes All

PROLOGUE

AMBER WONDERED if she'd ever grow accustomed to hospitals. She knew she'd never get used to losing those she loved. First, her mother passing away five years earlier, then her father three years after that.... And now, tragically, her dear friend was dying.

Getting up from the chair by the bed and walking to the window, Amber glanced outside, then back at the gaunt figure beneath the white sheets. Everything outside look so ludicrously normal. Inside the hospital room, everything seemed unreal. Outside in the Missouri hills, a warm summer surrendered to a colorful fall. Inside, pale life gave over to...

"Amber?"

Amber started at the agitated whisper. She hadn't expected...

"Yes, Francie," she said, already at the bedside. "I'm here."

"You take Kim."

Amber reached for Francie's frail hand. "We've already got that straight. You just rest."

"No. There's more."

Amber didn't know if she should encourage her friend to talk. Francie was supposed to be resting quietly. But all morning, Francie had been insisting there was "more". She obviously couldn't relax until she communicated her message.

Seconds ticked by.

"Tell me," Amber finally coaxed, squeezing Francie's painfully thin hand as tightly as she dared.

"You take Kim. Promise?"

"I promise. I'll take Kim."

"Kim loves you like a mother. Like she should have loved me."

"Francie," Amber pleaded. Francie's words tore at her. "Kim loves you, Francie. She's your daughter. You're her mother. No matter what happens, that will always..."

"No, no." Francie sounded impatient, anxious to collect her thoughts and go on. "It's right that you be with Kim."

Francie's confusion was natural, Amber thought. She sought her words, but it was Francie who spoke first, her tone surprisingly firm.

"Nate Fields is Kim's father. When he made love to me that night, we were only kids."

"I know," Amber said softly. As did everyone else in Francie's close-knit, riverside community. Nate Fields and Francine Gibbons had been no more than nineteen and seventeen respectively when Francie conceived Kim Gibbons. As Granny Maple had often said, Francie Gibbons had been too fancy and fast for the place she'd been born to, even at seventeen. And while Francie had never before admitted to a living soul that Nate was Kim's father, the truth was obvious to anyone, simply by looking at thirteen-year-old Kim. The strain of American Indian blood that gave

Nate Fields his arresting looks was apparent in his daughter's exotic beauty.

Tears seeped from the corners of Francie's closed eyes. "I've done a lot of things I shouldn't have."

"We all make mistakes."

For the first time in days, Francie smiled. "You're always too easy on me, Amber. I didn't just make mistakes, I..."

Amber waited. Francie had to know that neither of them had the strength for much more.

Finally Francie spoke again. "I never connected with Kim the way I should have. I left her alone too much. You'll be good for her, steady and stable. I feel good about leaving Kim with you. It's the only good thing in the mess I've made of my life. Leaving Kim with you. Really." She sounded so genuine that Amber was moved to her core.

Selfishly, desperately, Amber prayed that Francie had said what she needed to say. She hoped her friend had found some peace.

But then Francie's eyes fluttered open again, seeking Amber's face. Their bright green color contrasted sharply with her white skin and stunning red hair. A renewed urgency marked her ravaged features as she spoke.

"About Nate," she managed.

Amber stiffened. "Not now. You don't need to consider Nate Fields."

"You don't understand."

Except for a single encounter on a hot summer afternoon, Amber had barely known Nate Fields. Still, his neglect of Francie and his own daughter over the years told her all she needed to know. Swallowing her rush of anger at the man, Amber focused on Francie's barely audible words.

"Tell Nate I'm sorry. Tell him that Kim is his, and that I'm sorry I..."

Suddenly the surrounding equipment emitted a high-pitched shriek that brought medical personnel running. Francie never said another word.

CHAPTER ONE

FIVE MONTHS LATER, Nate Fields waited for a sense of victory to wash over him. After all, he had Amber Reinhart exactly where he wanted her. The pale winter light shone in through the windows of his lawyer's plush office, reflecting off the papers she was signing. The sound of her pen scratched softly in the hush of the onlookers.

Amber Reinhart's lawyers, the young and elder Messrs. Cox, were longtime friends of her family. As Amber completed her task, Nate's lawyer from Chicago drifted into a conversation with a second lawyer Nate had hired here in St. Louis. Amber's brother, Adolphus Brandenberger, excused himself and left.

Nate, however, remained where he was. He stood above the polished table, watching Amber sift through the documents, pen in hand. As much as he'd expected it, the sense of triumph eluded him. Amber Reinhart looked too damned vulnerable, too damned courageous, too damned composed. The only pleasure he'd have on this day was the simple one of seeing her again.

Arms akimbo, Nate thumbed the undercurve of his lower lip. His eyes passed down the row of caramel-colored buttons punctuating her stylish cream suit. Spectator pumps in caramel and cream covered a neat foot that edged from beneath the corner of the table. As she bent over the last of the papers, the brim of her caramel hat hid her perfectly arranged nut-brown hair and her brown eyes. But he could still see the flawless, peachy skin, the straight little nose, the ripe lips, polished in soft rose. Her movements, he noted, were still as elegant as the rest of her. Amber Reinhart had been a rich man's daughter and an even richer man's wife, and she looked it.

Well, he thought, she wasn't rich any more. In fact, she was struggling to make ends meet. His purchase of her family's brewery would keep her afloat for only a little longer. With her half of the proceeds she could complete the renovations on the family estate. She was turning Allswell into a horse farm. Or so he'd been told. The price they'd agreed on was fair, and it would give her a breather. But not for long.

Just as she finished with the last paper, her younger lawyer, Ray Cox, rushed over to her. Cox sent Nate a stiff look, then sweetened his voice for his client. "That does it," he said, assisting her up from her chair. "The hard part's over."

Nate could understand Ray Cox's desire to protect his client. The Cox family had done business with the Brandenbergers for generations. Still, Cox's attitude rankled. The idea that Amber Reinhart might need protecting from Nate was both true, and...well, not so true. Nate, too, felt protective. He wished he could be the one to take her by the elbow and guide her to where the other lawyers stood talking.

But that was impossible. Unfortunately, it was also the whole point. Nate Fields might have made a success of his life. He had certainly just bought out the

Brandenbergers lock, stock and barrel. But that didn't make him their social equal, worthy of offering his solicitude to Ms. Reinhart. Nor did he want to be so soft as to *want* to assist her so desperately. He'd returned to St. Louis precisely to get over Amber Reinhart—to put his memories to rest, once and for all.

Nate joined the group that was endeavoring to pass the last moments comfortably. Four lawyers and two clients on opposing sides made for stilted conversation. Ray Cox continued to maneuver Amber away from Nate. By planting himself between the two of them, the lawyer kept Nate from getting a clear view of her. But even though she avoided eye contact with him, Nate thought she seemed to be holding up all right. He wondered why Dolph had left. His apparent abandonment of his sister also rankled. But then, as Nate remembered, Dolph had never shown much interest in her welfare.

"Well," said Nate's St. Louis lawyer. They were in his office. "From what I understand, Ms. Reinhart wants a few private words with Mr. Fields. If you'll follow me, there's a smaller office where you can speak privately."

Nate's heartbeat deepened into a slow, reverberating thud. When he'd first heard of this request a few weeks ago, he couldn't imagine what she wanted. He still hadn't figured it out. But if she wanted to talk to him, he was willing enough. He didn't expect any hysterical diatribe. He'd always known Amber Brandenberger to be fair, reasonable—as elegant as she looked. Only his own body betrayed him. He felt surprisingly unsteady.

"We've changed our minds," Ray Cox said, exactly as Nate moved to open the door for Amber.

Nate's Chicago lawyer, Bernie Hirsh, snapped to. "What do you mean you've changed your mind? Ms. Reinhart asked for a few minutes with my client, and he's agreed. What do you mean you've changed your mind?"

Cox turned to Bernie calmly. "I realize it was my client who made the request. She still wants to talk to Mr. Fields. But since our original request, my father and I . . ."

"This is ridiculous," Bernie interjected.

Nate's exasperation equaled his lawyer's. For weeks, he had wondered what Amber wanted with him. He was looking forward to finally finding out what it was.

"I'm telling you," Cox insisted, "my father and I have discussed Ms. Reinhart's wishes, and we can't allow her to go into some private meeting without representation."

"Representation?" Bernie parroted. "Don't you mean protection? Ms. Reinhart does not need protection from my client. Ms. Reinhart and Mr. Fields have known each other since they were kids."

"Not precisely," Ray Cox asserted. "Besides, this meeting involves a legal matter and, as Ms. Reinhart's lawyer, I insist on sitting in."

Nate realized that Bernie knew only the particulars Nate had told him. From the time Nate had been ten and she eight, their paths had often crossed. But they'd hardly been friends. Nate had come from the wrong side of the tracks. Amber Brandenberger had been raised on the hilltop estate. Nate was a product of the small, riverside community of laborers who had slaved in her father's gravel-dredging operation beneath the bluffs. Except for one, hot summer afternoon, they had barely even spoken to each other.

But Bernie had also struggled up from the ranks of the disadvantaged and, as soon as Nate had told him about his upbringing, Bernie had understood. Now the scrapper in Bernie took offense. Nate would be treated with the respect he deserved or Bernie Hirsh would know the reason why.

Silence filled the room. They all recognized they'd reached an impasse. Nate looked at Amber and, seeing her obvious discomfort, made an offer he wouldn't have made otherwise.

"It's all right," he said. "If Mr. Cox wants to sit in, so be it."

Bernie sent Nate a dumbfounded look. Nate ignored it. Instead, he allowed Ray Cox to reclaim Amber's elbow, to step out of the office and into the hallway ahead of him. The three of them followed the host lawyer to another smaller, equally posh office.

When Amber sank onto a couch, Ray Cox perched beside her. A secretary served them coffee. Nate went to sip his by the single window. He'd give Amber a minute to gather her thoughts. Hell, he'd give himself a minute to gather his own thoughts. He'd been thinking about this moment for so long. And now, it had been spoiled by Cox.

Still, Nate couldn't blame the lawyer. It was quite obvious that the man had an interest in his client that went beyond their lifelong family connections. Ray Cox watched over Amber with a casual ease that Nate envied. Cox seemed as comfortable with Amber as her equally refined former husband would have been.

Shaking off personal thoughts of Amber, Nate collected himself. He'd indulged his emotions enough for one day. It was time to get hold of himself. He was good at what he did. He'd become a successful businessman through hard work and careful thinking. If there had ever been a time for clearheadedness, it was now.

AMBER PRAYED for the afternoon to be over, and yet the worst of it had only begun. She'd never felt so frustrated, or so frightened. She might lose Kim, just as she'd lost the brewery. And to the same man.

Amber's emotional overload was exacerbated by her natural inclination to avoid conflict—to smooth things over no matter what. If only Ray Cox hadn't insisted on sitting in on her talk with Nate, she thought. If only she'd had the forethought—no, the guts—to put her foot down with him. His possessiveness irritated her as much as did Nate Fields' unreadable expression. The animosity between the men was palpable.

She took a deep breath. Ray Cox was about to expose the most precious thing in her life to a man who might consider himself her enemy.

"Thirteen years ago, Francine Gibbons gave birth to a baby girl. Do you remember Ms. Gibbons, Mr. Fields?"

Nate Fields stood by the window, coffee in hand, his dark, stunning features clearly delineated. In his very expensive three-piece suit, he looked remote and unapproachable. If he was surprised by the subject, he didn't betray it. When his gaze swept to her, then back to Ray Cox, Amber thought she saw a flicker in his black eyes.

"Yes," Nate said. "I remember Francine Gibbons."

"Last fall, she died. Ms. Reinhart was with her and, before her passing, my client and Ms. Gibbons agreed that Ms. Reinhart was to take the child and raise her as her own. Subsequently, Ms. Reinhart gained temporary custody, and the child is living with her."

Silence. Amber could almost believe that Nate Fields really had no idea where this was leading.

Cox cleared his throat. "Because there was no father named on the birth certificate of this child, she was given her mother's name. My client and I have filed a petition for adoption. Of course, we have every reason to believe the petition will be granted. Francine Gibbons assured Ms. Reinhart that there are no longer any close blood relations on her side of the family."

Cox paused. Amber watched Nate Fields by the window. She twisted her hands together in her lap. She couldn't imagine what was going through the man's head. Nate Fields had left Francie almost three months into her pregnancy, and yet Amber wondered if Nate could actually be unaware of Kim's existence. Ever since that day five months ago when Francie had told her to tell Nate she was sorry, had told her to tell Nate he was Kim's father, Amber had been questioning her own assumptions about Nate Fields. Could he truly be unaware that Kim was his?

Ray Cox's voice interrupted her thoughts.

"My client and I have placed a notice of adoption in the newspapers. Naturally, we want to be sure the petition isn't contested. The truth is, I advised Ms. Reinhart against approaching you. She insists, however, that she wants everything aboveboard. She especially doesn't want trouble from you. Even though you don't have any legal claim—I mean, what with the birth certificate not naming you as the father and your undeniable abandonment of your daughter—my client feels you have a right to know about the girl. But beyond that, she also thinks the girl has a right to know about you."

Another silence stretched out. Nate just stood there, immobile.

As Amber knew, Nate had never seen Kim. When he did, he certainly would not doubt that she was his daughter. Kim looked just like him. A resemblance that strong couldn't be coincidental.

The tense, strained silence persisted. Amber looked at Nate, but his gaze was unreadable. She watched as he moved to set his coffee on a table. Each action was a study in masculine grace.

Tugging at the sharp press of his chalk-and-gray pinstripe suit trousers, he sat down on a couch across from where she sat with Ray Cox. For a moment, he just stared at her. He smoothed his full lower lip with his thumb.

What in the world was the man thinking?

"Ms. Reinhart," he finally said, his voice low and soft. "Did Francie Gibbons actually tell you I was the father of this child?"

"Ms. Reinhart doesn't have to answer that," Ray snapped.

When Amber found herself on her feet, she didn't know who was more surprised, she or the men whose gazes followed her as she paced within the close con-figuration of the couches.

"Look, Ray," she said, "this formality is ridicu-lous. Why can't we just talk this through like I've wanted to all along?"

"You forget, Amber," Ray insisted, his voice insis-tent, "that we..."

"No, I don't forget," Amber said. "I remember. I remember very well." She straightened her shoulders. "Although Nate and I were never exactly friends, we've known each other all our lives. I simply don't see why you won't let me talk to him. I think there's some sort of misunderstanding here, and.... Well," she added, facing Nate, "yes. Francie told me you're Kim's father. She told me on the day she died, just before she lost consciousness for the last time."

Amber heard the renewed pain in her own voice, sensed the empathy in Nate's steady, black regard. She forced herself on. She knew she wasn't saying things the way she wanted to say them, and she went to her purse, which rested on the coffee table. With jerky movements, she withdrew a photograph and handed it to Nate. "Francie didn't need to tell me Kim is yours. Anyone who knows you can see right away that Kim is yours."

At last, a reaction. Nate studied the picture. His tight reserve dissipated, his broad shoulders slumped. He sat for a long time, the photo pinched between his thumb and forefinger, his stare finally focusing on something besides Amber.

She knew the face he now studied as well as she knew her own. Kim's was a sober face, unnaturally sober for someone so young. Her long black hair, as shiny as satin, hung in soft waves to her waist. Her eyes, which shone as green as her mother's had, were the only characteristic that spoke of Francie. The high cheekbones, the deep-set eyes, the stunningly chiseled features were undeniably those of her father.

"Well," Cox said impatiently, snatching the photo from Fields's fingers, "I'll serve my client as well as I can. You can decide on your course of action when you speak to your own lawyer. Ms. Reinhart insisted on telling you about the girl and her place in my client's life. Now you know."

Before either she or Nate could exchange more than brief goodbyes, Ray hustled Amber out of the smaller office and back into the hallway. But Amber didn't mind. She desperately needed to regroup. She certainly didn't know what to make of Nate, or of their brief encounter. In any case, it wasn't a matter of winning or losing. Not to her mind. Claiming Kim and selling Nate the brewery had been coincidental. Not tit for tat.

And while selling the brewery had been difficult, Amber knew she had to let go of the past. If she was to build a secure future at Allswell for both Kim and herself, she had to keep her head above water financially until her growing business in American quarter horses was solid. Though she realized what a blow it was to Dolph, she was grateful to have the brewery to sell.

Dolph, she suddenly thought. She and Ray had reached the entrance to Nate's lawyer's office.

"I guess Dolph left while I was signing the papers," Amber murmured.

"You aren't surprised, are you?" Ray asked.

She didn't answer.

Ray's father, who had been a close friend of her own father, waited to give her a hug. "I know this doesn't seem like a happy day for you, my dear. But in the long run, the sale is for the best."

"I only hope Dolph sees it that way," she said.

Mr. Cox patted her shoulder comfortingly. "Dolph'll come around. He'll see he had his chance at rescuing the brewery. And while he didn't exactly ruin it... Well, we all know the challenges the small breweries in this town are facing. In its day, Black Forest Beer was very popular. It had a loyal following that stuck by it longer than most premium beers. But then, things change, and you and Dolph have had more than your share of bad times. Now, it's time for some good times."

Amber forced a smile. "I'm certainly ready for the good stuff."

"That's our girl, eh, Ray?"

Ray smiled down into Amber's eyes. "That's our girl." Switching gears, he motioned to the door. "I know you have your car, but I don't like the idea of you driving. Not after what we've just been through with Fields."

"No, I can drive."

"I can take you anywhere you want to go. Dad's given me the afternoon..."

"No," Amber insisted. "I promised the Hewletts I'd drop by on my way out to Allswell."

"But are you really sure?" the elder Cox added.

"I'm sure."

Ray was frowning and apparently on the verge of arguing with her again, but Amber cut him off with as much patience as she could manage. She had learned a lot of hard lessons lately, and the hardest had been to finally say no—to finally draw her limits with people who might otherwise take advantage of her easy nature. Ray Cox had a tendency to push her when she didn't want to be pushed. In the past, she might have allowed him to do what he wanted if only to please him—to be nice.

Amber's soft smile tilted wryly. *But those days are gone,* she told herself. She wasn't "nice" anymore. Not in the old sense. She was a new Amber. Over the last five years since her mother's death she'd learned a lot. Not even for old family friends like Ray Cox and his father would she be the same one again.

With a final wave to Ray from across the parking lot, Amber climbed into her car. The Mercedes-Benz had been a wedding present from her ex-husband. It was the last accoutrement of real wealth left to her. Or rather, the car together with Allswell. And while she might be forced to sell the car, she'd hang onto Allswell for as long as she could.

Turning onto the street, Amber breathed a sigh of relief. It was Friday, the meeting was over, and she was looking forward to a relaxing weekend. As she drove, she thought about Nate Fields. She didn't need to guess why he and his lawyer, that brash Bernie Hirsh, hadn't followed her out of the building. They were probably in conference—probably discussing what Nate would do about his daughter.

Amber couldn't imagine what he was planning to do. Her memories of Nate Fields were as enigmatic as the man she'd witnessed today. Oddly enough, she'd also felt his compassion today. And his offers had been fair, right down to the last negotiations.

She knew he was a hard businessman. His reputation had preceded him all the way from Chicago, where he made his home and operated a nationwide business. He was a partner at Coldsdon and Fields, a respected real estate development company that specialized in the preservation and restoration of historic buildings.

The premises of Black Forest Beer would suit him well. He planned to turn the site into an office and apartment complex. But Amber didn't want to consider her family's lost brewery facilities. Not today while the wound still smarted. Not today when she knew Dolph was hurting. She needed to focus on something much more important—her relationship with Kim Gibbons.

Kim. She loved her so much. Every time she looked into those shiny green eyes she thought of Francie. She missed her. And yet, in a sense Francie's child continued to bind the two of them together.

Inevitably, thoughts of Kim also led Amber back to thoughts of the girl's father, Nate Fields. Amber remembered Nate as a gangly boy. And today, despite the impact the man had made on her, the boy lingered poignantly in her memory.

Still, she didn't want to think about her clearest memory of Nate Fields. Not with the possibilities that stretched ahead of them. And not with the additional emotional challenge of stopping by the Hewletts's. Only after that could she return to Allswell, lick her wounds and start over again.

AMBER PULLED into the curving drive before the large, Georgian-style house just off Lindell Boulevard. She couldn't help heaving a sigh. The house was almost as familiar as her own. Her family had been close to the Hewletts since before she had been born. The Hewletts had not only introduced her to her husband, but had supported her through her mother's death, her amicable divorce and then her father's passing.

Even so, Amber knew the Hewletts didn't really understand the inner transformation those events had worked on her. She was no longer the protected, rather shallow, rich man's daughter she had been. But these old family friends cared about her, and she owed it to them to let them see she was all right.

Lillian Hewlett welcomed her into the entrance hall. Like Amber herself, Lillian was thirty-one and single. Unlike Amber, Lillian was basically complacent and comfortable with her life.

"How are you?" Lillian asked, a frown marking her long, palely attractive face.

Amber gave her a squeeze. "I'm fine. It's over."

"What about Kim?"

Amber smiled softly. "Nate Fields now knows about me and Kim."

"Well, tell me! What did he say?"

"Actually, he didn't say much. But then, neither did I. Ray Cox did most of the talking. I guess I was in such a state that I . . ."

Lillian took Amber's hand. "Come on. Mother and Father are waiting to hear." At the door leading into the living room, Lillian paused. "You haven't mentioned Dolph."

"He left right after I signed the papers. I guess he went home to his apartment. I'll call him later. He sure won't remember to call me. He probably has his nose in a book already. Anyway, we're both resigned—it's just the residual feelings."

Lillian looked unconvinced. She'd always been close to Dolph. But when Lillian didn't press her about her brother, Amber felt relieved. Especially today.

"You do know Warner is staying with us, don't you?" Lillian asked. "He stepped out for a minute, but he'll be back soon."

At the mention of her ex-husband, Amber nodded. "Your mother told me he's visiting."

"Well," Lillian commented as the two entered the living room, "this is turning out to be a big day for you."

The room was long and broad, with casements piercing one wall at regular intervals. Outside, the sun shone overbright. Inside, a fire in the hearth beckoned. Howard and Phyllis Hewlett sat by the fire, he with a newspaper, she with her knitting. Despite the opulence of the surroundings it was a homey scene. The Persian carpets, the portrait over the mantel, the mahogany furniture felt familiar to Amber.

"Ah, Amber," Howard said, putting down his paper and coming over to kiss her cheek. Taking her hand, he led her to a chair across from his. Lillian joined her mother on a couch.

Phyllis smiled and set aside her wool and needles. "I've been so worried about you," she said. Amber could read the concern in the woman's narrow features. "Tell us, how did it go?"

Amber shrugged. "As well as it could have, I guess. The lawyers hung over us like ghosts, and I signed the papers."

"And what about this Nate Fields? How did he react to the adoption?"

Amber briefly described the meeting. Her audience listened intently. And while their hostility toward Nate bothered her, she wasn't up to either explaining her feelings, or defending him.

She looked up just as Warner entered the room.

"Kitten!" he exclaimed, striding toward her with a small parcel in his hands. As always, Warner Reinhart looked wonderful. He dressed impeccably. He was older than Amber—closer to Phyllis's age, in fact. Warner was her cousin. His wealth, his polish, and his soft charm remained undiminished by time.

Amber hadn't seen him since her father's funeral, but she knew they'd always share the same, sad bond.

He bent, cheerfully bussing her cheek. "They didn't rough you up too badly, did they?"

Again, Amber absorbed the warmth in Warner's gray eyes. His silvering hair, his patrician features, the scent of his expensive cologne defined Warner.

"I'm okay," she replied, accepting the package he handed her. "What's this?"

"A smile for a rainy day," he said, looking pleased, even a little smug.

"Then I can't open it now. The sun's shining."

She glanced at the others. They were smiling, too. They evidently knew the secret of what she held. Opening the smooth silver paper, Amber gasped. A slim, old-fashioned volume of poetry emerged from the wrap. It was a book of her own poems, *Remnants of Memory*, an endeavor she'd almost forgotten.

"We thought you could use some good news," Warner said, lounging elegantly in a chair. "As with the first volume, Howard had this one printed by the university press."

Amber didn't know what to say. Writing poetry was an activity she associated with her old self, not with her new one. Really, she hadn't felt the urge to put pen to paper for well over a year.

Still, looking around the circle of observers, she knew she had to say something nice. They just didn't understand yet what a different person she'd become. Nor did they probably want to understand. A young woman, struggling with her identity, struggling to keep herself financially afloat, was an alien entity to this family so like the one her own family had once been.

Smiling, Amber thanked Howard. "After *Skipping Stones And Remembering*, I'm surprised you could get this one published."

Howard pointed out that her first volume had met with a modest reception that justified the university's hopes for this one. "Of course, if you'd get out to some of the readings, if you'd do a few interviews..."

"No," Amber said, tempering her interruption with her soft smile. "A working girl like me has neither the time nor the energy to peddle poetry."

Everyone laughed. Obviously, no one was taking her seriously. Amber wanted to run. If Warner hadn't looked sympathetic, ready to listen, she might have.

Later, when it was time for her to go, he walked her to the door, out into the cooler, darker afternoon. The sun had disappeared behind more typically gray February skies and the wind had picked up. Even so, the two of them lingered beside her car in the curving drive.

"Are you sure you're all right, Kitten?"

Amber noted that even the wind didn't dare ruffle his hair or tinge his cheeks. This man was inviolate. At least, on the outside. On the inside, Amber knew better than anyone his major flaw. Warner Reinhart was loving but incapable of sexual desire. He was asexual, largely impotent. The experts called it inhibited sexual drive.

Amber's pitiful discovery about her husband had dawned slowly and painfully. It had been hard for them both, and it still hurt. Amber could see by Warner's search of her face that things hadn't changed. He continued to both accept what he was and to remain helpless to change it as well.

"How's your grandmother?" she asked with a grin. They both loved his freewheeling, expatriate grandmother.

"She's fine. After I leave here, I'll join her in Deauville. I've been thinking about translating *Remnants of Memory* into French, and trying to find a publisher for it in Paris. What do you think?"

"I guess I don't know what I think anymore. Not about my poetry. If you like it, do what you want." She grinned. "And if there's any money in it, please let me know."

"So, I ask again, Kitten, how are you? You know you can always come to me. For money, for anything."

"Yes, I know. And I thank you. But really, Warner, I have to do this on my own. I have to stand on my own two feet. I think at some point we all have to learn that. It just happens to be my turn."

"And you're doing all right? Howard and Phyllis bemoan—"

"I know Howard and Phyllis are worried. I do the best I can to reassure them. But, in the end, they can't comprehend what it's like to be without copious amounts of money." Again Amber grinned. "I hope they never have to find out."

"I hope *I* never have to find out," Warner quipped, also grinning.

"I'm sure your granny will keep you safe." With one hand on the car door handle, Amber smiled at him more wistfully. "You've been part of my learning experience, Warner. I learned tolerance and kindness from you. I'll always love you for that."

"You didn't have much of a choice, Kitten. You either learned tolerance and kindness, or the means for murdering me."

Amber popped open the door. "Those days weren't all that bad." Her departing smile was sweetly cunning. "Besides, I hate the sight of blood."

CHAPTER TWO

WHEN HER MOTHER DIED, Amber had realized she had to extricate herself from her painful marriage to Warner Reinhart. Then she had moved home to Allswell. Her father had been shaken by her mother's death, so to think of him rattling around alone in their old country house—when she'd also been rattling around without purpose on her own—hadn't made sense to her.

At first, she'd thrown herself into her former social routine with the same effort she'd expended on her poetry. Neither had done her much good. Nor had her father improved. She had been glad she'd been with him then. His health was steadily declining, and he had needed her. But, once again, the nagging demand to grow and to change had pushed at her. She simply hadn't been satisfied as she was, and the sources of her dissatisfaction went beyond the dreadful blows she had been dealt over the past few years.

She had always loved horses. She rode well and had a fine touch, an affinity for the animals. These talents, which she'd always taken for granted, included a sharp eye for both a horse's good and bad points. Gradually, she'd tied these skills together. The idea of starting a breeding and training facility for high-quality American riding horses flowered. The idea became urgent when she learned about her father's dwindling resources. After he died, she and her brother had discovered the financial mess their parent had kept from them. Perhaps, from himself.

So Amber had thrown herself into the stables. In the meantime, Dolph, who was a year younger than she, stepped in to run the Black Forest Beer brewery. Unfortunately, while Amber had gained a little ground at a time, her brother had mismanaged the brewery to near bankruptcy. All along she'd known he was trying, but...well, finally something had to be done. Her efforts to hang on to Allswell, the only property from their old life that she really wanted, became her obsession. Just as Scarlett O'Hara was tied to Tara, Amber comically thought herself bound to Allswell. Only, it wasn't really a comedy at all.

The threat of losing the estate had kept Amber going. She had traveled all over the world; yet turning into Allswell's wrought-iron gates, embellished with the oval logo for Black Forest Beer, always elicited the same sense of comfort. No matter what crises her life threw at her, Allswell remained her refuge.

A long, straight drive led to the broad circular driveway, in front of the house, which was surrounded by low boxwood hedges. The house, a genuine château, had been brought to America in pieces and reassembled on the cliffs above the Meramec River. Looking south from any window, one could see miles and miles of Missouri countryside, stretched out like a patchwork quilt.

This setting, now on the edge of St. Louis's exurbs, was not only picturesque but unique. For Amber, as for four generations of Brandenbergers before her,

Allswell meant home. As long as she felt she had a right to such a private preserve—a right she would earn by making it pay for itself—she'd hang on to it for dear life. Developers like Nate Fields—who looked for exactly such intriguing, historical properties—would not trespass at Allswell. Not while she could hold on. Selling the brewery allowed her to hold on for a bit longer. That bit of time, she hoped, would be enough to get her horse farm going.

As she climbed the broad steps of the veranda, which wrapped three sides of the house with a pierced balustrade, Kim came out through the large front door. Amber caught the girl in an embrace. Amber knew she had to treat Kim with care. At thirteen, Kim was as skittish as any colt in the stables. She had been through too much. Only now was the tall, lanky teen gaining some sense of security. She'd obviously been waiting to hear Amber's news about "this father" of hers. This father she wanted deeply to know.

Of course, Kim was also putting up barriers against the likely rejection Amber had warned her about. Amber's heart wrenched. Looking into the girl's green eyes, she read expectation mixed with caution.

"Are you all right?" Kim asked, her nose already reddening in the chill air. Dark clouds rolled overhead. Light sifted through the open door. The contrast of house and elements always seemed more stark on the hilltop.

Amber found her soft smile. "I'm fine. It went just fine."

"And Uncle Dolph?"

"He's okay. I'll call him later. Come on," she said, shepherding the girl inside the house. "It's too cold to talk out here."

The peace of Allswell enveloped Amber like a blanket. In the enormous double-story entry of the rustic structure, Amber shucked off her coat. A grand staircase, as rustic as the house, led up to a balcony that framed the lofty hall on three sides. The major upstairs rooms opened off this balcony. Beneath them, the rooms of the lower floor opened off the entry. The house was filled with fireplaces and an eclectic collection of furnishings that her family had accumulated over three generations. Everything was familiar, a lot was fine, all of it was dear to her.

Amber and Kim walked back to the cozy rear parlor that was their favorite retreat. Here, the single fire in the house burned. The couch was comfortable, the Persian carpet lay lush and inviting across the gleaming dark planking of the floor. Dropping her coat and purse, Amber hugged Kim again. "I suppose Etta Fay has supper almost ready."

"Almost. She's been watching for you, too."

Amber smiled wryly. "I'm glad she's busy cooking, or she'd be in here, wanting to put in her two cents."

The pair sat down on the couch together.

"So, tell me," Kim urged.

Drawing a breath, Amber collected herself. "Everything went as I told you it would. I signed the papers, and we have Allswell for a little longer. I met your father, and he looks like I told you he'd probably look. The last time I saw him he was only nineteen, so of course he's changed. Still, he's pretty much the same." Amber stroked Kim's cheek and hesitated. While she and Kim were invariably honest, honesty could be brutal. Even so, Kim seemed eager, and Amber went on. "We talked then, and I showed him your picture. Actually, neither he nor I had a chance to say too much. Not with Ray Cox there."

"I can just bet."

"He didn't say anything, sweetheart," Amber finally admitted. "I don't know what he was thinking. I would imagine he wants to confer with his lawyers first, and I'm sure he was surprised by the subject being brought up the way it was."

The girl looked simultaneously downcast and composed. Amber and she had discussed the possibilities, and this had been one of them. Kim asked the question Amber expected. "Does he want to see me?"

Amber considered. "As I say, we didn't get specific. Not like I'd hoped we would. Ray Cox discouraged personal communication. He didn't want anything revealed that could be used against us later." Amber pushed a long strand of black satiny hair back over Kim's shoulder, noting the tinge of pink in her cheeks. "I wish I could tell you more—something we'd both like to hear. But you and I, we're straight if we're nothing else, right?"

Kim nodded. At that moment Amber could have ripped out Nate Fields's heart. *If* he had one. "So? What went on here today?"

Kim also pressed on. "The usual. When I came home from school, Gnaw raced up from the woods to meet my bus. After some pats, he ran down to the stables. I did some homework and practiced a little. But not much. I couldn't..."

"I know. You probably couldn't concentrate." Amber's gaze skipped to the cello, resting against the chair in the window. Kim watched her. "Do you go to Granny Maple's?"

This finally brought a smile from Kim. "Where else?"

"Did you get anywhere with her?"

"No. She says she doesn't want a phone jangling her nerves. She still said no, even when I told her all the stuff you said I should say."

"Stuff I've already said."

"Things like we'd feel better if we could reach her. And if she needed us, she could call. But she still says no. And she won't get her roof fixed, and she won't go into the hospital for tests. The same old story."

They both worried about Granny Maple. The old African American woman was the heart of the small riverside community where Francie and Kim had been born. Granny Maple was as stubborn as a Missouri mule. She was aging, growing too old to hold onto her independence. But Granny Maple insisted on living alone. And while everyone loved her, and people were always dropping by to check up on her, Amber, and especially Kim, worried about her. Whenever Francie had left town, gone off somewhere seeking something she'd never found, Granny Maple had taken care of Kim.

"I'll go down and see her tomorrow," Amber said. "I'm sure she won't listen to me anymore than she ever does, but I can't stop trying."

"I know it's because she doesn't want you to pay for her telephone."

"Well," Amber admitted with a sigh, "she has her pride, and I can understand that. But I'm also afraid for her, just like I know you are. We just have to remember that the way she's behaving has nothing to do with how she feels about us. Some people, when they get older, have a hard time letting go of their independence." Amber winked and patted Kim's hand. "We'll just keep nudging at her until she finally gives in."

"I hope you don't mind, but . . . since it's Friday, I told her I'd spend the night. You don't mind, do you? I mean, after today, maybe you don't want to be alone, and . . ."

Amber chuckled. "No. I'll be fine. She needs you tonight. And I think you sort of need her."

Kim nodded. "I feel close to her. I feel like, well, like I'm close to her because I know she was close to my mom. When my mom was a little girl."

"Yeah, Granny Maple's always taken people to her heart, and that means into her home. She even took care of your father for some of the time when he was growing up."

"I know. She tells me stories about him. She says he's good. That's why I keep thinking he'll . . ."

He'll love you, Amber thought, filling in the words Kim couldn't say.

Impulsively she gathered Kim into an embrace. "Just take it one day at a time, honey. That's all. Just today, and then tomorrow. One day, the sun will break through."

Amber wanted desperately to believe her own words.

Etta Fay, a large matronly woman who Amber admitted was the real mover behind Allswell, came in from the kitchen. Fists on her hips, she asked, "Well, how did it go?"

Amber thought that if she had to recount her meeting with Nate Fields even one more time, she'd scream. But she didn't. Patiently, she described the meeting as she and Kim and Etta Fay joined Mick, Etta Fay's husband, in the large, old-fashioned kitchen.

Mick Spillby and his wife had proven to be godsends. While Amber's parents had always hired people from the river community whenever a job came open, Etta Fay and Mick had wandered in one day when she'd been a child and hired on themselves. Etta Fay handled the house with vengeful efficiency. Mick, who'd originally been meant only to look after Amber's father's few riding horses, had grown into the position of trainer and overseer at the burgeoning Black Forest Stables. Where Mick hardly ever spoke, Etta Fay talked enough for both of them.

It being Friday, Etta Fay and Mick left right after dinner, not to return until Sunday night. They owned a cabin on one of the local lakes where Mick liked to get away and fish. Kim left soon after, leaving Amber alone with her thoughts.

Later, padding around in creamy silk pajamas, Amber let out Gnaw. Gnaw was an Irish setter, a large dog with silky, auburn hair and overactive hormones. Good-natured, he welcomed everyone and everything around him with tongue-lolling joy. His exuberance, in fact, made him nearly impossible to live with, even with acres to run in and a house that was above average size.

She was on her way back through the kitchen when the phone rang. Absentmindedly, she picked it up.

"Amber?"

"Yes."

"Nate Fields."

Amber didn't know why her heart began to pound. "Yes?" she repeated.

"I'd like to talk to you."

"I have some time now."

"No. I mean, could we go out? For a cup of coffee or something?"

"I'm afraid I'm..."

"You're undressed?"

Somehow, the question, asked in his low voice, sounded suggestive. "Yes—er, no. I'm relaxing, that's all."

"After today, we can all use some relaxation. But it's important that we talk."

When Amber hesitated, he went on. "Look, I know you'd rather have your watchdog with you, but I'm not up to waiting until we can schedule another meeting. Frankly, Cox has never been cooperative, and, like I say, we need to talk."

Amber could well imagine that Ray Cox had been uncooperative with Nate Fields and his organization in the past. If she had felt she'd had the choice, she wouldn't have involved Ray, either. She certainly didn't look forward to another meeting like the one she'd had with him and Nate that day. Along with the resentment it had produced, their confrontation hadn't settled anything.

"All right," she heard herself say. "But, if you don't mind, could you come out here?"

Now it was his turn to hesitate. "I don't know if I should. I think there are things we have to get straight, and..."

"You don't need to worry that you'll run into your daughter," Amber said sharply. "Kim's spending the night away."

When he still hesitated, Amber couldn't figure out why.

"Well," he said. "If you're sure, I'll drive out. I'm all the way downtown, so it'll take me about forty-five minutes."

"That's okay. I'll be here."

"Good. Forty-five minutes."

"And Nate?"

"Yeah?"

"Her name is Kim. I'm sorry that Ray didn't speak of her as he should have."

There was another pause, then: "Uh, yeah. Forty-five minutes."

Amber dropped the phone into its cradle. Forty-five minutes to shore up her defenses. She was glad Kim wasn't at home. Amber would meet Nate Fields on her own. She'd figure him out for herself first. She didn't like what she knew of him. Except for his business success, she couldn't admire him. Any confrontation with him would require considerable effort.

And yet, Amber knew she'd have to confront Nate Fields many more times in the future. If there were any chance for Kim to have a positive relationship with her father, Amber would encourage the contact. But first, she'd determine whether or not he was a safe person for Kim to know.

Everything Amber knew about Nate Fields warned
her that he was anything but safe, especially his abandonment of Francie. Still, a picture of the boy he'd
been—gangling, dark, watching her intently—kept
surfacing in her mind. That picture, together with a
deeply ingrained faith in human nature, kept a slim
hope alive. Maybe she had misunderstood him. Maybe
Francie hadn't been straight with him. Maybe he'd be
good to Kim.

NATE FIELDS WHEELED IN through the wrought-iron
gates at Allswell.

"God," he muttered under his breath. "The place
hasn't changed a bit."

The old feelings rushed at him: the old yearnings
and anger, the old disgust with himself for feeling
those yearnings. He hated his uncontrollable attach-
ment to this place. And yet, in this place he recognized anew the needy boyhood self he'd turned his
back on years ago.

Gingerbread gatehouses still stood sentinel on either side of a long drive that led to the house through
a wide, winter-dead lawn. Cruising slowly down the
drive, Nate's eyes narrowed as he searched for alter-
ations. There were none. Allswell rested as it always
had, nestled atop the cliffs above the river he'd known
by heart, set in a woods that had been cultivated for
decades to look perfectly natural. An enormous sloping roof overhung the veranda, trimmed along its
edges in white gingerbread, as were the balconies and
windows. Stained in the same deep brown, the house
looked timeless and dark.

At the age of nineteen, Nate had left here without a single regret. As a man of thirty-three, he realized now that it was because of Allswell that he'd chosen the work he did. Allswell, old and laced with a single family's history—also threaded through decades of the area's history—also intertwined with his own history. Allswell composed the deep bass notes of his ongoing composition.

Nate found himself as frustrated with this latest revelation as he was with the rest—with his past and with the ties to the past that he couldn't seem to cut. He also knew Amber Brandenberger stood as the focal point of his resentment. He had hardly known her, and yet he had never forgotten her. Not entirely. That a shallow, rich man's daughter could maintain such a hold on him was perhaps rationally explicable, but frustrating for a full-grown man.

Nate admitted it. He had always wanted what she represented. *But he'd gotten that.* Now, why in hell couldn't he get over her? It wasn't as if he had been in love with her. He'd returned to St. Louis on impulse—unusual motivation for him. When he'd seen that her father's brewery had come up on the market, he'd acted within the day. He'd put in a bid. He'd made an offer few could refuse. He could afford to.

So, why did he still feel like some dirty kid standing on the outside looking in?

And now, this latest blow. Amber Reinhart claimed that Francie's daughter was his. And that picture of the girl . . . well, it had also struck him to his gut. The girl did look like him. But Francie had also told him she wasn't his. All those years ago, when Francie's condition had become obvious, he'd asked her if the

baby was his and she had said no. Emphatically. The
baby was Kenny O'Donnell's. Or so Francie had spat
at him.

But that photo...such a sober, heartrending photo.
Since seeing it, Nate hadn't been able to think of any-
thing else. As little as he wanted to, he had to talk with
Amber Reinhart again.

He parked his rental at the foot of the broad stairs
that led to the veranda and gazed for a moment at the
closed door. An army of memories and feelings as-
sailed him. His plans for a quick, sweet revenge had
doubled back on him. He was only too well aware of
the irony that iced the bitter tangle of his emotions.

He got out of the car, and just as he reached the top
of the stairs the front door cracked open. Amber
Brandenberger peered at him.

"I thought it must be you," she said. "But it took
you so long to come up the drive that—"

"I'm sorry if I frightened you. I was trying to look
at the house."

A wind swept up, a reminder that it was cold and
dank and February."

"Come in," Amber said, stepping back inside.

Nate had never been in the entrance hall. Not precisely. When he'd had his first look at Allswell's interior, he'd been fourteen and Amber Brandenberger
twelve. He'd been on his way up the grand staircase,
on his way to her bedroom.

The home's rich interior had been assembled much
as the interiors of fine, English country houses had
been. Each object held a meaning, recalled a particular event. Nate's adult eye now appreciated what he'd
only sensed intuitively as a youngster.

"This way," Amber said. "I've got a fire going in the family room."

At the sound of her voice, Nate turned his attention to the elegant woman who preceded him. As always, this particular woman made him feel very large, very male, very gauche. None of that had changed, either.

She was wearing a neatly tailored pair of stone-colored slacks and a soft, white shirt buttoned to the throat. Her nut-brown hair, beautifully cut, swept casually across the nape of her neck. She had the looks he invariably sought in other women. Just as Allswell set the standard for the architectural style he hoped to achieve in his own work, so the lady of Allswell epitomized the type of woman that habitually attracted him. Here was elegance beyond price. Here elegance had been refined over many generations and with a great deal of money.

Surprisingly, the room they entered was, compared with the rest of the house, ordinary. A fire crackled on the hearth. On the couch, a book lay open amid the folds of a gaily-patterned afghan. Beneath a window, a cello cozied up to a chair. A pile of schoolbooks were haphazardly stacked on a buffet. Papers littered a table.

"Would you like a cup of coffee?" Amber said.

She was posed in the doorframe. A picture of caramel buttons against a natty cream-colored suit, the one she'd worn to the lawyer's office that day, came to Nate's mind. Despite the casualness of the room, Amber Reinhart remained all buttoned up.

"No thanks," he replied. "Going out for coffee was an excuse."

"Please" She indicated the couch with an eloquent gesture. "Sit down."

Before she swept up the book and the afghan, Nate noted that she'd been reading poetry. By Keats. He also smelled her perfume. Expensive.

Placing her things on one chair, she perched neatly on another, just across from him and the fire. Firelight touched the smooth swing of her hair, glowed along her cheek. Her dark brown stare, her soft voice, remained cool.

Nate had meant to get right to the point but he didn't. "I've heard about your success at the stables. Congratulations."

"Actually, congratulations aren't in order yet, but we're hanging in there."

"Opening the stables was a great idea. You'll be able to both keep Allswell and preserve it intact."

She shrugged a slim shoulder. "I guess only time will tell."

Nate's next words surprised him. "If Allswell were mine, I'd do whatever I could to hold on." Her next little shrug spurred him on. "Look, about today. At the lawyer's offices, I mean. I was... your announcement about the baby, the, uh, girl, came as a shock. I know I didn't react much—say much—but I was..."

"I'd been wondering if you didn't know," Amber admitted, still somewhat cool. "Francie didn't tell me anything until the very last, and then I was thinking about, well, about the situation. As I recall, she said to tell you she was sorry. She definitely said Kim is yours, but the rest isn't clear in my mind."

"I can understand that."

"I think the important thing for you to know is that Francie was genuinely apologetic. She'd changed a lot over the five years she and I were friends. I don't know how much you know, but she worked here. When the stables began taking up more of my time, I hired her to do the paperwork. Francie and I became very close, as did Kim and I. When Francie said she was sorry, I'm sure she meant it. I mean, well, I guess she must have misled you."

Nate suddenly found himself on his feet. The cozy fire, the intimate conversation, was somehow too much. Being with this woman under these circumstances was especially too much. She was confiding in him as if they'd always been friends, *and they hadn't been friends*. He wouldn't have been allowed to be her friend.

And then there was the subject of the conversation. It sounded illicit—somehow squalid. "Not only did Francie mislead me," he managed to say, "she downright lied to me. When I asked her point-blank if the child she carried was mine, she told me no. In fact, she did more than tell me no. She acted as if I was nuts to even consider it as mine. In the light of our relationship, or rather, our lack of relationship, it was easy for me to think I was way out of line."

Looking down at her Nate saw Amber stiffen in the chair.

"As I say," she said, her voice crisp, "I'm sure Francie meant her apology. If you're in doubt as to whether or not Kim is yours, there are tests that can prove parentage. Kim and I have discussed the possibility of testing, and—"

"No." Exasperation edged his voice. Nate hated Amber to think he'd ever been involved in irresponsible sex. "No, the picture of the girl was enough. We don't need to go through the testing."

Allowing his gaze to linger on Amber, Nate felt himself relax. "Look," he said, "I'm here to offer whatever I can. Naturally, I've spoken to my lawyers—"

"Naturally."

He swallowed another flood of resentment at the tawdriness of the situation. "I've made arrangements for a trust to be set up for...Kim." There, he'd said the girl's name. The next came easier still. "I also want to help financially on a monthly basis."

Amber seemed brought up short by this, even a bit relenting. "Nate, I didn't tell you about Kim for the money. I'm not a wealthy woman anymore, but I have enough to support Kim and to make her comfortable."

"And my point isn't the money, either."

"Oh?"

Now she had him. He'd come to offer the money, and he'd offered it. Yes, he knew Kim was his child. But he didn't know about children—about thirteen-year-old girls. He should have known not to act on emotion, especially not in this place with this woman. Instead of rushing out here, not knowing what he thought, what he wanted, he should have thought this through. This was unlike him.

Obviously sensing his confusion, she spoke. "Maybe you shouldn't be so hasty. Maybe we could handle this through our lawyers. Evidently you want to assume some responsibility for Kim, but—"

"And what kind of responsibility should I assume?" He'd been asking himself the same question all afternoon.

"We both know it's up to you to decide how much responsibility you want. Within the parameters of my having custody, that is. I'm only saying it's reasonable for you to take some time before you answer that question. In telling you about Kim today, I did what I felt I had to do. Both for Kim's sake and for my own conscience. But how you react is up to you."

She sounded so damned reasonable. And he felt so damned unreasonable. It was Francie's lie. It was the house. It was Amber Reinhart. He was so damned attracted to her—to her softness. He'd always thought he'd cornered the market on control.

Nate simply had to move—to the window, to the table, to the cello leaning against the chair and squeezed in by the music stand. He knew Amber watched him.

"You're not the only one this is hard for, Nate. I had a horrible time deciding what to do. While Ray Cox assures me you don't have grounds for taking Kim away from me, I know the courts are unpredictable. A judge could throw out every argument of abandonment, of Kim's choice, of my five-year relationship with both her and Francie. A judge could find Kim's blood ties to you the only valid argument. And that possibility has been a terrible thing to discuss with Kim. She's lost her mother. She's only beginning to feel some sense of security with me, and—"

"Then why did you start this damned business?"

"As I told you, my conscience wouldn't allow me *not* to tell you. Especially when I knew I'd be seeing you with regard to the brewery sale. And above all, there's Kim herself. She has no one on Francie's side of the family who even knows her. Besides, when children become teens, they begin to feel the urge to move away, to be separate. Don't you see? Kim doesn't have anything to move away from. What little she's had has been taken. She has to know where she comes from before she can separate from it. The truth is, she and I are doing very well, but everyone has a right to know their own history. I'm not asking you to establish a relationship with your daughter. If you want that opportunity, I'll give it to you. But what I'm really asking you to do, is to say, 'Yes, Kim Gibbons is mine.' And even if you never see Kim, or talk to her, I can tell her that you know what she knows, that she's your child.''

Nate had stopped pacing at the other end of the room from where Amber remained in front of the fire. God, she had courage. And sense. And love. A wealth of love. To think he'd thought of her as merely a stylish woman with no depth. One emotion after another washed over him. There wasn't enough time to sort them all through, to define them. He heard his own voice, hushed and unexpected.

"What's Kim like?"

Finally, Amber smiled a soft, knowing smile. "You saw her picture. She's like you."

"No, I mean, what's she like. What's a thirteen-year-old girl like?"

"What's a thirty-one-year-old woman like? Or a thirty-three-year-old man? Kim's a complicated human being. She's less sad about Francie, but she's still confused. She doesn't like the horses much, but she loves her dog. She goes to the local middle school, but that might change. She's intelligent and sweet, and yet she's shy. She doesn't make friends or trust easily. That worries me. She plays the cello. In fact, she has a gift for playing the cello. She's studying with a teacher at Washington University, and her teacher claims Kim should move on soon. I'm looking into music schools up east, but..."

"But?"

Amber immediately looked soft, as vulnerable as he felt. "I don't want Kim to go so far away. Not when we're just finding each other. Still, I have to stick by that motherly instinct I'm learning. No matter what I feel, I have to do what's best for her."

Nate's eyes met Amber's soft brown ones in a steady stare. On top of all the rest, she was telling him something else. She was speaking to him of parenthood.

The chasm of fatherhood suddenly yawned open at his feet. Abruptly, unexpectedly, like an earthquake rending the ground beneath him, everything had changed. This was not a matter of checkbooks and lawyers, of responsibilities and decisions. This woman was showing him something that was way beyond his ken. The wellspring of emotion that he'd suppressed years ago was also threatened by the quake. He was afraid to feel it. It would drown him. He was the last person to know how to handle emotions.

Amber seemed to be collecting her thoughts too. Although Nate could be sure there was more, she'd revealed a lot to him. Almost visibly, she gathered herself together. The intimacy was gone from her voice and expression, and he felt suddenly bereft.

"Are you planning to be in the area for a while?" she asked. "Or will you oversee the remodeling of the brewery from Chicago?"

"I'll be here. I always do my jobs hands-on."

"Well then, you have some time to think this over. Not that you can't think in Chicago, but . . ."

When she didn't suggest that he see Kim, he was grateful.

"Where are you staying?" she asked instead.

"In the Landing. Near the brewery."

"Your job sounds exciting and—well, it must be interesting. Creative and . . ."

He felt himself grow equally remote. He'd known not to drive out to Allswell, and yet he hadn't known how to stay away. Goaded by his own sense of inadequacy and the coolness seeping in between them, Nate plucked up the fur-lined trench coat he'd worn over his slacks and shirt. "I'd better go."

"Yes," she agreed, "you'd better."

CHAPTER THREE

"WELL, SUGAR LUMP. You may as well tell me. You didn't send our Kimmy off to Beaver's just because you think I need fresh milk in my icebox. You know as well as I do that Beaver'll keep her, tease with her, for as long as he can."

Turning from the window with its view of the Meramec River, Amber gazed into the wise and wizened face of Granny Maple. Patches of smooth brown skin about the woman's brow and cheeks contrasted with the crinkles around her eyes and mouth. Still, even with her grizzled hair and plump figure, Granny Maple didn't look her seventy-plus years.

Amber smiled. "You think I'm going to lecture you again. About getting a phone, about going to the hospital for tests, about letting me send someone to work on your roof."

The old woman got up from the table, fussing with their teacups and sticky plates. As she often did when visiting Granny Maple on a Saturday afternoon, Amber had brought bakery goods. She, Granny Maple and Kim considered them a treat.

"There isn't much difference," the woman observed, "between rattling your points off like a list and arguing them. I know what you want. I can see the day coming."

"All I want—all any of us wants—is for you to be safe."

"Well, I'm not so old that I can't go on here like I always have." Obduracy showed in Granny Maple's shoulders and voice. "I'll tell you when I'm ready for the poorhouse."

Amber knew to drop the subject. The woman who was the heart of the river community on the banks of the broad, flat Meramec had spoken.

Granny Maple was a strong woman. She'd been hammered strong and pure by life, like the finest gold. Amber knew that one day the old woman would take leave of this life on her own terms. Amber simply dreaded the thought of her leaving.

"But there's something else, isn't there?" Granny Maple prompted.

Again Amber turned from her study of the slow-moving river, the strip of cottonwoods and sycamores in which the string of river houses perched along the banks. Granny Maple finished washing up the plates and wiping down the table. Her tiny premises, one main room with two small bedrooms and a little bath, sparkled with years of attention. That everything was worn—that stains marked the ceiling where it would drip again when it rained, that the stuffing of the large, cushy chair in which the woman sat to crochet was oozing out at the seams—was a condition she bore with a dignity anyone had to admire.

Granny Maple sat down in the cushy chair and peered at Amber over her spectacles. She had picked up her hook. The floss she would weave into lovely, lacy tablecloths threaded her brown fingers. Her tablecloths earned her part of her living.

But Amber knew that Granny Maple's real purpose was to delve into Amber's own thoughts. One did not escape the wisdom here. Amber, like others, had grown to depend on the love she'd found here in such a pure concentration.

"Kimmy's been chattering, you know," Granny Maple prodded.

"About Nate Fields?"

"Who else?"

Amber moved to the chair facing the old woman's. She sat down with a sigh. "Why do you think Francie lied to him about Kim?"

Granny Maple sighed, too. "Heavens, Francie always served her own whims and purposes, even when she was a little girl. Not that that didn't make her as lovable as the others, but..."

"Tell me about Francie when she was little. Did you take care of her a lot?"

"Off and on, like most of the others I've collected around me. Times down here have always been hard, and the children, the family life, suffered the most. But Francie was the image of her mother. The prettiest little thing I ever saw. She was always moving, dancing—restless. And wanting. You couldn't give that girl enough. One cookie would never do. Francie wanted as many as you'd give her, and she'd wheedle until you finally said yes. Her problem was that no one could resist her."

Amber remembered Francie differently. To easygoing Amber, Francie had seemed a red-haired spitfire. Whenever Amber had crossed Francie's path, which hadn't been often, Francie had chased Amber off.

Amber recalled their initial encounter. She'd happened on Francie and her friends playing in the woods along the river beneath the bluffs. Amber had been riding her pony. The girls' hurtful response to her gave Amber her first inkling of the differences between people, differences that could make people resentful and angry. Francie's jealousy of Amber had lasted for many years.

Amber had gone off to college, then to New York. Only when she and Francie had met again—when Amber had been looking for someone to help with stable business—had they spoken. At first, their relationship had borne the marks of the past. But gradually, they had become friends. Where Francie might have been resentful and needy, she'd also had a tough fairness about her that had appealed to Amber. It seemed impossible that they would have become as close as they had in the time they had.

"And Nate Fields?" Amber asked. "You kept him some, too, didn't you?"

"Not as much as Francie, or Kim. I've had Kim the most. Francie had no more sense of being a mother than some cats. But with Nate it was different. When he and his father came here, Nate was around eight or so. His father did heavy work, like lead mining down in Bonne Terre and working the barges along the Mississippi. The gravel-dredging operation drew Gerald Fields to this area. But, of course, that place was on its last legs by then." Granny Maple studied her hook and thread. "After the gravel works folded, Nate's father left him for long periods. I had him for awhile, but as soon as he was old enough he started working part-time at Beaver's General Store and...well, Beaver's always had a soft spot for Nate. And then Nate also earned his keep. He worked hard, studied hard. He deserves what he's done with himself.''

Amber thought of the boy who had haunted her memory here of late. All too often, however, she thought of Nate at nineteen, of that afternoon in the cave when he'd no longer been a boy but a man—when she'd had her first taste of womanhood. Not ready to face that recollection, Amber looked at Granny Maple. The old woman was still watching the white thread inching through her leathery brown fingers.

"And you," Granny Maple said, surprising Amber, "were also a sweet little thing. I always thought of you as one of my children. Yes, even rich little girls can seem neglected, you know." The woman chuckled softly. "I remember that day so clear, when you came up on me fishing by the river. I sat on the bank, and your pretty dappled pony shied away. Remember?"

Amber chuckled, too. "I sure do. After that, I started looking for you. You've always drawn children like a Pied Piper."

"And that seems funny, doesn't it?" As she reminisced, the old woman's voice waxed more wistful. "Mr. Maple, my husband, was a fine man. He worked hard all his life, conducting on trains. He didn't give me any children, but he gave me love and this house. If it wasn't for my children, for my memories of him, I'd have been alone a lot."

With that uncanny ability she had for reading the thoughts of others, Granny Maple zeroed in on Amber's major anxiety.

"You don't need to worry where Kim's concerned. You're doing the right thing. She wants to know her daddy."

Amber sat back on her chair, thinking. "None of this would have happened if Francie had told Nate the truth in the beginning. Even if he hadn't married Francie, he would have supported her and Kim as he'd been able. Even knowing him as little as I do, I know that much."

"Yes, he would've sent money."

"Then why did Francie lie to him?"

"At the time, Francie was after a young man named Kenny O'Donnell. They had their ups and downs something awful. From what I heard, Francie told Kenny the baby was his. But instead of getting him to marry her, Francie's news sent him packing. By that time, Nate was gone, too. I would imagine Francie's pride kept her from admitting what everyone could see simply by looking at Kimmy. I mean, it was obvious that Nate was the father. But once Francie took something into her head, she stuck by it no matter what."

"What amazes me is that Francie and Nate...well, you know. They hardly seem the types to be compatible."

Peeking at Amber over the rims of her glasses, Granny Maple chuckled. "Compatible? Heavens, sweetheart, compatibility has nothing to do with Nate and Francie! They were young, and all the girls went for Nate. And while Nate didn't think one way or the other about Francie—and he was certainly busy keeping himself in school—well, young men have their weak and needy moments. Not that that's an excuse. It isn't. The only excuse is that we're all human, and that we're all young at the wrong time in our life."

"It's difficult to imagine that Nate was ever *that* young," Amber scoffed. "He seems so hard."

At last, the old woman paused to look directly at Amber. "But he isn't hard. No matter what he seems, Nate is as soft as butter."

Amber would have asked more about Nate, but Kim came in. Carrying a slim carton of milk, the girl tugged herself out of her coat. As she put the milk in the small refrigerator, her long hair swung like black satin to her waist.

Amber noticed that Kim was built like Nate had been at the same age. She was tall and thin rather than slender. Amber knew she'd change, just as her father had. But in the meanwhile, Kim had that gangling awkwardness that was painful in someone so vulnerable.

Kim's eyes shone a shiny green. She perched on the arm of Amber's chair, looking affectionately at Granny Maple.

"It's sooo cold out," Kim said. "I can't believe it, Granny Maple, when you say spring's just around the corner!"

Granny Maple chuckled indulgently. "Oh, but spring *is* around the corner, sweet pea. And a lot of other good things, too."

The old woman's quick knowing glance was for Amber.

THE REST of Amber's Saturday afternoon ran in familiar grooves. After checking the stables, she settled into the comfortable couch in the family room with a stack of business periodicals. She had to keep an ear to the phone. Her secretary had the weekend off, and horse sales could pick up any time.

Amber had hired another woman from those who lived along the river. The young mother needed the job and was working out well. Still, Amber missed Francie's ability to second-guess her needs. Amber's new employee didn't give her quite the same freedom to be at the stables. Nor on the phone, selling.

Restless, Amber couldn't keep her mind on horse-trading news. Thoughts of Nate Fields, of their meeting the night before, kept intruding. If anything, their evening encounter had been more emotionally trying than their earlier meeting at the lawyer's office. Amber didn't know what to think of him. Nor had he said what he intended to do about Kim. At least, beyond his offer of monetary support, both for now and in Kim's future. Still, that offer had to mean something.

On the other hand, Amber had to put herself in his shoes. When he'd left Missouri for his sophomore year at college, he'd obviously put his life at the river community behind him. To be confronted by the reality of a daughter so many years later had to be a shock.

Only hours after finding out about Kim, Nate had arrived at Allswell. He'd considered the matter for long enough to make an offer of support. But he hadn't made any other offers—the offers of commitment and acknowledgment that Amber considered more important. She had to remind herself that he was a loner. He'd been a loner all his life. That kind of man wouldn't want a daughter. Still, he hadn't said that. And further still, Granny Maple claimed he was, despite his appearance and reputation, "as soft as butter."

A picture of Nate at nineteen, of his deeply-cut features illuminated by the scant light filtering into the cave below the bluffs... his face had been contorted with wanting.... They'd both been wanting.

Amber forced her thoughts to the sales sheets in her lap. She could not afford to let that bit of the past encroach. She had to stay sharp. Her adversary was as sharp and closed and unaccountable as she was the opposite.

Amber was in thought when the phone rang. She picked it up.

"Amber?"

That voice. "Yes, Nate."

"I've been thinking." A pause, then, a cryptic laugh. "Hell, that's *all* I've been doing."

Amber waited. She didn't know what to say.

He plunged on, confidentially. "I wouldn't know what to do with a girl of thirteen. I know she's better off with you, so don't worry that I'll contest the adoption. But I still want to support Kim financially. As I told you last night, I'm having a trust set up. You'll get a copy of the papers. You'll also receive regular monthly checks. I've tried to think about cello lessons, and, well, I don't know what she needs, but I've talked with some friends of mine in Chicago who also have a little girl. If what I send isn't enough, let me know. You've met Bernie Hirsh and he's handling everything. You can always reach me through him."

Again he paused. Amber's mind ran the gamut from confusion to relief. Kim would be hers. But Kim wouldn't know her father. Nate Fields was stepping out.

He was also talking. "For the next six months or so, I'll be in and out of St. Louis. Mostly in. If there are any problems—if you want to reach me, it'll be easiest now. Like I say, it's hard for me to know what a girl needs—what she'll need in the future. I also know her needs will change. If ever . . . well, feel free to call me. Anytime."

Unaccountably, Amber felt sadness thickening in her chest and stinging her eyes. Nate Fields was bowing gracefully out of their lives. She should have felt relief—this had to have been hard for him, too. The lonely little boy, the fighter who'd grown up on the banks of the Meramec . . .

"Amber?"

"Yes, I'm still here."

Once again, a pause stretched out. Once again, Nate spoke softly into Amber's ear. "I know you'll take good care of Kim. She'll do well with you. I trust you, Amber."

Amber barely controlled her voice. "I promise to take good care of her. I love her."

"I know you do. Tell her, uh, tell her I know she's mine."

"I will."

"Bernie Hirsh will be in touch."

"Okay."

NATE HUNG UP THE PHONE. Across the hotel suite, a pile of papers and plans waited for him on a desk. But

Nate was drawn to the St. Louis riverfront. Missouri had an abundance of rivers and streams, springs and fast and slow water. No one knew that better than he. Thoughts of the Meramec, of his earlier days wandering around eastern Missouri with his dad, were all tied up with the daughter he'd just agreed to leave behind.

It's for the best.

Nate was accustomed to silence and hotel rooms—to curling sheets of blueprints, to stacks of paper and, especially, to hard work. He wasn't used to thirteen-year-old girls and soft, loving women. He knew for a fact that he'd be bad for both.

Staring for long periods out at the view didn't help, either. The riverfront scene, the gigantic stainless steel monument that was simply referred to as The Arch, the historic bridge designed by James Buchanan Eads, the cobbled slope leading to the collection of equally historic riverboats—its beauty was lost on him.

On impulse, Nate shrugged out of the crewneck sweater he wore over a white oxford-cloth shirt and jeans. He grabbed a tweedy sport jacket, then, the worn trench coat he'd had for years. When he wanted to, he could dress with as much polish as anyone, but most of the time he didn't want to.

Outside the hotel, the air struck him as a chill reminder that winter hadn't surrendered yet. The stiff wind, rushing up off the river, up through the narrow, steep cobbled streets of the area known as Laclede's Landing, felt as cold as any he'd experienced in Chicago—a city known for its wind. He found his rental car and climbed in.

Within forty-five minutes, Nate was looking at a different river—the Meramec. And at a very different community. It wasn't quite like stepping back into boyhood, but almost. Nate felt his spirits lift at the sight of the river. Guiding his car along the road that ran along the bottomland, past the strip of houses in the woods fronting the river, was both a new and a familiar experience. Most of the structures, which were lifted a story above the ground on stone walls, were in better shape than he remembered. The usual collection of cars and pickups, of boats, with and without motors, littered the drives and waited beneath the houses.

Beaver's General Store, which was both a grocery store and the community meeting place, stood across the road, not as high, on a cinderblock foundation. Oddly enough, Nate realized that, more than any other place, Beaver's was where he'd come from. He'd already spoken to Beaver on the phone, and didn't know why in hell he was here. He got out of the car and went inside.

Now everything looked the same. The crowded interior was small, almost claustrophobic, with loaded shelves and narrow aisles. Nate could recall stacking those shelves and swabbing the aisles with a mop. Beaver worked the small meat counter at the rear of the store, while another employee, most likely an employee with blond hair and fleshy curves, ran the checkout. A bachelor, Beaver had an eye for the ladies.

Going directly to the meat counter, Nate waited until Beaver looked up.

"Nate! You old dog! I didn't think you were coming!"

Nate smiled cryptically. "Neither did I."

"Whatcha mean? Hell," Beaver added, laughing, "I never know what you mean."

Wiping his hands on a white apron already smeared with reminders of his trade, the portly, balding Beaver maneuvered from behind his meat case. "Take over for me, will ya', Mabel, honey?"

"Okay," Mabel-honey called back.

Nate knew where they were going. Beaver had a back room. He had a refrigerator full of beer and a table for playing cards. Once, a radio and cot for Nate had also occupied the room. They were gone now.

"Sit down, sit down," Beaver said, going to the fridge and taking out two long-necked bottles of beer. Nate relaxed, savoring his old friend's hospitality, open affection and gruff humor.

"So," Beaver said, sitting at the table across from Nate. Nate had done his homework at the table. "I thought we'd had our little talk day before yesterday. Was there something you forgot to tell me?"

Nate accepted a beer. He couldn't help noticing the label. A gold oval, struck with three green fir trees on a sloping mountainside, looked both familiar and old-fashioned.

Beaver noticed him examining the label. "Would you believe it? You buying out Black Forest Beer? You buying out the Brandenbergers? Don't it seem amazing?"

Nate nodded. "Yeah. It's amazing, all right. But you know I'm not going to brew beer. I'm—"

"Yeah. Rehabbing the old place. Like you said. But still, it's amazing."

The pair took a long swig.

"Still goes down smooth," Beaver said, swallowing. "And *you* own Black Forest Beer. You *own* it."

Nate couldn't help chuckling. Who better to share his triumph with than Beaver?

"I knew you'd do it one day, buddy." Studying the bottle, Beaver lapsed into nostalgia. "But I sure hate to see the last of this beer. It's always been a good beer, no matter who owned it. Ms. Reinhart sent down a few cases as a thanks for a favor I did her. I'm gonna save them for as long as I can. Won't be getting good beer like this anymore."

Nate hedged. "Speaking of Amber Reinhart, how's she taking it? Have you heard?"

"Well, she don't talk to me about anything that's personal. She's tight with Granny Maple, though. But then, Granny Maple don't gossip, either. From what I've heard, I think she's doing pretty good up there. She's making the old place into a stable, you know. Raising horses."

"Yeah, I do know that much. But what about her brother, Dolph? Doesn't he do anything?"

"Nobody knows what Dolph Brandenberger does, now that the brewery's gone. He's not a bad guy, I just don't think he's got much sense. Most everybody says they lost the brewery because of him."

Nate knew better than that, of course. Small breweries were almost extinct, even in a big town like St. Louis, where they once proliferated. They simply couldn't make a profit anymore, unless they were local and had a loyal following. And Black Forest Beer had been too big to survive on merely local sales. Caught in the shift of demographics, it had been finally squeezed out. That wasn't Dolph Brandenberger's fault. No, what Nate couldn't understand was why the guy didn't help his sister, with the horses or with Allswell.

"When you drove in," Beaver interposed, "did you notice how Ms. Reinhart's dismantling the tower at the gravel pits?"

"No, I guess I didn't notice."

"She is. And it's a good thing, too. It was a terrible eyesore. Rusted out and dangerous. We're all glad it's going. It's the last reminder of what this place used to be." Beaver chuckled. "Hell, we've even got a few yuppies moving in!"

"Yuppies?"

"Yeah. People who like to come down from the city on the weekend. They fish and putter around in boats. It's funny to see 'em meet up with the old-timers, but it's good for business. And it's damned good for the area. They keep up their places. As long as they don't buy us out altogether, we like to see 'em. I mean, those of us who want to stay on do."

"I didn't think there were many of the old-timers left."

"Oh, they're here, all right. Plenty of 'em. Of the elder ones, at least. It's hard to leave, both economically and...well, once you get the river in your blood, you can't get over it easy. Besides, what with Ms. Reinhart providing us with more work, more of us can stay on. A few have jobs at the stables, a few work the grounds. She's got old Murray and his sons farming the riverbottom property, planting crops that are grown organically for the health-food stores. She figured out there's money in it. She's a hard worker, that one. And smart as a whip."

Silence stretched out. Nate disliked talking about Amber Reinhart. Finally, he changed the subject to another difficult one. ''I guess you haven't heard anything more about my dad?''

''Naw, just what I told you. He's still working as a mechanic in Flat River. Doin' all right, last I heard. I'll tell you if I hear anything more.'' Nate watched Beaver take a long drink of beer. The guy never changed. He had the proverbial heart of gold. ''I sent him the money, like you said,'' Beaver added. ''But I didn't hear anything. I also saw to the hospital bills for Eddie Conyers' little boy. You know—''

''Yeah, I remember Eddie,'' Nate interjected. ''In high school, he was my best buddy.''

''Of course, Granny Maple won't let me lend her the money to fix her roof. I keep telling her I've got it, just like I tell the others who I think might need it. Really, Nate, you oughta let me tell some of these folks where I get the money they need for this and that.''

''No, that's part of the deal. You just let them go on thinking you've got a few extra bucks to lend them when they're strapped.''

Beaver chuckled. ''They think I get it from my winnings when I play poker at this table. People! They're funny, ain't they?''

Nate nodded, savoring his beer.

''Are you gonna see Granny Maple?''

''Not this time. Maybe later. I'll be in town for a few months.''

Beaver nodded, then excused himself. Mabel-honey called from the checkout.

Nate wondered why Beaver had never mentioned Kim to him. He supposed the river community had seen the child as Francie's, not his. Anyway, they were people who basically minded their own business. They gossiped, of course. But along the river, a man's life was his own.

Nate nursed the last of his beer. He could hear Beaver talking and laughing with somebody. A customer, probably. Nate would leave soon. For now, his gaze wandered around the old room. Once this had been home. When he'd been a kid. When he'd first seen Amber Brandenberger. She'd been cute as a button then. And while he wouldn't have known how to define it, she'd already been sophisticated.

She'd been around eight, and he ten. She'd come into the store with her father to talk with Beaver about something. Nate's own dad had recently flown the coop, and Nate had barely gotten used to fending for himself. He remembered being conscious of his worn clothes—of his tattered T-shirt, of his jeans that had been too short and too white from so much washing. Oh, he'd always been clean. Granny Maple had seen to that. But his hair must have been too long, and he'd been holding a broom he'd been using to sweep the stoop.

She had stared at him. But then, he'd stared at her. She'd stuck out her tongue at him. First he'd been mortified, and then so angry he'd stomped off. Nate had to smile at the memory.

Ever since yesterday evening, when that grown-up little girl had showed Nate a picture of his own girl, emotions had rocketed through him. He'd returned to St. Louis to buy out the Brandenbergers. He'd longed to feel the satisfaction of that. He had also wanted to see Amber, and then to forget her once and for all.

Now he had bitten off more than he could chew. While he knew he'd made the right decision in leaving Kim with her, he also felt something he didn't want to define. He didn't know what to do with a child, and he never would. But that didn't seem to matter, either. After only one night of pacing the floor, he'd decided to give up Kim. And yet he admitted he could no longer go back to his old life. He thought he'd never be able to lose himself so completely in his work again, and his work meant everything to him.

When Beaver turned in through the door, Nate drained the last of his beer and stood up.

"You ain't going, are you?" Beaver asked.

"I think I will. I've got things I have to do."

"Yeah. You're a big man, now."

Beaver's broad face with its teasing grin glowed with soft pride. Nate clapped his mentor on the back. An awkward clap on the back was the best show of emotion and gratitude Nate could muster. Here, he thought, was another good reason to give up Kim. Children needed hugs. They needed a warmth he didn't know how to give, if it existed in him at all.

Amber would be good at hugs. She had revealed her loving nature to him last night in her cozy back room at Allswell. How could he have thought she was merely a shallow woman?

Finally leaving Beaver's, Nate found it had grown dark and cold. He was hungry. He stopped by a bar he'd frequented as a teen. He remembered them serving sandwiches and they still did. He drank a couple more Black Forest beers. He watched the people he didn't know. As a youth, he'd often patronized the bar; now he didn't recognize a soul.

Outside again, the air hit him like a brickbat. He felt angry and he didn't know why. He also thought he was a little drunk. Usually, he didn't drink much, and the beer had gone to his head.

No one waited at his hotel room, he knew. He slumped in his car, letting his head clear. He thought he might go back into the bar and order some coffee. But he didn't. He twisted the key in the ignition and listened to the car warm up.

Allswell was only minutes away. The clock in the dash showed eleven-fifteen. He hadn't realized it was so late. He drove through the iron gates and up the long straight drive anyway. The old house waited as dark as sin. Nate jerked the car to a stop and, getting out, slammed the door. He rather thought he bounded up the steps two at a time, because doing so made him slightly dizzy. When he pounded on the front door, he was breathing hard and swaying slightly. The lights switching on nearly blinded him. He blinked to clear away the red lines threading in front of his eyeballs.

Focusing, Nate saw Amber standing in the doorway. She was dressed in creamy silk pajamas, with a short half-robe of the same fabric thrown over them. Her hair was disheveled and her face was clean of make-up. She looked sexy. She looked surprised. She also looked as irritated as hell.

"I want to see Kim," he blurted out.

She stood there, looking at him.

"I want to see Kim. Just once. Just once, I promise. And not right now—not this minute." Was that his raised hand, seconding his pledge?

She stood, holding onto the partly open door. Something told Nate he wasn't making sense, that he might be scaring her. He didn't like that. He started to apologize, and then to leave.

But she opened the door wider. "Come in," she said so softly he couldn't be sure he heard correctly.

CHAPTER FOUR

AMBER'S THOUGHTS RACED. To open her door after eleven at night and find Nate Fields looming on the veranda—well, if not drunk, then unusually unsteady—was disturbing enough. The intensity of his stare pierced her to her core. But to hear him demand to see Kim, after he had told Amber that he didn't intend to have any direct contact with her.... Well, dammit, it was confusing, exasperating and, yes, frightening, too.

On the other hand, Amber didn't fear Nate Fields. The ties of childhood precluded that. But his standing there, outside the door, his gaze locked with hers, forced a decision. She was tired, but, well, the wind catching in his rumpled, fur-lined trench coat revealed his jeans, his equally rumpled white shirt, his tweedy jacket that didn't quite suit him.... He made her think of a lost dog.

Of course, his stare made her aware of other things—of her silk pajamas and robe, of her thrown-together appearance. She never felt so vulnerable as she did with this man.

He followed her into Allswell's large, dimly-lit hallway.

"I'm sorry. I know it's late. It's just that, uh, I've been thinking about what you said. About Kim."

The softness of his remark, the abrupt switch from intensity to almost boyish shyness, moved Amber.

"Come on," she murmured, indicating the large kitchen at the rear of the house. As she went along, flipping on lights, her silky night things rustled in the quiet.

"You aren't here alone, are you?" he asked, the edge back in his voice.

Flicking on the bright overhead light in the kitchen, Amber set the kettle on the stove. "On the weekends, I'm usually on my own. Kim's with Granny Maple."

He nodded, frowning as she lit the burner beneath the copper kettle. "I don't cook, but I make instant coffee. Does that sound okay?"

Again he nodded. He looked concerned. "It's too isolated out here for you to be on your own."

"Like I say, normally I'm not. Only on the weekends, and then just for a night or so. I have a couple who lives with me—"

"Are the Spillbys still here then?"

"Yes."

She motioned to the large table planted in the center of the room. Crossing her arms on her chest, she leaned against the counter closest to the stove.

Everything in here was wide, white woodwork, cabinets with sparkling glass doors, and black and white tile stretching across the countertops and the floor. Only the copper pots and pans, hanging in neat formation, the plants lining the sills, added color. The stoneware mugs Amber took down from the row of cabinets were thick and white with shiny black rims. The kitchen had been assembled years ago, and even if Amber had wanted a change Etta Fay wouldn't have let anyone near it. Allswell was a throwback. Its four inhabitants liked it that way.

Amber watched Nate slip off his trench coat and toss it over the back of a chair. He sat down, his movements masculine, fascinating and somehow discomfiting. Although she'd smelled alcohol on him, she now wondered if he was feeling unwell.

Nate turned his attention to a professional examination of the room. Amber could tell he liked it, too. It was homey, charming, unique. She wondered if he mentally ticked off changes he would make, given the chance.

Instead he surprised her. "It's great. Just like I remember." He even sounded pleased.

As far as she knew, Nate had been in the house only once. She'd been twelve and he fourteen. At the time he'd been humiliated and covered with mud. But she refused to remember that now. Recollections of the boy who'd been cheated of his childhood had to be ignored. Amber had to stay sharp when dealing with this man. She didn't really know him, and to define him through her memories of him would be a big mistake. She had to think of Kim.

Indeed, it was the adult Nate who evaluated Amber with eyes as black as night. Before she could help herself, she reached unsteady fingers to the top button of her creamy silk wrapper. Trying to ignore his unreadable stare, she slipped the top button into place still thinking about Kim. Her scattered thoughts allowed Nate to speak first.

"I'm sorry if I woke you. I guess this is pretty impulsive. And you don't have to worry that I'm drunk. I had a couple of beers, and although I'm not used to alcohol—well, I don't know what's wrong exactly. This's been a shock. I was up last night, trying to decide what to do. This afternoon, when I told you that I trust you to raise Kim, I meant it. I still mean it. It's more that—''

The kettle called. Welcoming it, Amber turned and poured the water into the mugs. The brown crystals dissolved into fragrant coffee, and she handed one to Nate at the table. ''Do you use milk or—''

''No, no, just black.''

''It's decaff—''

''This is great. Thanks.''

Amber slipped onto a chair on the other side of the table. Nate stared into his coffee, and Amber studied him.

Like Kim, he was tall, and, at his stage, well-formed. Amber realized that father and daughter weren't traditionally handsome, but both had the exotic, ethnic looks favored by high-fashion photographers. Their mixed blood was a stunning, even a mesmerizing, advantage.

''When I said you'd be better for Kim than I, I meant it,'' he said suddenly. ''But something else you said stuck with me. I can't get it out of my head. Your point about Kim's need to know where she comes from—*who* she comes from. I understand that.''

Amber was torn between sympathy and a desire to tell Nate to leave things alone. But the sincerity marking his sharply sculpted features convinced her to listen.

''I know what it's like to be illegitimate,'' he said. ''I never knew my mother.''

Nate's admission was so candid, so emotionless, that it ripped at Amber more fiercely than if he'd showed pain. She couldn't reply, and he observed her levelly, unmoving, his hands absorbing the warmth from his coffee mug.

His fingers, she noted, were strong, masculine fingers. His skin was naturally darker than hers. Darker even than Kim's. A generation darker. His eyes were also truer to their shared heritage.

"What I'm trying to say," he continued, "is that I think I should meet Kim. I think we should see each other at least one time. I think that could be important to her."

"So do I."

Kim and Nate were blood. Amber saw with relief that both she and Nate were coming to grips with reality—the reality of what Kim needed.

"The fact is," he added, softly, his eyes studying her, "I think she should hear me tell her that she's mine."

Amber felt his emotions, his confusion, like a lump collecting in her own throat. She was equally confused. Equally floored. No one had ever reached her like he did, and she couldn't for the life of her explain why.

But then, they were both tired and struggling with the same bafflement. When he looked at her uncertainly, she thought the intensity of her own emotions might make her cry.

"What's your opinion?" he asked quietly. "I mean, not about my meeting her. I'm convinced that's right. I just don't know what I should say. I mean, about the.... I'm grateful you're adopting her. But is it enough that I tell her that and let the rest go? I'll be damned if I understand what my part should be.''

"I don't see any hard-and-fast rules here. To show her you care enough to meet her, that you want to at least know her.... Well, it's probably more than she's expecting.''

Nate looked dubious again, his expression withdrawn. "I don't want to raise her hopes. Just because I recognize her need to know me doesn't mean I can help her. I'm not good at this. I never will be. To get her hopes up...for her to believe I can be there for her...well, I'm more worried about that than anything.''

Now, Amber felt a tinge of resentment mixed with her confusion. She couldn't imagine having a child like Kim and not wanting more than a single meeting with her. Where were the man's feelings?

She didn't know whether to rant or to cry. Only the pain in his dark eyes kept her from doing either. "You should see Kim, talk to her,'' she said finally.

Nate sipped his coffee.

They'd each done the best they could. Beyond that, Amber didn't want to go. When Nate looked at her again, she could sense his weariness.

"I'd better leave,'' he said.

Without thinking, she replied, "You shouldn't drive all the way back downtown tonight.'

He seemed puzzled. In the middle of getting up and reaching for his trench coat, he paused.

"I mean...'' she said. *God, what did she mean?* He couldn't stay with her. Not even on a couch. She just didn't want him to drive. *Don't let people drive drunk.* That was the rule, and she still didn't know how much he'd had. "Maybe you should get a room in Concord village. There's a little motel—"

"No, I'm fine."

"Or I could call a cab. Of course, a cab takes forever to get out here."

When Amber rose too, Nate moved toward the hallway leading through the house to the front veranda.

Amber didn't know why she was so anxious for him, but she was. She started after him, when a scratching noise at the back kitchen door halted them both.

"What's that?" Nate asked, instantly alert.

"It's all right." With a smile, she reached for the knob. "It's only Gnaw," she added, letting in the silky-haired menace. "Kim's dog."

The large, immature Irish setter bounded in. He knew no strangers, and Nate was no exception. Before Amber could react, the hulk planted his paws on Nate's shoulders. Gnaw stretched his full length, his tail wagging furiously as he sniffed and licked at his new friend's face.

Losing his balance Nate stepped backwards. His head rammed into the doorjamb behind him with a thud that could be heard even above the happy whines of the dog.

"Dammit!" Nate exclaimed, holding a hand to his head.

By then, Amber had pulled Gnaw off. "I'm sorry! Usually, when he comes in at night, he's so tired from running all day that he's manageable. Really, I didn't think. I—"

"It's all right." Nate's voice sounded slightly strained. He'd gone a little white around the mouth. He looked ill.

She tugged Gnaw by the collar in the direction of the porch. "Here. I'll put him out until you leave."

"No, I can find my way—"

"No, no." *This was getting more and more awkward.*

Closing the porch door, she returned back to Nate. He was leaning against the doorjamb, rubbing at the back of his dark head, then at his neck. His trench coat was draped over his arm.

"I'm fine," he said. "Really."

She stood directly in front of him. "I don't think you should drive."

Slowly, he brought his hand down from his neck, down to where his fingertips could graze her jawline. His eyes were intense, black, holding her immobile.

"I must admit I'm a little shaky," he said softly. "Maybe I'll give Beaver a call."

She considered this the perfect solution, and wanted to say so. But her mouth, her brain, refused to function. She felt the tentative touch of his fingertips along her tingling skin. His gaze glided over her face, measuring it and remeasuring it.

"Being worried about is nice," he said slowly. The tips of his fingers moved on down, down to the top button of her silk wrapper, the one that remained fastened at her neck. "You're all buttoned up," he murmured. "Yesterday at the lawyer's office, you had caramel-colored buttons, and they were all buttoned up, too. Right up to here," he whispered, his index finger touching the silk-covered button.

Only two layers of thin fabric separated Amber's skin from his.

Amber was dizzy with sensation. Nate Fields. Nate Fields could do what her husband hadn't been able to do. Nate could make love to her. Nate had been making love since he'd been a teenager. She wondered how many women he had pleasured with his well-cut lips and his large, dark body. For some reason, the unbidden thought thrilled her.

One day, long ago, Nate had awakened Amber to her own sensuality. Feelings her own husband had never been able to arouse in her. Fleeting images of what could be possible with Nate ...

Nate tilted his head. Very gradually his face dropped nearer to hers, his shadowed eyes half closed. He bent to taste her bottom lip, to rub it with his. His move was slow and sexy, but not intimate. Amber knew enough to recognize the difference. She wondered if he sensed her need. Or was he simply responding to a need of his own?

At that thought, Amber stepped back, bumping into the other side of the doorjamb. She walked away and briskly snapped on a light in the family room.

"You can call Beaver from here," she said, indicating the phone. "I'll go upstairs and pull on something to follow you down to his place."

Nate tried to protest, but she put up a hand to silence him. She kept moving. She had to. Almost out of the family room, she glanced back and saw him watching her, his expression puzzled. How could Nate know she was a complete novice at the games men and women played?

NATE PACED the cozy family room at Allswell. It was after midnight, and he was feeling worse and worse. His head ached from when the dog had rammed him into the kitchen doorjamb. And while he wasn't feeling the effects of the beer anymore, he supposed his state was more emotional than physical.

He knew he'd allowed himself to become unusually agitated. That Amber wanted to follow him to Beaver's added to his turmoil. On the other hand, he realized she was right: he wasn't up to driving into the city.

And then, there'd been that little kiss, that little pass he'd made over her soft lips. He was a mature man, and in the overall scheme of things tentative kisses meant little. *But it had seemed so sweet.* Of course, she'd merely felt sorry for him, and he wasn't accustomed to having someone care. Why couldn't he just leave it at that?

"Because it was so damned sweet," he muttered, peering out the glass-paned doors that opened onto a small balcony.

Besides, there'd been something else. Something as needy in her as in him.

Beyond the mirroring windows, the night was pitch black. He'd forgotten how dark the country could get. He disliked the idea of Amber following him to the river community below the bluffs in the dark. That she rattled around at Allswell on her own bothered him enough.

Allswell. It never changed. He remembered stories about it, told by the old-timers along the river and the local farmers. That one day, long ago, when old man

Franke had carved out the circular drive with his mule, Jackson, had become a local legend.

"Sorry," Amber called, interrupting Nate's memories.

Taking in her appearance, he felt unreasonably affronted. The intimacy of her silky, cream-colored pajamas and mussed hair was gone, replaced by utilitarian jeans, sweatshirt and jacket. Her attitude, as well, was newly formal.

"I'm ready," she said, reinforcing the distance she'd already put on with her clothes. "I'll go out the back way. My car's in the garage. You can drive yours around, and we'll take the road down the bluffs."

"I'm all right," he said stiffly.

But she didn't buy that. She swept out.

"And what about locking up?" he called after her, following her into the hallway.

"We hardly ever lock up. This is the country, remember?" she replied over her shoulder. "Besides, I'll be back in a few minutes. Everything'll be fine."

Disgruntled, Nate went out the front door as he was told. By the time he'd coaxed his cold vehicle around to the back of the house, she had lights on, shining from the kitchen porch and the large, four-car garage. Back here, a smaller cobbled courtyard mirrored a similar one at the stables beyond. Here, too, iron gates set in stone walls were emblazoned with enameled ovals depicting the logo of Black Forest Beer.

Finally, Amber eased her old Mercedes out of the garage. Nate fell in behind her, his headlights cutting through the night, carving slices of a scene he knew by heart. Beyond the stables and the broader open ex-

panses of quiet paddocks and pastures, a large woods
waited. The woods blanketed the bluffs that stood
over the river and the small community below. Once
again, as far as Nate could tell by the beam of his
headlights, nothing had changed.

Entering the woods felt like entering a fan-vaulted
tunnel. As the two cars wended their way down the
narrow curving road, bony branches scraped overhead. The people who had worked at Allswell had
used this road to go back and forth to their own
homes. The trip reminded him of Allswell's ties to the
past.

When Amber reached the bottomland at the base of
the cliffs, she picked up speed. Nate kept up. Here,
woods thinned out along the side of the road that
paralleled the river. Houses, perched on walls and
stilts, and mostly dark now, nestled in the bare, de-
ciduous trees. On the other side of the road, Nate
again sensed the stretch of open spaces, of fields
owned by the Brandenbergers, waiting for cultiva-
tion. Fleetingly, he wondered why Dolph Brandenberger didn't seem to be involved.

Nate followed Amber's car into the parking lot at
Beaver's. Beaver had a tiny house just behind the grocery store. A porch light signaled that he was await-
ing their arrival. Parking next to Amber's car, Nate
shut off his engine and got out. When Beaver appeared in his door, Amber, too, got out of her car, although she left the motor running.

"Hey, there," Beaver called. "You all right, old
buddy? Hi, Ms. Reinhart."

The portly, balding Beaver was still dressed. The
blue flicker of a TV in the room behind him indicated

he'd been up when Nate had called. When Nate reached the porch, just behind Amber, Beaver clapped him on the back.

"Are you all right?" the man repeated, his gentle concern touching Nate as deeply as Amber's had earlier.

Nate shifted uncomfortably. Admittedly, he felt off, but he wasn't sick. "I'm fine," he assured his old friend.

"I didn't think he should drive back downtown," Amber explained with a smile.

"Come in, come in," Beaver said.

"No," Amber replied. "I've got to get back. But I do think," she added with a second smile Nate coveted, "it's time you called me Amber. I realize we've never known each other well. Not until lately. But you really should call me Amber."

Beaver grinned readily. "That's fine by me, Amber. And thanks again for the beer you sent. Like Nate can tell you, I've been enjoying it bottle by bottle."

Amber turned away. "When you found the people for dismantling the gravel pit tower, I appreciated it. The way I see it, we're in this together. 'Night, now."

Walking back to her car, she got in and changed gears. Nate and Beaver watched her reverse, the elder man rapping at Nate's shoulder again.

"You okay?"

"Dammit, I'm fine. Sorry," he quickly amended. "I just want to use your couch."

"Fine by me. I'll get you a blanket and a pillow. Nothin' fancy, you know."

Inside, the rooms were few and small but fairly tidy. When Beaver padded off, Nate collapsed on the couch.

God, he wasn't exactly sick, but he sure felt like hell.

"So, what's the matter, do you think?" Beaver asked, returning to switch off the television, and to drop a blanket and pillow next to Nate.

"Just tired."

"When you left here earlier, you said something about gettin' something to eat."

"Yeah." Nate let his head drop to the back of the couch. He peered up at Beaver's face, now only partially visible in the light of a single squat lamp. "I guess I'm not used to beer anymore."

The men stared at each other for a moment. Then Beaver announced he was ready to call it a night. Tomorrow was Sunday, and although he didn't open that day he usually went fishing or for a boat ride, even in the cold. No matter what the season, river people enjoyed the river.

"Why didn't you tell me I have a daughter?" Nate asked, surprising himself. Lord, he was losing it.

Beaver shifted his stout body on slippered feet. "So that's it. I was wondering."

"Why didn't you tell me?"

"What in hell? You know I don't interfere. I may gossip as much as the next guy, but I don't carry tales about those I care about. I care about you. I care about Kimmy. And I don't interfere."

Nate passed a hard hand over his forehead, across his hair and skull. His head pounded steadily now. "I'm sorry. I know you don't mess in other people's business unless it does some good."

Beaver also relented. "You remember how people are down here. Oh, maybe not so much anymore. But certainly ten, twelve years ago. Back then, Francie was saying the kid was Kenny's, and we let her say it even though no one believed it. She was runnin' on pride, and we let her. Nothing's ever been said otherwise. Not openly."

Nate nodded. He understood.

"So, Amber's gettin' it all out in the open?"

Again, Nate merely nodded.

"She's a good one, that one. And Kimmy?"

"She's been told."

"So," Beaver said, "whatcha gonna do about Kimmy now?"

"Hell, I don't know."

"Knowing you, I guess you're gonna pay Amber something."

"Yeah."

"Well, then, what else? No one expects anything else. Kimmy'll do fine with Amber, and you can go on with what you do. It's good for everybody. Better 'an what some kids have nowadays."

Nate rubbed his head again. "Yeah, I guess." But he still wasn't sure what to do about Kim—or about Amber.

CHAPTER FIVE

ON SUNDAY MORNING, Amber hoped to sleep in. Kim remained at Granny Maple's and Allswell was quiet. Amber decided she deserved a lazy morning, but when the phone rang she groped for it anyway.

"Amber? This is Lillian."

Amber stifled a groan. "Hi, Lillian."

"Are you still asleep? I didn't intend to wake you."

"No, no, I'm awake." *Shades of Mr. Nice Guy*, Amber thought, sitting up and trying to concentrate. She should have said, "Yes, I want to sleep, but I'll be happy to call you back." Still, her opportunity had passed. "What's up, Lillian?"

"Have you seen Dolph yet? Friday, after that horrible meeting with the lawyers and Nate Fields, you told me you'd see Dolph."

Amber might have anticipated that this topic would be raised. "No, I've called him, but I haven't seen him."

"And what did he say?"

If Amber hadn't heard the concern in her friend's voice, she would have slumped back into her large four-poster, in her large bedroom, and gone back to sleep. She liked Lillian. Lordy, she'd known her forever, and she heard the worry.

"Lillian, I think he's fine. He's just being Dolph. You know how Dolph is."

"Yes, but this is different. He blames himself for the brewery going under. I think you'd better go see him, make sure he's all right."

Good Lord, how many times had she gone around and around with Lillian Hewlett like this? Why in the devil couldn't she just say no? But instead, Amber answered as always, "*Yes*, Lillian..."

OF COURSE, Amber couldn't say no to Lillian. She just couldn't. On top of everything else, Lillian's call aroused Amber's feelings of guilt. While she had spoken with her brother, she hadn't expended any real effort. He had said he was okay, and she had accepted that.

After hanging up the phone, Amber got out of bed and dragged herself to the bathroom. She had the same room, or rather, the same set of rooms she'd always had at Allswell. Since her return home after her divorce, she'd redecorated, changing the pinky, girlhood colors to soft apricot, cream and jade.

She had retained the fine antique furniture, the mahogany four-poster and chairs and bureau and dressing table. In her sitting room—or, as she now called it, her private office—a large window overlooked the western countryside, and her desk sat squarely in front of it.

A large bath and a dressing room completed her suite. The rooms were comfortable and commodious, but more than that, they were home. She couldn't help loving them.

She also couldn't help fearing she might lose Allswell one day. She invariably worked until she was exhausted, winning no more than a single month at a time. The sale of the brewery would give her a bit of leeway, but she couldn't coast. Not even for the weekend.

Still, she'd steal a little more time today. She'd visit Dolph. She'd even be nice and call Lillian afterwards. The evening she'd share with Kim. Tomorrow, she'd get back to work.

With that neatly decided, Amber also determined to sweep any thoughts of Nate Fields out of her head. She decided to discount the brief kiss he'd given her. Even though that kiss had awakened startling possibilities, that, too, she'd put out of her head. She had enough on her mind, and the ball with Kim's name on it was in Nate's court. That was all she needed to know.

Casually dressed, Amber drove into midtown to see her brother. He lived in an old high-rise apartment building, a block or so from Forest Park in the University City area. He'd lived there, in contented bachelorhood, since he had graduated from college and returned to St. Louis to work at the brewery with their father.

Adolphus Brandenberger was a year younger than Amber, and she'd always accepted him just as he was. Some considered him eccentric, reclusive and thoroughly inept. And, to be honest, he was. He answered his door in his slippers and robe, his hair, which resembled hers in its deep, nutty-brown color, ruffled from sleep. She immediately felt the old desire to mother Dolph.

"I brought some doughnuts," she said. He took the sack with his free hand; the other held his glasses and Sunday morning paper. "So, you like plaids, do you, Dolph?" she said, smiling. His pajama top and bottoms clashed wildly with the multicolored grids on his robe. "I'll have to remember that at Christmas."

Sweeping on by him into the vestibule, she entered the musty, book-lined living room, stepping carefully around the stacks of books piled on the floor. A large pleasant room, it presented the usual mess. Dolph had maid service, so the room wasn't so much dirty as cluttered.

Also, neither a television nor a radio could be heard. Dolph's apartment rested utterly quiet. It was a sanctum, a retreat organized for reading. Magazines, periodicals, car manuals, cereal boxes, anything printed: Dolph read it. He regularly walked to the nearby university, devouring the contents of its libraries and bookstore like a bookworm through ancient paper.

Needless to say, for all his unprepossessing appearance, he had a very high IQ.

"I haven't made coffee yet," he said, trailing after Amber through the dining room and into the kitchen—the doughnuts, his glasses, the newspaper still in his hands.

"I didn't think you would have," Amber admitted, stopping in the middle of the kitchen.

Because it was never used, the room was immaculate. Dolph didn't prepare meals. He simply ate when he realized he was hungry, usually at the diner down the street. In fact, that's where they normally met when Amber gave him a call to remind him of her existence.

"Do you even own a coffeepot?" she asked, her gaze running over the empty countertops.

"I don't think so."

"Then why did you say you hadn't made coffee *yet?*"

"Uh, did I say that?"

Amber heaved a sigh. "I should have brought some. I knew it."

Opening the refrigerator, she held her breath. Empty. Clean, well-lit, but empty. "You might as well unplug this," she said, turning to him.

"You mean, uh, it's plugged in?"

"Oh, Dolph. You're barely functional. You should at least have some milk or orange juice. People need liquids. How about a few cans of soda? Or some designer water? What do you drink when you're at home?"

He shrugged, his hands full. "This and that."

Amber's heart wrenched. At thirty years of age, her brother was like an old man. She simply didn't know what to do. She knew that Dolph cared about her. And she loved him. She wanted him to be happy—*to do something.*

What was it with Dolph? He was a rabbit cast into city streets, helpless and lost. And now, well, his half of the money from the brewery sale would keep him going, but....

She examined him more closely. In his own way, he was really quite cute. "Dolph," she said gently, "are you still upset about the brewery? You realize we had to sell it, don't you? We didn't have a choice."

Dolph smiled disarmingly. "No, Amber. I don't understand. Why don't you explain it to me again?"

Oh, yeah, he was cute all right. Amber backed off. "Sorry. I don't mean to mother. It's just that I'm worried about you."

"But there's nothing to worry about. I'm fine."

But you aren't fine, you dolt! She wanted to shake him. But shaking him would do as much good as shaking a pillow.

"Okay, okay," she said, forging on to the next topic. "Lillian called me this morning."

His bewilderment was reflected in his brown eyes. "Lillian?"

Patiently Amber waited.

"Is she worried, too?" he asked feebly.

"Of course she's worried. Why haven't you called her? You know she phones me when she can't get what she wants from you."

"I, uh . . ."

"Just say you'll call her, will you?"

"Okay."

"And when you do, for heaven's sake, make it clear that you're all right. You know I've never wanted to interfere in—in whatever it is that you two have had going since you were kids. But please, Dolph, talk to her so she leaves me alone."

"We haven't had anything going since we were kids."

"Then what was all that near-engagement business, not once, but three times?"

"Was it three times?"

"Okay," she said, marching past him. "I'm leaving. But I'm warning you," she added, pausing at the kitchen door, "if you don't call Lillian and convince her you're all right, I'm coming back."

Sometimes, Amber thought as she pulled the apartment door shut behind her, *self-assertion is damned satisfying.* It was too bad she only managed it with Dolph and Lillian.

On her drive out to Allswell, she grappled with her worries about her brother. If he could only find a niche for himself. But then, how could he? All the information Dolph had filed away in his dusty brain was obscure and impractical. If his own father hadn't employed him at the brewery, he would have been fired time and again. Dolph fit the corporate world no more than he did the blue-collar rank and file.

At one time, Amber had thought he might teach at the university. He had loved rattling around Washington University. But he had never settled on a subject. Then a career in research had been suggested. But Dolph wasn't organized enough to be a researcher.

Amber sighed. She supposed she should let him be. Her parents had. But then, her parents had neglected them both. She and Dolph had always needed more than their parents had provided. Both children had been sent to the best boarding schools, and they had always had all the material comforts that money could buy, but their parents had always remained emotionally distant from them.

Their mother had been a born socialite. She'd been one of the ladies who lunch and entertain, one who tends herself as an occupation. Amber's clearest memories of her involved shopping bags and waiting chauffeurs and quick pecks on the cheek.

It had been Allswell that had given Amber roots and stability, she reflected as she drove through the gates. It was no wonder she loved it.

The sight of Gnaw rushing out of the woods and heading pell-mell for her car greeted her. He jumped on her as she got out.

"Down, down, you big lummox! I swear, Gnaw! As soon as I have time to find an obedience school or maybe an oriental gourmet— *Down!*"

With a final lap of a tongue to her cheek, the setter dashed off, back toward the woods. Gnaw chased mail trucks, delivery trucks, school buses, all small animals—anything that moved on wheels or feet—with the same exuberance. He intended no harm. He was simply having fun.

Promising herself she'd do something about him, *soon,* she went inside just in time to hear her message machine in the family room.

"I guess you're not there. If you will, I'd appreciate a call back. My number—"

Amber grabbed the receiver. "I'm here, Nate. I just got in. I didn't hear the first part of your message."

"Oh, hi. I, uh . . . I've been thinking."

"Are you feeling better then? Last night you looked a little green around the gills."

"No, no, I'm fine. I'm at work, in fact. But I thought I should drive out this afternoon. To see Kim."

Amber hesitated. She didn't know what to say. Her feelings were ambivalent. Still, if he wanted to see Kim . . . "Are you sure you're up to it? Have you had enough time to think about this?"

"My God, I can't think about anything else until I get this straightened out."

"You've only known about Kim since Friday and this is Sunday, and I—"

"No, I want to get this over with." The finality in his voice silenced her. His next words were spoken softly. "One favor, though. Would you sit in? I've never talked to, well, to any child, really. I have no idea what to do."

Amber softened. "I'm sure you'll do fine. Kim's a great girl. Ever since I first told her about you, she's been looking forward to meeting you."

"I guess she's always thought Kenny O'Donnell was her father, huh?"

"I don't believe Francie ever said that to Kim. Not exactly. But Kim must have heard something about both you and Kenny. She's been with Granny Maple a lot. Not that Granny Maple would gossip, either, but..."

"I understand. It's all so damned awkward. So damned—I don't know. I'm only afraid I'll make it worse."

"No. That's exactly why I wanted a fresh start. I had to wait until Kim recovered from her initial grief over Francie. But now it's time to begin with a clean slate. I'm convinced of it. I have been for a while now."

"Yeah, well, I'm glad she has you. I only hope I don't screw things up."

"You won't," she assured him. "What time can you come?"

"Is later this afternoon all right?"

"Anytime's fine. I have to pick her up in a little bit."

"Well, maybe I'll drive out sooner."

"Okay."

In spite of her assurances to Nate, Amber felt uneasy as she hung up the phone. She couldn't help feeling he was rushing things.

At least, the house would be quiet. Etta Fay and Mick wouldn't be back until evening. Nate didn't need an audience when he met his daughter for the first time.

Later, when Kim climbed into the Mercedes outside Granny Maple's stilt house, Amber took a deep breath. This was what she had wanted.

A fresh start for Kim.

The truth out in the open.

A possible relationship with her father.

Glancing at the girl beside her, she took the next step.

"Your father called me this morning."

"He did?" Kim exclaimed. Hope radiated from those shining green eyes.

"He wants to visit."

"He does? When?"

"He'll be here sometime this afternoon. Is that okay with you?"

Kim didn't hesitate. "Yeah, sure!"

Amber reached over to Kim's long, frail fingers. She got a squeeze back in response. Amber was always amazed that Kim had the strength to play the cello. To press the tight strings against the fingerboard, to achieve the right grip on the bow, required great strength in the hands, and Kim's hands felt like a collection of twigs to her.

Then Kim met Amber's eyes. "I'm okay," she said, her expression still bright.

Amber's heart sank. Kim had grown up too fast. She'd gone through too much. The likelihood that Nate Fields might be what the thirteen-year-old needed seemed remote.

But it was too late to think about that now. As she turned into the drive, with Gnaw racing along beside the Mercedes, Amber glimpsed Nate's rental car in her rearview mirror, approaching the iron gates to Allswell.

THE FEBRUARY AFTERNOON light was harsh, emphasizing the dark exterior of the house and its enormous overhanging roof. The sun shone starkly on the expanse of dead, brown grass that extended to the lookout. The latter, a flat space at the very edge of a bluff just beyond the house, afforded a splendid view of the river below and the countryside beyond.

Nate followed Amber's car into the circular drive in front of the veranda. His heart thudded deep and hard. He got out of his car, shoving his fists into the pockets of his coat. He thought he might look a tad scruffy for meeting his daughter. *His daughter.*

Ahead of him, Amber stepped out of her car, while a tall, dark-haired girl struggled with the dog that had pinned him to the doorjamb last night in the kitchen. God, had it been just last night? This was all happening too fast.

Leery that the red-furred menace might target him next, Nate greeted Amber with a sideways glance. And sure enough, as she returned his greeting, the dog lunged delightedly in his direction, fur flying, tongue lolling. Only Amber's sharp command made the dog veer away, to dart past Nate and off toward the stables.

"Sorry," Amber said, as they faced each other.

Apparently, Amber's uneasiness matched his. Then, his anxiety was compounded. The slender girl in a knitted cap, casually dressed like Amber and himself, came around the Mercedes to join them. Nate sensed her hesitancy.

Fortunately, Amber remained composed enough to speak.

"Kim, this is Nate Fields."

Kim stretched out a finely-boned hand, and Nate took it, his eyes meeting the deep green of hers. The contact hit him like a blow to his belly. While she was shorter than he, her build was similar. Her hair—long, black strands falling from beneath her cap—was the same color as his, although her skin was fairer. Her eyes were as green as Francie's had been. But the rest—her expression, her reticence, her frame and features—were his own, rendered with a youthful feminine delicacy.

Kim's picture hadn't prepared him for this reality. This was his daughter. He was responsible for her existence on the earth.

Amber's voice penetrated his reeling senses. "I just picked up Kim at Granny Maple's. You remember Granny Maple, don't you, Nate?"

Surely, his brain had turned to mush. "Uh, yeah." He thought to release Kim's hand. "I remember Granny Maple. How is she?"

Kim smiled at him shyly. When she spoke, fairly levelly, his heart did a flip-flop. "She's supposed to go into the hospital for some tests, but Amber and I can't budge her from her house.''

Amber smiled encouragingly at both Kim and him. ''What Kim is saying, in a nice way, is that she's as stubborn as ever.''

As if he were thirteen, too, Nate shifted his weight. ''I'll have to, uh, drive down and see her.''

''Why don't we go inside?'' Amber said.

But they were distracted by a pickup coming up the drive and swerving to a halt beside them. Nate recognized the Spillbys as clearly as if he'd seen them yesterday. Mick greeted Nate with a warm handshake from the cab window of his truck, while his wife jumped out and rushed over to them.

''Nate!'' Etta Fay exclaimed, hugging him firmly against her ample figure. ''By gosh, I haven't seen you since you were nineteen! It's high time you came back.''

Nate didn't know what to say. He mumbled a greeting.

Again, Amber saved him. ''What are you two doing home so early?''

''Got that guy picking up Firefly today,'' Mick explained. ''Got to thinkin' he might have some trouble. Firefly's never trailered too good.''

''That seems a shame,'' Amber replied.

''Naw, naw, I'd rather be here than worry about it. See ya later, Nate. Kimmy, honey.'' With those words, Mick drove off in the direction of the stables.

Nate turned back to Mick's wife. He could read the warmth in Etta Fay's eyes. She was genuinely glad to see him, and he realized again that he'd neglected some people who'd cared about him at one time.

"You sure have filled out nice," Etta Fay said, her gaze running him up and down appreciatively. "Lordy, lordy, how many times did I sit you down at the kitchen table, right here at Allswell, and make you eat something? I'm glad you're not so skinny anymore."

Nate realized that Amber couldn't have known that he'd ever sat down at her kitchen table. And while Etta Fay would never intentionally embarrass him, he was embarrassed.

"See, Kimmy, honey?" Etta Fay said. "You'll fill out just as nice as your daddy has. Just wait and see."

Daddy. Nate cursed himself for his thoughtlessness. He should have brought something—some candy, a stuffed animal, something.

Again, Amber intervened to prevent an awkward moment. She herded them into the house. There, all of them got out of their coats, and Etta Fay finally retreated to the kitchen.

Nate drifted after Amber and Kim into the family room. With a fire newly lit and crackling on the hearth, it felt as cozy as ever. But the scene actually heightened his unease. This house had always been a problem for him. And this woman, too. He was always on uncertain ground at Allswell.

And now there was Kim. Sitting across from him on the couch with Amber, she observed him steadily, with some apprehension. Emotion continued to compound emotion. They threatened to overwhelm him.

Amber was making small talk about Kim's life, but he couldn't seem to keep up. She was explaining Kim's cello studies. What in hell did he know about classical music? And then Amber talked about Kim's school and her music teachers and her dog, of course. It was all foreign to him, as if he'd been dropped into a dream.

Once again, he had to hand it to Amber. She carried on like a trouper.

"No, no coffee, thanks," he heard himself say.

He wanted to run.

"Look, uh," he began, forcing himself to face Kim.

He'd learned to face boardrooms full of people. He knew how to sell an idea, or even a whole project, but he had never confronted anything like this in his life. All he could remember was the relief he'd felt that day when Francie Gibbons had told him that the child she carried was not his. Gazing at Kim's slightly flushed features, he wished he could grasp something solid, say something perfect.

The impact of his own selfishness, of his having put the pregnancy so completely from his mind, blocked his ability to function. However, he'd started, and he had the attention of the two pretty women who observed him, waiting for the gems to fall from his lips. With a deep breath, he plunged ahead.

Looking right at Kim, he said, "I, uh, I'm happy that I've gotten to meet you today. I think you're a beautiful young woman, and you have all the talent and…well, all the wonderful qualities any man could ask for in his, er, daughter."

Nate heard his heart pounding. No wonder Francie had been unable to tell him the truth. He wouldn't have wanted to hear.

"I'm happy you have Amber," he managed to say, "and I'm glad about the adoption. I can see the two of you are good together. I know you'll make a go of it, and . . . Well, if you ever need anything, Amber knows how to get in touch with me.''

His meaning was clear. He was finalizing a chapter he hadn't known he had written. He was, none too neatly, trying up the loose ends. At least for himself. The rest he'd leave to Amber and Kim.

He felt wretched. The void in him had never gaped so wide and empty. He felt helpless to do anything about it. He couldn't possibly belong to anyone. He never had.

With a final demonstration of true grace, Amber let him off the hook with a few kind words and an arm around Kim's shoulders. Kim smiled shyly but said nothing. Oh yeah, they'd do fine together. He only wondered if he would ever be fine again.

As he abruptly departed Allswell, he thought the house and all it represented to him had taken its final revenge. Now, he could never leave it completely behind. His daughter, his blood, was tied to it as surely as were the darkest corners of his own soul.

CHAPTER SIX

AMBER HAD COAXED Granny Maple into the Saturday afternoon sunlight, to walk with her and Kim along the river. The elderly woman leaned heavily on Amber's arm, rocking into her next step and shifting her weight rhythmically with every movement. Ahead of them, in the area that had been set aside as a community park, Kim wended through the trees. Soft light glimmered on the river surface, filtered through the newly budding leaves, brushed the grass beneath their feet a luminous green.

"Are you sure you're warm enough?" Amber asked.

Although Amber worried about the woman's general neglect of her health, she wouldn't nag her. Not on such a pretty day.

"I'm fine," Granny Maple said, "I'm glad I came now. I don't like to go out unless I have to, and this is very pleasant."

"When you're ready to go back, tell me."

"Don't worry about me, lambie pie." The old black woman's grin dimpled her cheeks. "You know I'm not shy about saying what I think."

Amber chuckled, glancing ahead to check on Kim's progress.

"So, how's she doing?" Granny Maple asked.

It has been six weeks since "that weekend," as Amber thought of it. That weekend in February, when they'd sold the brewery and Nate Fields had come and gone from their lives. Granny Maple knew they hadn't heard from him since, and here, the first signs of spring burst into life around them.

"Kim and I talk," Amber said. "And I know you keep talking to her, too. She acts as if she's doing fine. But then, that's the way she always is. She's had to grow up too fast, and she's learned how to control a lot. Sometimes I want to grab her and hug her tight. I want to tell her to let her bottled-up emotions out. And yet, when she talks to me, she seems fine."

"I know what you're saying, but don't worry. It's just that the wound is still fresh."

Comparing Kim's experience with Nate to a wound upset Amber. Even so, Kim must be hurt. To meet and part from a father she'd never met before, in so short a time...

The parting had been so final and so clean. Oh, he'd said all the right words, but...

"And you, sweet pea?" Granny Maple looked at her shrewdly. "You've never told me much about how you felt that day. Are you ready to talk about it yet?"

"It's not how I feel, but how Kim..."

"I know that. But you were affected, too. You've just been holding on for Kimmy's sake."

Amber watched the grass passing slowly beneath their feet. Granny Maple's sturdy shoes matched the well-worn appearance of her own boots. Lately, she was always in boots and jeans and bulky, handknit sweaters.

"It wasn't so much what *I* felt that I remember," Amber finally admitted. "Of course, I tried to protect Kim, but...oh God, it was horrible for Nate. He looked like an animal struggling in a trap. For Kim's sake, I was angry with him. But for his sake, I was relieved to let him go. And, boy, did he go."

They walked a bit more before Amber began again. "His checks have started coming. Very regularly, each month. I've also gotten the papers from his lawyer, Bernie Hirsh, about the trust."

She paused again for a few more steps. "That day, Nate was really sweet to Kim. He told her that he could appreciate what a wonderful girl she is. He let her down easy."

"You're just upset that he had to let her down at all."

"Yes, and I really do know he had to do that. He felt he had no choice. But still, there's a part of me that's so mad at him."

There, she'd finally said it.

Granny Maple nodded. "Mmm-hmm. And I'm sure you also understand why he felt he had no choice."

Amber heaved a sigh. "Intellectually, I do. He never had a family, so he can't know what a family is. He's had to build himself, from the ground up, and to build that part of himself that would enable him to be close to people must seem impossible. Besides, I gave him the choice as to how much he'd be involved in Kim's life, and I can hardly go back on that by disapproving of his decision. I guess it's more that I don't see how he can turn his back on a girl like Kim. I know it's all very emotional, and I'm trying to be patient, but....

Well, I guess it's just easier for him to ignore the whole situation.''

"Oh, but he isn't ignoring the whole situation."

Amber stopped short. The old woman smiled up at her.

"No, no," Granny Maple assured her, "I haven't heard any more from him than you have. But I know that boy of mine. He's wrestling with this like you wouldn't believe! Oh no, even for all of six weeks, he's not ignoring this. And he certainly hasn't forgotten.''

Amber had other concerns about Kim—worries about how she was adjusting at school and her apparent lack of friends her own age. And then, there was the business about her cello lessons. But she didn't voice them. She and Granny Maple had begun to move forward again.

They neared the large, low structure that overhung the edge of the river. The community had erected an open-air pavilion just last year. Kim stood inside on the empty floor, leaning on the farthest balustrade and watching the river's soothing waters flow by.

At Amber and Granny Maple's approach, she pivoted to look at them with a happy smile. She helped the older woman up the stairs and onto one of the benches running along the sides of the quaint, airy building.

"I can't believe it's almost May," she said, gaily twirling herself around the pavilion. With matching grins, Amber and Granny Maple observed from the sidelines.

Amber chuckled. "It's not quite April, and you're thinking it's almost May."

"I love May Day River Day. It's always so much fun." Sobering somewhat, the girl wound down to a standstill in front of Granny Maple, who tugged her coat more closely to her. "Do you think I could ask my dad to come?"

Amber exchanged a look with her companion, who also seemed stunned into silence.

"Oh," Kim said, sensing their apprehension. "I know he's busy. But he's still in town. Etta Fay says he'll be in town a while longer. Besides, he knows a lot of people who'll be there. He likes Beaver. And you, too, Granny Maple."

"I know that, honey lump. But he has to be awfully busy."

"Yeah," Kim said, more subdued. "I'm sure he's very busy. He has to finish his job here so he can go back to Chicago. Building stuff is always important."

Amber heard the hero worship in Kim's voice. She also saw her attempt at putting on a brave face. It comforted Amber that Granny Maple shared her own feelings for this bright, courageous girl. But Amber's mixed feelings about Nate Fields now crystallized into a single truth. The sooner he left St. Louis, the better.

BLACK FOREST STABLES grew almost faster than Amber could keep up. As with any burgeoning enterprise, she'd learn to deal with one aspect of the business, only to find that in the process she gained insight into other areas as well. And, of course, that experience was critical. When she'd started, she'd known nothing about business or handling money or anything else except horses.

Still, she'd gained as much from her mistakes as from her successes, so she supposed she was doing something right. Fortunately she had help with the basic office work, and Mick had all but taken over at the stables. In addition to the training, he oversaw the day-to-day routine.

Amber pursued buyers. She also kept up with the market, attended shows and auctions, and chose the horses they bought. Recently, she'd decided to get into breeding, and that had become her latest challenge— although nothing much would happen now until next year.

Amber was busy. She put every ounce of energy into building on what she had. Hers was a complex, competitive business, and what she did made her happy.

Naturally, her own routine was flexible. She courted clients when she had the opportunity. But, the one thing she never missed, no matter how busy her schedule, was the horses' exercise runs. Every day of the week, she handled at least one run along the pathways through the bluffs and along the riverbanks beneath.

Amber's time spent with this horse or that was as important to her personally as it was for keeping her in touch with the animals she owned. Whenever she could, she hung out at the stables simply because she liked it there.

The oldest stables had been a part of the original Allswell. They surrounded a cobbled courtyard, complete with a circular watering trough in its center. Inside the stables, the familiar Black Forest Beer logo adorned the barred stalls. The same oval was imprinted on the doorknobs in the house, the mantels over the fireplaces, and, of course, on the front gates. The place could legitimately be called baronial; the St. Louis beermakers of generations past had been called barons and had spent their money accordingly. One felt the aristocratic shades of the Brandenbergers most clearly in their oldest stables.

"So," Amber said to Mick. She'd just ridden into the courtyard on one of her more recent purchases, and slipped to the ground. The red gelding, Jazzer, stood behind her, his flanks quivering from their hard ride. She'd put him through his paces, and gotten a sense of his disposition. "What do you think of him?"

Mick's eye was as keen as her own. "He's a little rough around the edges for a pleasure horse. A little jumpy for someone who don't know what's up."

"Yeah, I think so, too. But he's got potential. His gaits are smooth."

"Oh, he's got potential all right. I'll call Jim to walk him out."

"No, I'll walk him out." Amber started a first circuit of the courtyard, leading the horse around until he cooled down.

When she had the time, Amber liked the mundane routine. It gave her further opportunity to evaluate her horses. She had to know each individual horse in order to match it up with the right buyer. She cared about that, and figured it was worth the effort in the long run. She wanted to satisfy people. Her business would grow if she built a reputation for going the extra mile.

Turning to face the great animal, she talked to him and watched for his response in snorts, twitching ears and glancing eye contact. He was a good fellow, if, as Mick said, a bit jumpy. She'd have to give him time.

"It's all right," she crooned. "It's all right, Jazzer. We're nearly finished. I know you're new here, but it's all right."

The late March sunlight came and went, highlighting the deep reds in the horse's satin coat. Then Jim came for Jazzer and led him away. At that moment Ray Cox's car pulled into the old-world courtyard. Amber struggled to control her irritation. For all the years her family had been acquainted with his, Amber simply couldn't like Ray. Worse, she recognized his attraction to her. At least, since they'd both been divorced.

Ray Cox got out of his expensive car, dressed, as usual, in an expensive suit. Amber waited. Her English riding boots—constructed at a London bootmaker's from a wooden last they kept for her there until she was ready for her next pair—matched Ray's attire in quality. But that was all that did match. Her outfit that day consisted of blue jeans and a jonquil cable-knit sweater that Granny Maple had made for her. She was dressed for comfort, not style.

He smiled at her, strolling in tasseled loafers to join her at the watering trough. Ray was fairly nice-looking. He had admitted to Amber that his receding blond hair bothered him, but he kept himself in good shape.

"Etta Ray said I should drive on back," he said, flicking the tip of her nose with a finger. The familiar gesture tested her patience.

As he gazed around the square and the stables, his pale blue gaze hardened disapprovingly. Ray's origins, in tradition and money, equaled Amber's, but he considered himself beyond caring about such things.

"I haven't been back here in years," he said. "Doesn't change, does it?"

"I like it."

"Yeah, well, I realize you like it. You probably won't be able to keep it, though. I mean, I've heard how hard you work out here. But even with the sale of the brewery, to turn this place around and prevent it from bleeding you dry is asking too much."

Amber kept her mouth shut. She longed to ask Ray why, if that was the case, he and his father, and even Howard Hewlett, had offered her the loan she'd needed for her start. While she admitted they were loyal to her, they weren't stupid men. Now, she was glad she had turned them all down and gotten the loan at the bank.

"So, what brings you all the way out here?" she asked, not bothering to hide her impatience.

"I thought I might coax you into having dinner with me."

"You know that—"

"Yeah, I know, I know. You're too busy. You have Kim to think about, and she's still a little unsteady. I've hard all that before, remember?"

He smiled unconvincingly. Nor did he hide the annoyance in his voice. Amber kept quiet. She'd let him say what he wanted to say so he'd leave.

"Actually," he added, "I got a call from Nate Fields and I thought I should tell you about it."

Amber turned to him sharply. "Nate Fields? Why didn't he call me himself?"

"Believe me, he wasn't happy to go through me to get to you. He said something about calling here and having Kim pick up the phone. He was afraid he might upset her. Or something like that."

Amber could tell that Ray had probably treated Nate as badly as usual.

"What did Nate want?"

"A private meeting with you."

"But—"

"Now, now, don't get all protective. It's not about Kim. This time he says he wants to go over some stuff he's found at the brewery. In the president's office. Private family memorabilia or something. He wouldn't get specific, not with me. But he mentioned the portraits. You know, from your great-granddaddy on down."

"But I thought all of that was part of the deal to sell the brewery? His people said they wanted to keep the president's office intact. They want to retain the flavor there because they have to dismantle almost everything else."

"And that's what I thought, too. I said as much to him. But he insists on seeing you. At the brewery. In the president's office. As soon as it can be arranged. Naturally, I told him I'd sit in."

"No." The word came out easily this time.

"That's what I told him. I said you wouldn't want to."

"No, I mean I'll see him, but I'll go on my own."

Ray had been slouching, his hands in his pockets. He pulled himself upright. "Oh no, oh no. I can't allow that. Not on your own. We've dealt with this guy before, Amber. You've seen what he's like. If he gets his chance, he'll cut out your heart and eat it for lunch.''

"And what makes you say that, Ray?"

He seemed a little surprised by her unusual heat. Too surprised, maybe, to reply before she plunged ahead.

"Have you ever heard anything about Nate Fields to indicate he's anything but what he appears? He's a good businessman from a reputable, if not a downright admirable, firm."

"My, God, Amber! You and I have known each other too long not to say what we think. Nate Fields may have made something of himself, but we both know where he comes from."

"And where does he come from, Ray?"

He forced a hard little chuckle, apparently hoping to knit them together. "You know what I'm talking about."

"No, I don't. What are you talking about?"

"What in the hell's the matter with you? First, it's this damned stable idea, and you running around like you know something about doing business. Then, you adopt some kid from—well, from the same place that bred her half-breed father. You won't go out to dinner with me. You hardly have two words for my parents when they give you a call. What is it with you? You've never been like this."

Amber felt her time had come. "No, as you put it, I've never been like this. I've never been allowed. I've never been able to do what I want to do, and to say what I want to say, and to be what I want to be. Well, I'm telling you something, Ray Cox, and you'd better listen. For the first time in my life, I feel good about myself. And if you don't like it, it's too damned bad.''

Ray reacted as though Amber had struck him. She saw him visibly recoil. When he spoke, however, his tone verged on condescension. ''Look, Amber. I know what you've been through these last years. We all know what—''

''No, Ray,'' she said stoutly, not giving an inch. ''Who I am needs no excuse. Who anyone is, including Nate Fields and Kim Gibbons, needs no excuse. Either you accept me as I am now—as a hardworking woman with a purpose and a life I've chosen for myself—or you don't.''

Silence.

Meeting his eyes unflinchingly, Amber saw that he really didn't know what to think. Nonetheless, he tried once more.

''All right. All right. Whatever you say. Just one thing, though. Let me, as your lawyer and your friend, go to the brewery for this meeting with Nate Fields.''

''No.''

Evidently, Ray still didn't believe what he heard. With a helpless shrug, he backed off. ''Well, okay. I'll tell Dad. But he won't like it any more than I do.''

When Amber didn't budge, he turned and walked back to his car, shaking his head. Amber watched him maneuver his car through the tight space of the courtyard and leave.

Her shout was pure glee. ''Y-Y-Yes!''

She'd never felt anything like it. The mouse had roared.

CHAPTER SEVEN

IN THE CENTURY BEFORE, St. Louis had been a natural spot for brewing beer. The Mississippi, with its network of tributaries, provided both fine-tasting water and a ready means of cheap transportation. St. Louis's central location in the Midwest guaranteed a limitless supply of the necessary grains. Caves under the city offered cool storage, and the immigrant German population supplied the know-how for the brewing process.

The premises of Black Forest Beer had been established in Laclede's Landing, right on the river. The warehouses there, in the oldest commercial parts of St. Louis, had, in more recent decades, been renovated to serve smaller businesses. Apartments, nightclubs and restaurants made the area just north of the cobbled riverfront popular again.

Likewise, as the Brandenbergers had established themselves as one of the major beer-making families, they had also become one of the threads weaving through the city's history. In the last years, the turn-of-the-century facility had been designated a historical landmark.

The overall appearance of the structure remained both solid and charming. Maroon brick, dressed in white limestone trim and punctuated by forest-green

woodwork, stood intact, despite the passage of time
and changing tastes. Because the brewery was a landmark, its original flavor had to be retained when it was
remodeled, and Nate, of course, had agreed.

Nate was willing to admit—at least to himself—that
the project at the Brandenberger brewery was as much
a matter of the heart as it was of the head. The Brandenbergers' presence was as clearly felt at the brewery
as it was at Allswell. And nowhere was this presence
more distinctly felt than in the president's office on the
Landing.

From the earliest stages of planning the renova-
tion, the decision had been made to keep that one
room intact. They didn't mean to use it merely as a
showcase for the rejuvenated complex of offices and
shops and living quarters, but to rent it by the hour for
meetings, as a sort of exclusive touchstone to the past.

In his weeks spent on the premises, Nate had begun
to wonder if he haunted the room or the room haunted
him. The space brought to the surface his deep inner
turmoil over Amber Brandenberger and his past—and
now, his daughter, too. Every day, at some point, he
found himself there, absorbing the atmosphere, indulging the feelings the room evoked in him. He could
almost believe he stepped into the last century by entering its wood-panelled walls. That was part of its
appeal. He loved the dark richness of the paneling and
the oriental carpeting, the ornately carved furniture
and the imposing desk firmly rooted in the middle of
the room. The bar with its patinated brass appointments, its beveled mirror and even its spitoon emblazoned with the oval logo of Black Forest Beer
conjured up images of days gone by. Nate could al-

most hear the Brandenberger gentlemen talking with each other.

But it was the enormous stained-glass window that made the room unique. Purposely set in a southern exposure, the glass glittered at the least hint of sunlight. A masterpiece of the art, the familiar Black Forest Beer signature glowed through it: a gold oval surrounded a trio of green pines set against a hillside and a backdrop of blue sky. Above it all the name of the brewery blazed in red, old-world script. Whether in darkness or daylight, the window demanded attention. In the light, it dazzled.

Here, on a sunny spring day, Nate waited to meet his nemesis. The portraits of Amber's great-grandfather, grandfather and father looked aloofly on.

Nate knew only his own dad, and him just barely.

He recognized what he should have felt at that moment. He should have felt that he had triumphed. After all, he'd taken possession of the very heart of the Brandenberger empire. But the murky corners of his soul taunted him. He couldn't wait to see Amber again, and he admitted it. He had never expected to see her, only to take advantage of an opportunity—an opportunity that should have fulfilled his wildest dreams of finally proving his worth to the Brandenbergers and their kind.

Somehow all that had changed. Guilt had superseded victory. The burden he now carried mocked him most deeply of all. He had a daughter. He had a daughter he didn't have the guts to take care of. A daughter who had fallen to the care of a Brandenberger.

Logically, he knew his daughter was better off with Amber. But the feelings persisted. Irony wrestled with guilt. His single goal for today was to sort out as many of the newer complications as he could.

He stood in front of the window, letting its patterns of colored light fall on his face and on the shoulders of his sharpest three-piece suit. The clear glass edges permitted him a view of the parking lot below. The lot was filled with the pickups and paneled trucks that denoted a workforce.

He was early. He vaguely noted the loud ticking of the large, pendulum clock. The rhythm punctuated the ongoing round of his thoughts. His resistance to her was ingrained, practiced. He had come home to prove to himself he could forget her. He had always wanted what she represented, always wanted a woman just like her. Although their incomes had flip-flopped, he still felt like a beggar on the outside looking in. He hated himself for continuing to want.

Indulging the pain, Nate finally allowed in the memory of the incident that had started it all when he was fourteen and Amber twelve. Her dad had put out word along the river that he was looking for a laborer. Nate's dad had volunteered.

Mr. Brandenberger had wanted the top of one of the bluffs cleared and leveled to form a lookout, a place to walk or to ride and enjoy the view. The trees and underbrush had already been cleared, and the stone wall that guarded the edge had been finished. Mr. Brandenberger had hired Nate's father to smooth the ground in preparation for a spring planting of grass seed. The flat round space would remain open, wind-swept and romantic, like so much of the damned place.

Gerald Fields had borrowed the necessary tractor, a particularly rusted-out reminder of its former self that spit fumes and smoke. The late winter day was gray. The ground was sodden. Nate, his dad and the borrowed tractor barely made it to the lookout above the river before the contraption quit on them. Scanning the expanse of deeply uneven ground, Nate realized that this wasn't the afternoon to begin their project, especially with cantankerous equipment.

At that point, Nate became aware of Mr. Brandenberger and his daughter. They had come out from the house to watch the proceedings and stood at the grassy edge of the mire, huddled in their expensive coats. Nate's own coat was threadbare, an embarrassment. He jutted his chin defiantly.

Focusing instead on where his father muttered curses over the insides of the tractor, Nate tried to ignore their audience. With a wrench in the same hand that had elevated the hood of the broken-down tractor, Gerald fussed and fiddled, barely muffling his curses. Gerald was unusually good with motors, but he was having no luck that day.

Gerald Fields, tall and raw-boned, remained a determined man. Nate knew his parent's stubbornness mirrored his own. Nate's next glance at Mr. Brandenberger, and particularly at his fragile daughter, prompted the words he should have known better than to say: "It's too wet out here, Dad. The ground's too muddy, and it's sure to rain some more."

"Shuddup!" Gerald retorted just as the motor coughed into life, choking its noxious exhaust into the stiff breeze.

Immediately, Gerald was back on the seat, working with the gears and coaxing the gasping machine into the mud. Nate stuffed his hands into the pockets of his ratty plaid coat, trying not to think about the damp that seeped through to his bones.

It took only minutes for the tractor to get bogged down. If Nate hadn't been so embarrassed by his father's pigheadedness in striving against such ridiculous odds, he might have allowed himself to gloat. As it was, a furious glance from his father kept his smirk in check. In fact, Gerald's sharp command mortified him.

"What in hell are you staring at, buttwipe? Don't you have enough sense to help?"

Ignoring the Brandenbergers, Nate jogged out into the mire. His expensive sneakers, the best things he owned, were quickly coated. Still, he kept his eyes and his burning opinions to himself. At the tractor, he figured how to jump on, how to hold tight as Gerald floored the accelerator. Amid tremendous clouds of exhaust and noise, the old tractor dug itself in deeper. Gerald switched gears so suddenly that the vehicle jerked violently in reverse. Nate was tossed into the muck.

Not surprisingly, Gerald exploded with a stream of invective. "You're so dumb you could be dangerous! No help at all! None! Zero!"

When Gerald ranted at Nate to get back on, he glared at his father scathingly. Knowing that his face was beet-red, and that he'd catch hell for it later, Nate slogged to the edge of the muck. On the dead grass, he shucked off his shoes, then strode toward the drive. For all the put-downs he'd suffered, this one hurt the most. And it had to happen in front of the Brandenbergers.

Heart pounding, Nate barely heard a second voice mingling with his father's harangue.

"Nate, stop! Please, stop!"

Swinging around, Nate cut his pursuer with a sharp glance. Amber Brandenberger was running after him like a puppy, panting. "Whadda ya want, kid?"

"Your arm's bleeding."

Nate stopped. They had nearly reached the boxwood hedges that made ornamental circles in front of the large Brandenberger house. He looked at his arm. He was surprised to see that she was right. He was bleeding. Though not badly.

Unintentionally, his gaze caught in the calm regard of the smaller girl who watched him. "I'm all right," he snapped. "My arm hit the tractor when I fell off."

He swung around to resume his retreat, but much to his surprise, she followed him. "Please, Nate. Come inside. No one's home but me and my dad, and he's still out there watching your dad. I can wash you up."

Nate's wrath escalated. He didn't know how to handle the concern in this girl's eyes and voice. What did a rich kid know? Nothing! "Go away, brat."

Her stubbornness matched his. "I have bandages."

"I said to buzz off."

"No one will see. Just you and me. Besides, you're dripping."

Nate peered down at the blood that trickled over his muddy hand. He didn't care. What galvanized him was the look in those level, dark brown eyes. Amber Brandenberger seemed genuinely worried about him. Simultaneously, he despised the vulnerability her anxiety made him feel. And yet . . . and yet . . .

He didn't reply. He didn't need to. She had taken his hand and was tugging him toward the house, the house that was as renowned in the area for prestige and affluence as the Brandenberger name. Nate couldn't have said why he relented. Maybe it was his innate fascination with the unattainable. Maybe it was the girl. She coaxed him all the way to the house, up the steps to the veranda and into the hall.

All these years later, Nate could almost call up the same sensations again. A genuine amazement, an awe he'd seldom, if ever, experienced since, had suffused him. But Amber had forced him on. Softly. Firmly.

Only twelve, Amber hadn't known the sexual implications of her actions. She led him directly up through the entry to the running balcony and into her pink bedroom. Nate's brittle resentment had been shattered, only to come rushing back. The house, the girl, the suite of large rooms . . . He had seen paradise. He had also discovered his innate visual sense— an appreciation of style that had remained with him ever since.

In a way he had felt as if he belonged there. And yet, he had known only too well that he didn't. He'd plumbed the unfairness of his life. For nights afterwards, he had been drawn back again and again to the bluffs and to Allswell. He skulked around outside, staring at the lighted windows, imagining what it was like inside. He pictured what the family was doing. He thought about the daughter.

She had become his ideal. She had represented everything he'd wanted. He had both cherished her and resented her for stirring up yearnings inside him, for being so unattainable.

Soon after, Etta Fay had discovered him outside her kitchen in the dark. That had initiated his years of visiting Allswell without discovery by its family. Years of eating at the kitchen table, of listening to the sounds, of feeling the warmth and of absorbing the gentility, had spurred Nate to achieve all that he now had.

Lately he'd realized he had never really put all of that behind him. His choice now was to make his peace with the past. Today, he hoped to initiate that process. The peace offering he'd found to give Amber would be his first step away from loving and hating Allswell.

From the window, Nate saw Amber's car pull into the lot below. He smoothed his lower lip with his thumb and watched her.

She stepped out of her car in another tidy suit, this one navy with crisp white trim. The clean sweep of her rich brown hair was her most obvious attraction. Since he'd been back, he'd decided she was a beauty, but not an obvious one. That he hadn't put his finger on that any earlier wasn't surprising.

No, it took maturity for him to finally define what he'd merely sensed at fourteen. Still, his intuition had been right on. Her natural elegance made her what she was. Her eloquent little moves, her erect carriage and her ingrained sense of decorum were tempered by a natural goodness, a kindness, that she had exhibited both to him and to his daughter.

No wonder he had been chasing more obvious beauties with scant satisfaction. Amber Brandenberger was subtle, unique. She was a product of her family and place, and yet also vulnerable beneath her sophisticated exterior. That he realized this about her only now made another bitter pill for him to swallow.

Amber had disappeared from the lot below. Nate pivoted to face the heavily carved door across the brightly lit room.

She knocked.

"Come in."

He absorbed the blow of her abrupt entry, of her eyes engaging his, without so much as the flicker of an eyelash. After all this time, he still wanted her. He *physically* wanted her. But his desire was also complicated by what he was beginning to know about her. He respected her, admired her. If it had been possible, he would have liked her, too.

Oh yeah, he was maturing a mile a minute.

"Thanks for driving in," he said, walking over to shake her hand.

Her small hand in his nearly overwhelmed him, but he forced a casual smile. The smile, he could see, disarmed her.

God, Nate, but you've been an arrogant jerk!

"Come in," he said. "Sit down. I'm sure you know your way around the place."

"Well, yes, but it looks so different." Her gaze took in the large room. "Except for in here," she added, perhaps a tad reminiscently. "It's a good thing now that, once my grandfather was gone, my dad didn't use this office. That left it intact for you."

Nate dragged his attention from her lips to what she'd said. "Uh, yes. It's a rare space that got frozen in time. I think it's what convinced us to attempt the rehabbing."

Rather than continuing to study her, as he wanted to do, Nate moved to the desk and leaned a hip onto its highly polished surface. She watched. He went on. "I'm grateful you didn't drag Ray Cox along this afternoon. If I could've helped it, I wouldn't have involved him at all. But—"

"Yes, I know. He said you were afraid that if you called Allswell, Kim might pick up the phone."

His eyes locked with hers. "How is she?"

"Fine," Amber said softly, and immediately changed the subject. "How's the work here coming?"

"We're definitely under way. There haven't been too many snags. Since the outside has to be preserved true to the original, it's always interesting to revamp the inside while working within the constraints of doors and windows that can't be changed."

"It sounds complicated."

"It is. But I like it. It's challenging. And this is a really great place."

This time, he allowed his own gaze to follow hers over the room. When they looked at each other again, he was glad to see she remained unemotional. Although he wouldn't have blamed her if she had been upset, he didn't want to see her hurting. He didn't know how he would handle that. He knew that his abandonment of Kim had caused Amber pain. But it was also clear that the issue of Kim was settled. Nearly seven weeks of his silence on the matter had seen to that.

He spoke again. "Being here so much, and in this room in particular, I realized you and I have made some mistakes. Oh, not on your part, but on mine—on the part of my company. I should have seen that asking you to include the portraits of your family in the deal was way out of line, so I've arranged for you to have them back."

Amber seemed surprised. Then she surprised him.

"Oh, but I don't want them." She must have discerned his surprise, because she smiled. "I'm sort of putting the dynastic deal behind me. Allswell and I can't afford the old trappings. I have to make Allswell work now, make it pay for itself. When I see these portraits of the past generations of males in my family, I can appreciate the history, but not especially the men themselves. In fact, looking at them now, I only see that Dolph—my brother, that is—is missing. It doesn't seem fair."

She fell silent. Nate waited for her to go on.

She smiled. Wistfully. "I can remember everybody—by that I mean my dad, my grandfather, their secretary and me—searching for Dolph one day when he and I were kids. We found him under that desk you're leaning on. He was reading. That's what this place means to me—family memories. And for the most part, my family's gone. No," she added with a sigh, completely, unexpectedly open with him, "the old days are over for me. And I'm glad they are. You keep the portraits. They belong here, like the men who belonged here. Not at the new Allswell."

Nate was stunned into speechlessness. Amber chuckled. Unconsciously she moved her fingers to her throat, testing the top button of her suit jacket in a way that, to him, emphasized her vulnerability. As usual she was all buttoned up.

Fascinated, Nate watched her fingers, wallowed in the imagery, then heard her chuckle again. "I have this vision of my ancestors," she said, "all three of them, in their spiffiest business attire. That's what they did, you see—business. Not life. But they're looking down on me from somewhere, tsk-tsking to each other. I'm sure I must be in big trouble. I can almost feel it."

In what time they'd had together, Amber had never revealed herself to Nate so casually, with such trust. He seldom found himself at a loss. But he was lost. Lost in her, in the look of her, in the sweetness of her that he'd always known was there. He'd simply believed her sweetness had been buried in the realities of maturity and marriage and money.

Now he was riveted by her. Sitting as she did in this room, in the bright streamers of light passing through the art-glass window, he absorbed every detail of her. Of her exquisite profile, smooth skin.... He trembled. His ideal didn't exist; something better did.

Amber made another telltale move, a stroke of her top button.

"Tell me about Dolph," Nate heard himself say. He'd been wondering about the guy lately, enough to ask a few questions about him.

"Oh gosh, there's a subject! Dolph. He never really belonged here, but he seems lost without the brewery. I'd ask him to move in with me, but he hates

Allswell. And then, in about a week, I'd be at his throat."

"I've heard he's quite a brain."

"Oh yeah, he's that. All brain and not a practical bone in his body."

"I was reading an article the other day, in a Chicago paper. There's this guy in New York. His name is Hargrove Kandel, and the article said he's always looking for thinkers. He runs a sort of loose-knit think tank that matches up people with unique problems to people who might be able to come up with answers. Have you heard of the guy? Of Hargrove Kandel, that is?"

Now it was her turn to look taken aback, perhaps by his interest.

"No," she said, "I haven't heard of him. I don't have time to keep up with the TV news, much less with the newspapers."

Nate leaned away from where she sat. He stretched across the ornate desk, reaching through the controlled riot of color spilling in from the window onto its surface. It was time to get down to brass tacks, to his real peace offering, before final goodbyes. Picking up a ledger, he handed it to her. Then he moved back to the desk, trying to appear relaxed.

"I found that—" he explained, as, with a frown, she opened the ledger "—in this desk. In a secret compartment. Your people must have missed it, and I'm not surprised they did. I only located the compartment because I've...well, because I've been in here a lot. Anyway..."

Since she couldn't seem to grasp the ledger's significance, Nate went on. "It's a private accounting of money that.... Do you recognize the handwriting?"

"Yes, it's my father's." The light dawned. Nate wanted to make it easy, but he couldn't do much more than wait.

"I'm sorry," he said.

"You mean my father was stealing money from his own company?"

She sounded disgusted, incredulous. Nate forced himself to continue.

"As you can see, he started years ago. If you studied the figures, you'd realize that he never took too much too often. I doubt if his actions did the company any real harm, but I thought you should see the ledger. No one except myself knows about it. Legally, it's water under the bridge. But when I found it, I decided I owed you a glimpse of it before it's destroyed. I have a fire going in the little anteroom off the old private bathrooms, and—"

"No, no. I don't want to burn it. Not yet. I want to show it to Dolph."

Nate did not know what to make of that idea. "I don't see what good showing it to Dolph—or, for that matter, to anyone else—will do. I nearly burned it without telling you, but—"

"No, no." She still sounded somewhat distracted. But she also sounded sure. "I'm glad you... Thanks for keeping it a secret, Nate, but I'm going to show it to Dolph."

It took all of Nate's strength to hold himself at the desk and appear casual. He heard the clock ticking. He watched the light shifting, whispery soft, in the dark, rich room. The room had always felt and sounded exactly as it did at this moment. Steadily, time had led them to this point, to him behind the desk, to Amber sitting on a chair, recovering from the shock of the crime revealed in the ledger she grasped on her lap.

After what seemed several minutes, she seemed to remember he was there. "I guess I'd better go."

She stood, readjusted the ledger and her purse so she could shake his hand.

On his feet, Nate found himself towering over her. Once again, he felt her hand, slender and warm in his. Her skin shone tawny and golden against the duskiness of his. When he thought he also felt the soft rasp of calluses in her palm, he was surprised. But the handclasp was too fleeting. He focused on her upturned face.

"Thanks, Nate," she said softly. "I'm sorry this happened, but if anyone had to find the ledger I'm glad it was you."

With a sad smile, she turned and walked away from him. At the door, she glanced back before closing it. "Goodbye, Nate," she murmured.

Nate felt as if the world had been revealed to him simply to be wrenched away.

BARELY AWARE of her surroundings, Amber picked a trail through the mess of the remodeling at the brewery, back to the parking lot. She checked her watch, but the time didn't register. She had to look again. It was nearly three. All she could think was that she had to see Dolph.

Her meeting with Nate Fields in the old president's office seemed merely a sequence of vague impressions. Once he had handed her the ledger, and she had realized what she was seeing, she'd had only one thought in her mind. She had to get to Dolph.

On her way from downtown to Dolph's apartment she concentrated on driving. She felt as if she had discovered the key for easing her brother's regrets about failing the brewery. That Dolph wouldn't carry on the historic family tradition no longer mattered. Their own father's disloyalty to the Brandenberger heritage had freed Dolph in his turn. Amber glanced at the proof lying on the car seat next to her. She had to get to him, to show it to him.

She couldn't wait to say, "Dolph! Look at this! The brewery wasn't the be-all and the end-all, even to Dad! We loved him, yes. We respected him, yes. We did nearly everything he expected of us, yes. But look! He wasn't perfect either. See? He'd failed the place long before you or I did."

To Amber's frustration no one answered the bell at her brother's apartment. She almost jumped up and down in frustration outside his door. Just when she had this amazing, liberating discovery under her arm, Dolph would, of course, be missing.

But ringing the bell wouldn't conjure him up. In the corner of her mind, Amber suspected she was overreacting to the revelation of their father's crime. She and Dolph had always idealized their father, and here he'd been merely human after all. She simply had to find Dolph.

Back in the scant spring sunlight, Amber marched down the sidewalk, heading for her car. Where could he be?

This was so like Dolph. She'd have to go look for him, but where? In this area of St. Louis, the city was laid-back, a reflection of the nearby university, the art museum and the World's Fair park. Trees, especially big old sycamores, overhung the streets, puddling the walks with faint spring shadows.

Amber hardly noticed when she nearly collided with a male jogger. All she saw was his sweatshirt, with its scowling Washington University bear.

"Hey, sis, what's up?"

Dolph. He hadn't called her sis in years. Amber felt a rush of affection for her brother. As he steadied her on her feet, she beamed up into his brown eyes. He seemed so tall and lanky. So familiar. So Dolph. She thought she might burst into tears.

"Hi," she said. In her overwrought state, "hi" sounded silly.

Dolph eyed her curiously, wiping his face with the hand-towel around his neck. "I was just running in the park."

"I wouldn't have guessed." The intensity of her emotions almost threw her off balance. Her smile felt crooked.

"What's wrong?" The fact that Dolph actually noticed enough to say something, impressed her. Maybe now wasn't the time to discuss the ledger.

"N-nothing's wrong," she said.

He accepted that. "Can you come up?"

"For what? Something to drink?" she asked wryly, remembering his bare refrigerator.

"As a matter of fact, I bought some mineral water. The good stuff. I'll show you."

Amber hesitated. "No, I just stopped by."

"Why?"

"Why what?" Boy, now even she was doing the Dolph routine.

"Why did you stop by?"

"I, uh, had to go in to the brewery to see Nate Fields. He asked if I'd heard of someone by the name of Hargrove Kandel, and I thought I'd ask you about him."

"Hey, yeah!" A flicker of interest showed in Dolph's expression. He scratched his head. "I'd forgotten."

"Forgotten what?"

"Some people over at the university mentioned him to me. They said I might be able to get some kind of consultant work through him."

"Why in heaven's name didn't you tell me? Or call him?"

"Because he called me. A few times, in fact. That was when the situation at the brewery got hot and heavy, and I forgot to call him back. I meant to, but I erased his number from my answering machine a few times. I remember thinking I'd get it from these people I mentioned. At the university. Funny, huh?"

"More like ludicrous."

"Over the last month or so, I've seen articles on him. I should've remembered to call him, I guess." He looked at Amber. "I think I'll go up and see if I can find out how to reach him."

Having achieved that purpose without too much effort, Amber considered her next move. She won-

dered if he had called Lillian but was afraid to con-
fuse him by asking. Shaking her head, she gave him a
peck on his cheek.

"What's that for?" he asked.

"Go call Hargrove Kandel. Because if you don't,
I'm coming back."

Dolph started away from her, walking backward,
naturally. "Don't come back. Don't come back. I'll
call the guy, I promise."

Amber smirked in warning.

Dolph threw a kiss. "For Kim," he added, just as
the inevitable happened.

Dolph rammed into a woman who was balancing
her groceries while herding her two children in through
the lobby door. Amber watched him apologize, and
then take the woman's bags in his arms. Amber worried if the incident might be enough to distract him
from making his call.

She also remembered she still clutched the ledger,
and that he hadn't noticed. She hadn't told him, and
in spite of her earlier resolve, she knew why. Discred-
iting their father in Dolph's eyes wouldn't help her
brother, and she knew it.

She realized she was protecting Dolph again. And,
maybe, if he hadn't had this possibility with Hargrove Kandel she wouldn't have. Dolph needed to
move on now, and her news from the brewery might
drag him down rather than give him a boost. Besides,
why tarnish his memory of their father after all this
time.

More settled within herself, Amber allowed herself
to think about Nate Fields. That Nate was the one
person in the world to share the secret about her fa-

ther was both strange and somehow fitting. She could be sure that he would never tell anyone what he had learned. She trusted him that much. They might lead entirely separate lives, despite Kim. But no matter what happened, they would be forever bound together by the same sad secret about the last aristocratic Brandenberger.

CHAPTER EIGHT

AMBER PREFERRED taking her regular ride on one of her horses during the day. That way, she could share her evaluations of the animal with Mick when she returned. Her ride became an ideal mix of pleasure and business.

But there were times when she couldn't squeeze in her ride until later. One such evening, nearly two weeks after her meeting with Nate Fields at the brewery, she ended up taking out the newer gelding, Jazzer. At that point she wasn't interested in evaluating how his training was progressing. She simply wanted to enjoy the hour before sunset in her favorite, solitary way.

Along the level trail paralleling the river, she felt the great red stretching himself out. They'd turned back toward home, and he seemed eager to return to his stall and stable-mates.

After her rough day, Amber felt tired and a little edgy. The western sky, streaked dramatically with daring sunset colors and forbidding clouds, seemed ominous. It was very raw, very beautiful, but she had never liked storms. In the Midwest, they could blow up quickly and violently, especially in spring and late in the day.

At the pace she was riding through the thick woods along the river and below the bluffs, leaves blurred like tiny bits of chartreuse lace caught in the black webbing of the branches. The pathways were loamy and moist from other recent storms. For over a week, nothing had dried out.

Emerging from the woods, Jazzer labored, obviously tired. Amber reined him in so he could take the steeper grade up to the house more comfortably. His heavy steaming breath mingled with the fog that had already formed along the valley floor. Since he tended to be nervous, she talked to him soothingly.

His iron shoes finally struck the loose gravel of the back road. Amber pulled him up even tighter because he could lose his footing on the loose stones. She had to watch the ruts as well. Above their heads, the trees swayed, tickled by the first breezes of the oncoming storm.

Knowing that the horse would sense her unease, Amber continued to control him with steady hands and soft words. His ears, twitching back in her direction, indicated he was paying close attention.

In all of her time on the back road that ran from Allswell to the river community below, Amber seldom encountered traffic. The ruts were enough to tear out the undercarriage from any vehicle, especially that of the low-slung, jet-black Porsche that suddenly appeared behind her on the narrow climb. Jazzer danced on the sharp shoulder of the road, waiting for the slow-moving car to come abreast of them and pass by. But, even though she was unable to see behind the mirrored surface of the windshield, Amber knew it was Nate Fields driving the car.

Irritation overrode other emotions. When he finally pulled up next to her, she managed to greet him civilly. If he wanted to bow out of their lives, then why the heck didn't he do it? What was he doing here now?

"Should I drive by and wait for you at the house?" he asked.

No more than a couple of feet separated them. Jazzer's height put Amber much higher than Nate, which added to their discomfort.

Amber looked down at the intruder. "No, you'd better not go to the house. Kim's there."

When she threw Nate a sideways look, he nodded. She saw him examine her usual if somewhat incongruous attire. While she was wearing her expensive English riding boots, her gear was strictly Western. She wore workworn jeans and another sweater Granny Maple had made for her, a plain knit-and-purl pattern in a deep, almost black, blue.

When she saw him glance at the sky with a frown, she tried to reassure him. "We're fine," she said, tightly controlling Jazzer's reins.

The gelding tossed his head and stepped sideways nervously. Despite his evident dislike of the contraption moving beside them, Jazzer was avoiding the ruts with ease.

"Did you come to see Beaver?" Amber added with another glance into the sports car.

The wind was picking up, and if Jazzer hadn't been hemmed in by the car he'd have been all over the place.

"Look," Nate said, "I'll drive on up to the stables. I'll wait for you there."

Perversely, Amber wished he'd leave. At the stables, she'd be stuck with him. "No, no," she said.

"This is good for Jazzer. He needs to get used to dealing with cars."

Nate did not look convinced. "My problem is—" he said, raising his voice over the escalating rattle of the trees and the purr of his car, "—I got a note from Kim."

Her surprise must have shown in her face.

"Well, uh, it's not a problem exactly," he said, as if he'd been corrected. "It's more that I don't know what to do."

"What does she say in the note?"

"It's kind of sweet, actually." He stuck a few fingers in the pocket of his white dress shirt and pulled out an envelope. He'd obviously removed his coat and tie before driving out from work. "She's invited me to the May Day River Day. She says she's worried I won't come because of her, and she thinks I should see some of my old friends. According to her, they all want to see me, and she believes that, if I do come, we can make everyone feel comfortable. She says we can show everyone that we're fine. That we're friends with no... hard feelings."

As tightly as she controlled the horse she rode, Amber reined in her surge of emotions. She simply couldn't fathom how Nate Fields could walk away from such a splendid girl. She was losing patience with him and his so-called emotional disabilities. *Why don't you wake up?* she wanted to ask.

The wind-wracked treetops clapped above them together in bony applause. Beyond them, the sky hung like black draperies.

"So what should I do?" Nate asked.

Amber wanted to shout at him, My God, I don't know! But she didn't. Instead, she inhaled deeply. "All I want is what's best for Kim," she admitted and finally gave in. "Look, why don't we discuss this at the stables? Jazzer's having a rough time."

Nate nodded. "You go on. I'll stay here for awhile."

Relaxing her grip, Amber let the horse follow his instincts and head for home. With a threatening roar, the storm breached the bluffs. Startled, the gelding challenged her.

"It's all right, it's all right," she kept telling him.

He barely remained in check. She was determined to teach him that, no matter what, he couldn't have his head. His hooves pounded heavily. His breath gusted from his lungs like wind through a barrel.

They rode to the hilltop, from which they could see the stables. Large raindrops pelted around them, portents of the gathering squall. Amber and Jazzer all but took wing. She anticipated the cobbled yard. They had to slow down again. As the cobbles grew slick, they became treacherous for galloping horses and their riders.

At last they reached the vacant courtyard. Jumping down, Amber led the horse, his sides heaving, his eyes and nostrils wide, into the darker stables. No one met them. She had planned to ride in and take some time brushing Jazzer out and wiping him down.

She barely had him in his stall before the first flashes of lightning illuminated the deeply shadowed stable. Blue light reflected on the old brass bars that formed the upper halves of the stalls. The other horses rustled around them, knickering softly to her.

Amber crooned softly to them, but she concentrated on Jazzer. Removing his saddle and bridle, she slipped on his halter. It jingled familiarly at his chin.

By the time Nate came in, she was wiping down the horse. "There's a switch there by the door," she called.

Nate flipped it on. The light cascaded in warm, dust-ridden shafts.

The horses stirred uneasily. They sensed Amber's intense discomfort, and Nate was a stranger. Torrents of water sheeted the windows like curtains.

Nate leaned against the open stall door, observing while she finished with the trembling red. Her surest recollection of Nate was that he'd always watched her.

Finally, he broke the silence with a single, casual remark. "With that white blaze, he's a beauty."

She strove for an equal nonchalance. "He's young yet, but once he matures he'll be really fine. Right now, he's all muscle and instinct. He has a good heart, though, and that's what counts."

With a lingering pat, some murmured encouragement, Amber left the horse and walked toward Nate. She draped the towel on the stall door, closing it behind them. Then she led the way through the circles of light that spotted the wide center aisle, with Nate falling in step beside her. "We'll use the old tack room. Have you seen it?"

He shook his head.

"You'll probably appreciate it. Like my grandfather's office at the brewery, it goes the whole route in masculine gentility. It'll be dusty, but you'll get the effect."

The old tack room did indeed go the whole route. And it was dusty. English prints of the hunt punctuated paneling as dark and rich as that at the brewery. Old tack added a leathery touch. The seating consisted of overstuffed furniture upholstered in more, deep brown leather. Another desk and bar stamped the place as a peculiarly male retreat. The focal point of the room was a green marble fireplace over which hung the familiar logo, this time in oils.

"When it's damp like today," Amber said, switching on a tarnished brass lamp, "you can smell the ingrained tobacco odor."

She moved over to the fireplace. Dusty logs lay neatly stacked on the hearth. "Should I light it?" she asked. "Are you cold? It's the only source of heat."

Nate seemed about to reply in the negative when lightning zigzagged nearby, sharp and sizzling. The lamp went out, immersing them in complete darkness.

"I guess you'd better light the fire," he said.

Amber bent to strike a match under the wood. Nate moved forward to watch. Logs that had been laid for heaven knew how long, responded with eager snaps and pops.

Another nearby zap of lightning, a resounding clap of thunder prompted Nate to ask, "What about Kim? How does she feel about storms? It's overhead now."

Amber allowed herself a wry smile. "I'm the one who has trouble with storms, not Kim. Anyway, she has Etta Fay and Mick and Gnaw. They know I'm here with Jazzer, and they won't worry about me. So," she added, straightening from the crackling blaze and forcing herself to face Nate's dark gaze, "there's probably some old brandy in the cabinet. If you want—''

''No, no, I'm fine.'' He stood in the firelight, his hands in his pockets. He'd put on a dark-gray suit jacket. To Amber he looked like any man who'd just come home from work, the struggles of his day softening him around the edges and shading his jawline.

He was such an amazing-looking man.... But, no. Amber concentrated on the purpose of their meeting.

''When did you get this note from Kim?''

''Just today, at the brewery. I was so surprised that I... well, I guess I should have spent some time thinking about it before I came charging over to ask your opinion. I'm feeling really confused. I thought I'd...''

''You thought you'd made your position clear,'' Amber said, unable to curb the curtness of her tone.

He picked up on it. ''Yeah, you're right. I did everything I could to make my position clear. I thought a quick break would be best, and I made it as clean and final as possible. I don't feel good about it, but I still think it was the right thing to do.''

He paused, and Amber waited for him to continue.

''Hell, now I don't know what to do,'' he finally said, swinging away from her and rubbing the back of his neck. He was tired. And obviously in emotional pain. Once again, Amber found herself more on his side than against him.

He swung back to face her. ''Obviously you think that—well, what do you think?''

The firelight cast shadows where the storm left off. It still thundered above them. Flashes of lightning still lit the sky outside the windows, but the initial assault forces had moved away. Amber was relieved.

"I don't know what to do any more than you do," she admitted. "This note is a surprise to me, too. For all she's been through, I thought Kim was adjusting. She's mentioned you a couple of times since the day you came out and talked to us. She always speaks well of you, and refers to you as her dad. I still think it's just a matter of time. Of time and of keeping her life in balance in the meanwhile. She's strong and I know she'll make it. It's more the pain . . . and all the adjustments."

Because Nate didn't seem to have an answer, but continued to listen, Amber went on.

"I want to protect Kim, and the truth is I can't. Granny Maple says there's a point at which every parent realizes he can't protect his child from life. I guess I've reached that point, because while I want to wrap Kim in cotton, I know I can't. In my opinion, you've got to stick to your decision. Vacillating like you are will do more damage than making the break clean. Like you yourself said."

"And you think that's easy for me, do you?"

"I don't think any of this has been easy for anyone."

When Nate walked away again, Amber sank onto the couch facing the fireplace. The space illuminated by the fire was close and cozy. It felt safe from the passing storm, and even from the rest of the room. She sensed Nate pacing the area behind her. She absorbed the sounds, then the deep masculine timbre of his voice as he spoke in the dimness, trying to explain his feelings. Perhaps he was trying to explain them to himself.

"Kim's so great, and you're so great with her. I can appreciate that, but it also makes me feel inadequate. I simply can't be like you. I can't be with her like you are. When I consider the responsibility, day to day... Every day you have to do the right thing by her—the best thing. I don't know how to do any of that."

Amber's heart went out to him. She hadn't realized how badly damaged he'd been by the unhappy childhood Granny Maple had described to her. He had never been exposed to healthy, loving relationships. Not even to the superficial ones she had known. At his deepest level, he'd been sabotaged by the very people who had brought him into the world. And though Nate had voluntarily decided against being a part of Kim's life, Amber suddenly felt more sorry for him than for his daughter.

He collapsed beside Amber on the old leather couch. Stretching out his long legs to the fire, he dropped his head back and rubbed his forehead. Amber could see the struggle, but she also saw the man.

In the flickering light his skin was dusky and tanned. His hair was blacker than the farthest corners of the room, as were his eyes. As he gazed into the fire from his reclining position, his eyes became slits.

His deep-set eyes, his prominent nose, his high cheekbones, spoke of his Osage Indian heritage the most plainly. His mouth was sensual, constantly inviting, even when the rest of his features were implacably set. Simply relaxing next to her now, with his profile outlined in the firelight, he was the most attractive man she'd ever seen.

When he turned his head against the cushiony back of the couch, to meet her eyes, his soft gaze pierced her. "I think I should come to the river celebration. But..."

"I'm open to suggestions," Amber replied. "Just because I love Kim doesn't mean I'm an expert on what's best for her. I'm learning, too."

He turned to study the flames again. "Ever since you showed me her picture in that lawyer's office, I haven't been able to think about anything else. I can't even concentrate on the work that's always been primary in my life. The way I see it, if Kim feels she'd be comfortable on the same public ground with me, then I want to be there. I'm glad she's not embarrassed about her beginnings, and I want to support her in that. I want her to feel good about herself."

As Nate talked, stripping his emotions bare before her, a new understanding began to dawn on Amber. Nate knew how to care, after all. He had learned love along the river, through people who had loved him— people like Granny Maple and Beaver. Nate carried a legacy she doubted he recognized.

Her heart began to pound, to yearn in a direction she had discounted as impossible. Nate could care about his daughter. As Granny Maple had said, under his driven, intense exterior, Nate was as soft as butter.

"I think you're right," Amber said, her voice drawing his gaze back to hers. "I mean, there's nothing for Kim to be ashamed of. At River Day, she'll be on her own home ground. The people there will know her history, and what better place for her to start living with the truth of her past than with people who care about her?''

Nate's satisfied smile at her agreement touched Amber again. Oh, yes, Nate could love and be loved. He just didn't think he could. Best of all, if anyone could convince him how essential love was, it was Kim. His daughter could coax Nate into joining the human race. Amber's heart lifted. There seemed to be a solution for Nate, a solution that would come from the very source he had resisted the most.

Nate probably figured he'd see Kim this one more time, and then finally make the clean break they'd agreed on. But what if there didn't have to be a break? Did Amber dare risk Kim's progress by pushing the pair together?

She didn't know. But she did see the next step to take. ''Perhaps,'' she said, ''you should drive out to visit Kim some time before River Day.''

When he looked at her as if to say that wasn't in their game plan, she quickly went on. ''Maybe a trial run would be good. You wouldn't need to stay. Just give her a call and drive out. You can tell her you received her note, and that you'll come to River Day. That way, you can prepare her. Then, when she meets you in public, she'll feel less pressure. Also, in the meanwhile, she won't worry about whether or not you'll be there. After all, it's nearly two weeks until River Day...''

''Okay, okay,'' he said softly, an equally gentle smile playing around his lips. ''You've convinced me. I'll call. I'll come out. I'll say what you said.''

Lordy, when he did smile, intimately, the way he did now, it was glorious. She glimpsed it again, that fully sexual male. Here was a man who went to bed with women. He knew what to do. He probably did it with the incredible expertise he applied to everything else he did.

The realization swept over her with double force. For so long she'd been denying anything between them that now she was stunned by the strength of her feelings. What would it be like to make love to Nate Fields? What would it be like to see him naked and wanting? The thought was astonishing.

Amber had little sexual experience, and Nate would surely view her as terribly naive. She wasn't precisely a virgin, but she might as well have been. She'd never found much pleasure in the sexual act. She'd had a husband, but, with Warner, she'd always ended up frustrated.

With Nate it would be different. She knew it, and the thought, the possibility, wouldn't go away. Not in the soft light of the fire. Not in the seclusion of the old tack room. Not with a world, even the storm, far away. Years ago, when he was nineteen, Nate Fields had lit a flame in her that had yet to be fanned into life.

Amber thought Nate sensed some of what she was thinking. For some time, he had been staring at her, measuring her face, feature by feature.

"Hey," he whispered. "What is it? What's wrong?"

Oh, yes. Nate knew how to be soft, how to be in tune. It was astounding.

Amber's fingers fiddled with the top of her navy sweater, as if there were buttons there. But there were none.

Nate smiled at her habitual gesture. Reaching between them, he took her hand and laid it, palm up, between both of his, smoothing it carefully, unfolding it within his. He looked down, fingering the dappling row of calluses.

"You're different than I thought you'd be," he said.

She knew her smile had to reveal her confusion. "It's agreed around the stable that, when I'm cleaning a stall, everyone steers clear. I take out my frustrations cleaning stalls."

He smiled, too. "Do you have really clean stalls, then?"

"Immaculate."

"I'll watch my step. Bad pun, I know. But if I see you with a pitchfork, I'll consider myself warned."

He studied her, easing closer, his eyes drooping shut. Amber saw what was coming and grew still. She wanted him. She wanted him to kiss her. She wanted a glimpse of the possibilities that lay beyond.

The fire crackled, the rain pattered, and Nate's lips came down tentatively on hers. He was tasting her, waiting to see how she'd respond. She remained still, unresistant, focused, wanting.

Encouraged, he deepened the kiss. She could smell traces of his cologne, could feel his day's growth of beard and the soft flow of his breath.

She felt herself sinking into the old couch. He leaned over her warmly, weighing her softly down. He embraced her. His black eyes delved into hers from inches away, and apparently satisfied with what they saw, closed again.

His kisses were varied. Doubtless he knew what he was doing. Amber felt the escalations, the retreats, the subtleties. Nate pursued his own pleasure, but she could feel he also gauged hers. He wasn't so much losing himself, letting go, as he was learning her face and throat and lips with his mouth.

And then she realized he sensed her inexperience. She felt him easing back, not to quit, but rather to be sure of her pleasure. She'd been married. For three years. He had to know that. He spoke gently. "Are you all right?"

All Amber could think was that he must find her inadequate. Compared to him with his experience, she must seem like a kid. She pressed against his chest, and he moved back, still without releasing her.

"I don't think we should do this," she said. He stared at her questioningly. "I—I don't think it's a good idea. Not with Kim."

"Kim?" He seemed relieved that the issue was only Kim. "What does Kim have to so with this? We'll be careful. She won't know."

We'll be careful. He had said, we'll *be* careful. That implied that he anticipated there would be more times like this. Amber yearned for more, but she pushed him away firmly and stood up.

Yes, standing up was better. She could think. Avoiding Nate's eyes, she went to the fireplace. She certainly didn't need the warmth, but it had grown dark outside and she craved the comfort of its light. She wondered why the electricity hadn't come back on.

When Amber turned and looked at him, the anger she saw on his face astonished her.

"For God's sake," he exclaimed, getting up from the couch, "I wasn't expecting something here on the couch."

Amber was thrown off balance. He was insulted. "I know that," she managed to say.

"I'm civilized enough to take things one step at a time. I don't carry a condom and ravish unsuspecting women on dusty furniture."

Obviously, Nate had misinterpreted her action. Amber tried to think of something to say. "I didn't think you were..."

"You didn't think I was what? Looking for a pay-off?"

"No! I just don't think we should take any chances that could ruin things for Kim. If we get so we can't—talk—then it will be hard on her."

"This has nothing to do with Kim. This has to do with you and me. I thought I'd been wrong about you."

"I don't know what you're talking about. Wrong about me? In what way?"

He remained standing but said nothing. It was obvious he was not about to explain what he meant. Inwardly, Amber flinched, but she returned his stare.

It was Nate who finally relaxed his shoulders. He sighed. "Come on. I'll drive you up to the house."

Relieved that he was no longer hostile, Amber stayed where she was. "I want to wait until the electricity comes on. I want to check the horses."

"You shouldn't be alone down here in the dark."

"I'm staying."

He demonstrated he could be stubborn, too. "I'll stop by the house and tell Mick what you're doing. If Kim sees me, it won't matter now."

If she were to tell him to mind his own business, Amber thought, she'd sound churlish. Rather than fight him, she merely said, "Thanks."

With a wry smile, as if he saw that he hadn't really won, he nodded and left.

CHAPTER NINE

NATE WAITED until four o'clock the following afternoon before calling Allswell, and the wait took its toll. Luckily, neither Amber nor Etta Fay picked up the phone. The object of his call did. Kim.

"Uh, this is Nate."

"Oh, hi."

Her sudden breathlessness threw him off. Then, the sounds of construction began again, carrying into the old president's office at the brewery where he sat. He should have closed the door.

"Can you hear me?" he asked, above the raw squeal of an electric saw.

Kim giggled. "It sounds noisy there."

"It is." *Steady, Nate. Who's thirteen here?* "I thought I might drive out to see you for a few minutes. Would that be a problem?"

"No, that's fine."

"What about practicing? Or your homework? I know it's a school night."

"I've started, but I can always see you."

Oh God. He wasn't good at this. "I'll come out, then. It'll take about an hour. Rush hour, you know."

"That's okay."

"See you then."

Nate had been in shirt-sleeves and jeans all day. He threw on his trench coat. He was hardly going on a date. And yet, when he plucked up the armload of shell-pink tulips he'd chosen at the florist's, the music CD, the box of chocolates, and the cool glass ball with its snowy scene inside, he felt just like an old-fashioned suitor.

Oblivious of the remodeling debris, he found his Porsche, parked at the edge of the lot where it had been sitting in the sun all day. The warmth inside the car felt good. Although cloudless, the April day remained cool. A recent rain had left the air damp.

He had been feeling unsettled since his encounter with Amber the evening before. He'd been thinking about how he'd kissed her and how she'd kissed him back. Her kisses had been…almost tentative. Unique, like the woman.

When she'd left him on the couch so abruptly, he'd felt rebuffed, insulted. Just as he had once before. He admitted it to himself now. He had overreacted, and he'd been glad to see her again. He hoped to smooth things over. He shouldn't have pushed her.

He had thought that leaving downtown at four for the drive out to Allswell would be a good idea. But commuters already thickened the highways. The drive itself was not difficult—a stretch through the urban sprawl of the metro area, southwest, then out toward the first hills that curved down into the gentle, picturesque Ozark mountain range.

For all his years away, eastern Missouri still felt like home to Nate. Since he'd been back, memories had followed him everywhere. At the river community, he had learned to work hard and to keep his nose clean.

Early on, he had figured out that good grades and tireless effort were his tickets out. After the day that he'd been dumped by his father off the back of that borrowed tractor, he'd more or less given up on any relationship with the man. Shortly after that, Gerald Fields had left for good. Except for sending an occasional check, he'd abandoned Nate at fourteen.

But aside from that humiliating scene, acted out in the mud in front of Amber Brandenberger and her father, Nate's most important memory of his life along the river was of a day when he had been nineteen and Amber seventeen. He realized now that that day had been a watershed in many ways.

It had been a hot summer afternoon. He had had his first year of college under his belt, and was feeling angry about coming back and doing menial labor and living with Beaver. Even with scholarships, Nate hadn't been able to afford to do anything else.

That day, he'd been doing a heavy clean-up job along the river for another guy. Nate had to admit that the community had given him whatever work it could. In its way, it had also supported him, encouraged him, cared about him. At the time, he hadn't seen it like that. He'd had his first taste of college and of the life he wanted. He'd been anxious to cut the old ties and to move on.

As if to add salt to his wound, Amber had flown by him on a palomino horse. By then, she'd had a great golden mount which, to his mind, epitomized the differences between them. As always, he'd been both resentful and entranced. Even then she was graceful, a wonderful rider who looked completely at ease on a horse.

She had been such a nice girl that everybody, even down at the river, had liked her. He would catch glimpses of her through the thick summer growth in the woods, a golden girl on her golden horse. . . . And he would be filled with longing.

He was a virgin then. He had never had the time or the money for girls, and his frustration had nagged at him for over two years. Desire had churned in his young body as clearly as resentment. He was all too aware of the differences between himself and girls like Amber Brandenberger.

Still, his gaze had followed Amber's progress along the pathway that afternoon. He leaned into his shovel, feeling the sweat running down his bare torso, darkening the front and rear of his jeans. His heavy boots protected his legs from the dense underbrush he was clearing along the riverbank.

He was working beneath the bluffs, along a stretch known by the river people as the Big Bend. Although for the most part a lazy river, the Meramec threw itself into the bluffs and on around at the Big Bend. Here, the usually calm waters could be treacherous, even in the summer when the water levels were lower. Debris collected at the Big Bend, lurking below the water's clouded surface.

Nate knew that Amber always kept to the trailways, never taking any risk greater than jumping the occasional fallen tree. But under his unseen gaze, she veered off the path this time, urging her horse down the riverbank.

It was so hot that at first he thought she was going to offer her horse a drink. Since people usually didn't mess with the river at the Big Bend, he never imagined that she'd coax the large golden beast, with its creamy tail and mane and forelock, right into the river itself.

Nate soon realized that it was her intent to do exactly that. She was going to swim the river. At one time or another, almost every young rider in the area pitted himself against the challenge of the river that nurtured and sustained the community along its banks. Nate continued to silently watch. The palomino did what instinct told him, and swam. Heavy gear, rider and all, the horse churned heavily across the expanse.

When Nate saw them nearly reach the opposite bank and turn back, he almost returned to work himself. He figured they'd be all right. The horse didn't appear to be laboring, and part of Nate congratulated the youthful rider for confronting the Big Bend.

But then, something beneath the water spooked the horse, and he started to struggle. The fragile rider called to the gelding, and he tried, but he seemed to be stuck. Nate didn't stop to think. Ignoring the weight of his boots, he waded, then swam toward the pair. Concentrating on the floundering animal, he discounted the terrifying current.

Reaching the thrashing creature, Nate groped in the muddy water, searching for the source of the problem. He grasped a chunk of log. The nub of a branch had gotten tangled in the reins and was pressing against the horse's chest.

Amber had slid into the water. She clung to the saddle, talked to the horse encouragingly. Nate worked feverishly, battling the fear that knotted his chest and heart and brain. The powerful current tugged at him fiercely. He couldn't free the wet leather from the log. They all went under a couple of times, but with his last gasp of strength he finally managed to free the animal.

Somehow, with what strength they had left, the trio struggled to the bank. The horse heaved himself mightily out of the water and scrambled up the steep slope. Amber and Nate followed more slowly, panting. At the top, they simply stood there, staring at one another. They were stunned. They were soaked. Amber's mount shook himself with a great spray and jangle of harness, his saddle askew. He sounded like a great bellows.

Nate watched the horse, then turned to the smaller bedraggled form that had begun crooning to the animal. Amber had to be as scared as Nate had been. Yet all she thought about was the horse. That was, until she looked at Nate. She didn't cry, but such remorse filled her face and eyes that Nate felt sorry for her.

"Thank you," she said gravely, her hair plastered to her head and still dripping. "Thank you for swimming out. You were very brave."

Nate grappled with anger, but found he couldn't be mad at her. He was still gasping for breath. Even though he'd never owned a horse, he recognized the irresistible challenge of Amber's attempted crossing.

"You made your bones," he heard himself say.

"I almost drowned Sovereign, you mean."

"Well, this is a bad place to try it."

"This is the *only* place," she said, her eyes meeting his.

Yeah, that was part of the dare, too. "So, you did it."

"You're a strong swimmer."

Nate shrugged.

Finally he felt calmer. He noticed that the horse breathed easier, too. Sovereign stood, ground-tethered, his head drooping, looking as nearly drowned as the girl did in her soaking jeans, T-shirt and cowboy boots. Long brown hair, freed from the clip dangling at the rear of her head, clumped together. Beneath the lightweight cotton, her breasts, pert and small, moved slightly with every breath.

Above where they stood on the rubble pathway that separated the river from the bluffs, a cave yawned. On hot days, Nate ate his lunch in there. It was a familiar cave that all the kids in the area knew about, though their parents warned them to keep away.

"I've got a couple of beers in the cave," Nate said.

Amber peered at him, brushing a skein of nut-brown hair from an eye of the same shade. Her skin glowed with a golden summer tan, and he didn't think her so much beautiful as... he wasn't sure. Only his sensations were clear.

"I don't know," she said, seventeen, shy, cautious.

He felt rebuffed.

He drew himself up, aware of how much bigger he was than she, aware of his own soaked jeans and boots. They were both unsteady from the sudden cool and the shock.

Looking from Sovereign to Nate, from the sun glinting blindingly on the now-quiet river to the dark cave, Amber finally nodded. He took her elbow and helped her over the gravelly path. A large rock several yards inside the cave provided a place to sit. He'd sat there earlier, gazing out at the river, listening to it. She sat there now.

The sudden dimness, even just inside the mouth of the cave, forced Nate's eyes to readjust. He plucked a can of beer from a container of ice. Purposely, it wasn't Black Forest but an expensive competitor.

"You want one of your own, or will you share mine?"

In the echoing hollowness, his words sounded as a challenge. For her to share with him was a further step into intimacy.

"I'll share yours."

Coming toward her, over the rock-strewn floor, Nate studied her with satisfaction. Amber Brandenberger hardly had the maturity of a college girl, but he'd always been drawn to her and now was his chance. He'd be getting out of town as soon as he could, and he thought he might get some of his own back.

He took a long drink of beer, then handed the can to her. She accepted and drank without hesitation. He sat down next to her on the smooth slope of the rock. She returned the beer, and he drank again, squinting his eyes both against the hot sun beyond the dark cave and the cold liquid.

He took another long drink, and offered her the rest to Amber. She refused with a shake of her head. He saw that she was blushing, and he realized she'd been staring at his chest, watching his throat work as he'd swallowed.

Setting down the can, he pushed a strand of now-dryer hair from her forehead. She stared at her hands, knotted in her lap.

"Are you sure you're all right?" he asked.

She nodded, her eyes glued to her hands.

Gently, he reached down and tugged one loose from the other. When he lifted her hand, she glanced up uncertainly. He took it, pressing it to his chest. Embarrassed by the fierceness of his heartbeat, he hoped she didn't sense his own vulnerability. He wanted to be neither vulnerable nor to let it show. Especially not to Amber Brandenberger.

Gradually, Nate dropped his hand, but Amber's remained resting against his chest. Then she began to stroke him, moving her hand slowly down, nearly to the western-style buckle above the zipper of his jeans. She must have realized what she was doing, because she turned bright pink and jerked her hand away.

But Nate reclaimed it. Patiently he guided her hand back over his bare flesh, along his chest to one shoulder, across his breastbone to the other. He cupped her hand to his cheek, then coaxed it again, back to his chest and over his belly. He kept his gaze fixed on her face, watching the wonder there. He felt it himself.

Bending forward, he kissed her, lingeringly, right on the mouth. He kept her hand in his, pressing it to the warmth of his flat abdomen where his navel peeked above his jeans.

She didn't resist. He kissed her again and again, one arm around her, the other between them, his hand holding her hand to him.

Inch by inch he pushed her hand down, over the large sculpted belt buckle, over his fly. He closed her hand around him, jeans and all, moaning into her mouth. He thought she might let him. He wanted her more than anything he'd ever wanted in his life. He was hot and ready, and all he could think about was the way he needed her. Amber Brandenberger. No one else.

His thoughts splintered in a thousand directions. His body thrummed. He had a blanket for napping when it got really hot. The underbrush outside would offer privacy. He was sure he knew what to do.

But just her hand, right there, just there, was almost enough. Almost. Soft, sweet, elegant, brave, unattainable Amber Brandenberger. She let him rub at his need with her hand.

He was almost there, almost, when she started to tug away. He was desperate to keep her there. Before he could convince her to stay, before he could regroup and figure another way to go about it, she was scurrying out of the cave.

"Amber, dammit!" he called after her, nearly crazy with need. "You can't leave me like this!"

It was too late. He scrambled after her, tripping over the rocks on the floor of the cave. By the time he caught up with her, she was mounting Sovereign.

"Amber!" he said, hating himself for the pleading note in his voice.

She wheeled the palomino away, without even looking back.

"Amber, for God's sake!" The pain of rejection flared into biting anger. "You don't know what you're doing, do ya, kid? Scared, are ya? Well, I don't need you!"

The memory had the power to shake him, even now. Nate met his reflection in the rearview mirror of his black Porsche. There was no smile in his eyes, no sympathy for his youthful self.

"Who says anyone at nineteen with a hard-on has sensitivity and finesse?" he asked himself ironically.

That night, an equally confused, equally neglected, equally drunk Francie Gibbons had met up with him outside a local liquor store. She'd asked him to buy her some beer. Like Amber, she was only seventeen.

Although he had had enough sense not to buy her anything, he had shared some of his with her. Francie had been beautiful and fast. Everyone had talked about her on-again, off-again relationship with Kenny O'Donnell. That night, it had been off-again, and she'd been hurting and looking for company. Of course, that was still no excuse. In the end, their misery had not only found company but had conceived a child.

At thirty-three, Nate didn't consider it hard to believe. The last thing he'd been thinking about that night was contraception and protection, or even sleeping with Francie. It had just happened. And as much as he believed in taking responsibility for his actions, the phrase applied. It had happened. Once. And when it was over he'd been embarrassed enough to stay away from Francie for the rest of the summer.

Only when he'd heard she was nearly three months pregnant had he approached her. He'd barely gotten the frightening question out. When she'd all but told him to buzz off, that the baby was Kenny's, he had been more than happy to oblige. He had been relieved. A child would have kept him from getting away from the riverside community he hated. He'd left for his sophomore year in college and never looked back.

That he hadn't questioned Francie further, that he'd never bothered at any time since to verify whether or not the child she carried was his, had become an on-going source of emotional turmoil. Guilt. It rested on his shoulder like a darkly gloved hand.

Yet, the way he saw it, everything was working out for the best. Kim was with a loving woman who would be a good mother to her. The best that could be done was being done. His role was to let Kim know who he was. She had to know he recognized and accepted and supported her and her life with Amber. The guilt that he lived with, those inner whisperings that he was getting off easy, considering what he'd done . . . well, he had an answer for them.

He wasn't getting off easy.

As much as he expected his daughter's memories of him to fade as she grew older, he also knew he'd never forget her. Never. He would always know he had a daughter somewhere. A great daughter he had failed from the start. That could never change. Somehow, with time, he would have to learn to live with that.

Nate turned into the gates at Allswell. He expected to see Gnaw, his rusty coat flying as he galloped to meet him. The dog would bark at the wheels of Nate's car, then pounce on him when he tried to get out. The animal was an irritant. But somehow, the dog also added a homey touch to Allswell. Gnaw tore around the old country manor of the Brandenbergers as if it were an ordinary house.

When Nate did emerge cautiously from the car, still unbeseiged, he relaxed a little. His arms were filled with the bouquet of tulips, the CD disc, the chocolate box and the glass ball with its snowy scene inside. Facing the house, he contemplated donning a red suit and finding a chimney. He wondered if he'd brought too many gifts, or too few, or the wrong kind.

It was too late to turn back. The front door opened slightly revealing Kim behind it. She smiled at him, her smile erasing his earlier impressions of a sober young woman.

Nah, he thought, he didn't need a red suit.

"Hi," she called, keeping herself tightly wedged between the door and its frame.

Nate could see the reason. Behind her, Gnaw was raising a ruckus. The dog obviously wanted to make up for failing to greet him properly earlier. That meant, easily, a thousand extra licks to Nate's face. Before Nate could say anything or do anything, he heard Etta Fay's voice.

"Get down! Get down, you rascal! It's okay, Kimmy, honey. I've got him."

Kim smiled again. "You can come in now."

This time, entering the house did not unsettle him. The usual resentment didn't surface. Allswell was Kim's home, and for some reason, that made a difference. Etta Fay stood in the middle of the entrance hall, grinning at him while holding Gnaw stoutly by his collar. The big dog strained desperately, willing to choke himself for just one lap at Nate's cheek. But it was Kim who glowed. Her green eyes sparkled.

"This, uh... Well," he said nervously, handing out his booty as he went. "The tulips and the CD are for you, Kim. The candy is yours, Etta Fay, and, well, this—" he held up the glass ball "—is something I want to show Amber."

As Etta Fay exclaimed over the candy, Kim accepted her gifts shyly. Now, the dog lunged in the direction of the candy box. Excusing herself, and the dog, too, the older woman headed for the kitchen. "Thanks so much, Nate! It's so nice. But you won't have a minute's peace until he's on the back porch," she said, disappearing.

Nate was left with Kim. The entry closed in, suddenly quiet.

Kim still smiled. "Thanks for the flowers. And how did you know to buy this?" she asked of the CD disc. "Do you like Yo-Yo Ma?"

"No, I don't know anything about cello music. I asked a guy in the store, and he recommended it."

Kim didn't seem disappointed. "Well, this is great! And so are the tulips. We have all kinds of tulips here, but they're not as pretty as these are. Thanks."

"Is Amber here?"

"No. I told her you were coming, though. I think she went to Granny Maple's. Anyway, she'll be back at dinner. Can you stay until then?"

"Uh, no. I don't have long, in fact." Nate slipped the glass ball that remained in his hand onto the nearest table. "When Amber comes in, will you give this to her?"

"Sure."

Nate shifted his weight. "Maybe we could go for a walk. It's a little cool, but it's still light enough."

"Great! I'll get my coat."

In less than a minute, she was back, her jeans and sweater covered by a short coat and knit cap. Kim and Amber seemed to have an endless supply of knitted items. What's more, they always looked good. Casual, but really good.

"I'm ready," Kim said, since he stood like a post.

Out on the veranda, Nate wondered if he'd made a mistake in suggesting a walk. He didn't know why, but he wanted everything to be perfect.

Trying to concentrate on the girl walking beside him, Nate saw the day was almost over. The breeze cooled. Beyond the stables, the sun was setting over the top of the woods.

"Are you sure you'll be warm enough?" he asked, buttoning his own coat.

"Oh, sure. This is fine. Have you ever seen the lookout?"

Nate felt the sudden tightening in his gut, and he forced himself to relax. This was Kim. She was new at Allswell. For her, the lookout was neutral territory.

"I've been there," he said, "but I'd like to see it again."

Leaving the circular drive in front of the house, they stepped onto the wide expanse of grass. The lookout wasn't far. Nate discerned it clearly. The irony was incredible. Nate had been no more than a year older than Kim was now. The day of his supreme degradation had marked, at least in Nate's mind, the day that he gave up completely on his father.

His feelings so overwhelmed him that he thought he'd made another blunder. He should have talked with Kim inside. He should have just gotten this visit over with.

But no, he had to be the grown-up now. "So," he said. "I received your nice note, your invitation to May Day River Day."

"Oh, but it wasn't exactly an invitation! I mean, no one gets invitations. Whoever wants to go, goes."

"Yeah, but, well, I'm glad to hear that you'd like me to come. It's nice that you consider me that way."

"So you're coming, then?"

"Sure. I think it's time everybody sees that, uh, sees that I'm your father. I'm sure everyone'll be happy we've, uh, found each other."

God, the words were so hard. Nate wondered if the stress of getting them out showed. But Kim seemed delighted. Her cheeks shone pink, and her green eyes continued to sparkle. Long wispy black hair trailed into the breeze, out from beneath her colorful knit cap.

It was funny, but he couldn't remember how Francie had looked. He recalled her as being extraordinarily beautiful. Kim had none of that about her. She was pretty. Exotically so. Kim was no fiery beauty.

She plainly favored him, and that pleased Nate. Despite the separation to come, he'd always resemble Kim and she him.

His next question surprised him. "Do you like Allswell?"

Swaying as she walked, she glanced at him. "Oh, yeah, I love it!"

"Amber said something about you not liking the horses."

"They still scare me a little, but I love everything else. Gnaw and Amber and Etta Fay and Mick. I started coming here with my mom when I was about nine or ten. My mom worked for Amber. That's when Amber and I started to be friends. She always made me feel happy. Sometimes, she's so funny."

"Amber? Funny?"

Kim nodded. "She listens when I need to cry, but she's funny, too. We laugh a lot. Of course, she's always watching me, too. As soon as she comes in the door, she's asking about my homework and my cello and that kinda stuff. She bought me my first cello. Well, all my cellos, really. But my first one she bought for me when I told her I heard a lady play at school. My mom was still alive, then, and she let Amber buy a three-quarter cello. But I grew too tall so fast that Amber had to sell it and buy a full-size cello. Then, at Christmas, she bought me the one I have now. It's a pretty good one. She says she'll buy me a handmade cello when I'm ready, and a really good bow."

Reaching the flat space of the lookout, he and Kim meandered to the stone wall curving the side facing the river. The view was amazing. For miles and miles, scenic Missouri stretched to the south and west, displaying the Meramec River countryside at its best. To Nate, the view reminded him of the patchwork quilt of the English countryside.

Crossing her forearms on the wall, Kim leaned out to look down. "Just below us, in the bluff, there's a cave. All the kids who live down at Granny Maple's sneak off and play there. But I guess you know about it, too."

Nate nodded, the irony of his knowledge of the place almost forgotten in his sudden concern for her.

"I know kids like to sneak down there to play," he said, not thinking. "But it's very dangerous. The river cuts in too close. When the water's high, it floods the cave and isolates it. I hope you're not telling me you sneak down there."

Kim looked at him, the spark in her eyes dimming somewhat. Nate's heart fell. He'd come on too strong. Now he'd ruined everything. He'd known he would. But surely her safety—

"I've been there," she confessed somberly. "But you don't need to worry. I don't see the kids at Granny Maple's much anymore."

Inside Nate the pendulum of emotion swung again. Kim pulled a switch on him. She looked so...what? He couldn't read her at all. He only knew she'd reverted to the earlier Kim, to the one he'd seen in the photo. God, he didn't know what to say. He wished Amber would drive up.

"It's, uh, kind of chilly out here," he said. "We'd better go back."

On their way across the lawn, Kim's spirits recovered somewhat. From what Nate could tell. Hell, what did he know? She scared the daylights out of him. She seemed so fragile and he was all thumbs.

When Nate said goodbye and closed the door on his car, relief overwhelmed him. As he started the engine, he looked up and saw her standing in the door, waving slowly at him. He had to believe she was okay, that in spite of him, she was all right again. The sooner he got out of her life, the less chance he had of messing her up.

CHAPTER TEN

AMBER LIFTED the sweater from the box on her lap. She unfolded it and held it up, displaying its full length, admiring Granny Maple's artistry. It was a ski sweater with stylized snowflakes and reindeer in gray and black against a pale gray ground, in the classic style that Amber preferred.

"Kim will love it!" she exclaimed, smiling at her friend.

The older woman occupied her favorite chair in the living room of her stilt house. As usual she crocheted. "It looks kinda hot now. But by the time Christmas rolls around, it'll seem fine. I guess I finished it a little early," she added with a crooked smile. "That pattern was so interesting I couldn't put it down."

Having folded the sweater back into the box, Amber slipped her checkbook from her purse and wrote out the amount due. "Now, it's a matter of hiding it for the next nine months. Thanks again! It's perfect."

Granny Maple peered intently at the string-like thread lacing through her fingers and hook. "Tablecloths aren't nearly as much fun," she admitted with a sigh.

"If I can get you more sweater business, I will."

"I know that. But as you say, the weather's warming up, and people won't think about sweaters until fall again. The truth is, I didn't want to get so busy I couldn't do the ski pattern for Kimmy."

"I guessed as much."

Amber's smile for her friend was knowing. But the restlessness she'd been feeling flooded back, and she left her chair. Walking to the kitchen window, the one over the sink that gave a view of tufted grass, purple iris and flowing river, she also sighed. "It's clouding up. We've had an awfully wet spring."

"It can't be too bad. The people down here aren't following the river stages and the weather forecasts yet. I don't worry until I hear that kinda talk from Beaver." Granny Maple kept her eyes on her work. "I suppose Dolph will come to the river picnic."

"I haven't talked to him since that day Nate showed me our father's ledger. I still wonder if I should show it to him."

"That kind of news seldom does anyone any good, sugar pie."

"That's what I keep telling myself. Of course, I'm chomping at the bit to hear whether or not he called Hargrove Kandel. You remember—the man who links up independent thinkers with people who had difficult problems."

"Mmm-hmm, I recall the name."

"But I can't keep following Dolph around. It's taken me long enough to stop mothering him, and I'm determined not to call him, even if he never calls me. Which he probably won't."

Amber watched the water flowing by. Today, it reflected blue and green and gray, mirroring the sky that

clouded over, the leaves that grew larger each day.
"Still—" she heard herself say "—Dolph phones Kim
a couple of times a week. She's so excited about River
Day, she's bound to get him to come."

"And what about Lillian Hewlett? You said she was
phoning you about Dolph—as I recollect, pretty regularly for a while."

"Yeah, well, she's calling less. And she never men-
tions Dolph. Normally, that means they're either getting along, or not seeing each other. My guess is
they're seeing each other. But I don't want to ask. The
minute I show the slightest interest in them, I hear too
much. The next thing I know, I'm in the middle, wor-
rying about how to fix whatever's wrong. Oh, no, this
time it's going to be different. And the only way I can
make it different is to stay out of it."

When Amber turned back, she glimpsed the older
woman's quickly smothered smile. Granny Maple
knew Amber inside out. She knew how hard she
struggled to set her own boundaries—how hard it was
for her to draw a line when people she cared about
took advantage of her. She thought the older woman
might have cheered her progress. But Granny Maple
merely sat, her fingers going a mile a minute, smiling,
nodding and listening to every word. Amber assumed
her friend also recognized her restlessness.

"You know," Granny Maple said, intuiting the
cause of her unease, "Nate's going to do just fine with
Kim. I've told you before that, underneath all the
pride and intensity, Nate is as soft as butter."

As soft as butter. That phrase had been threading
through Amber's head since the night before. Since
Nate had followed her up the old back road to the

stables. Since he'd followed her into the old tack room and kissed her.

Nate had aroused her as he alone could. And now, today, at this very minute probably, he was seeing Kim.

When Kim had told her he'd called, that he was coming out, Amber had made excuses to give them some time alone. Still, she worried. While Amber was beginning to believe Nate might be good for Kim, she didn't share Granny Maple's confidence. Besides, Granny Maple had yet to see the full-grown man Nate had become.

Hadn't he been insulted when Amber had pulled away from their shared kisses? When she'd stood up from the couch, ending their slow, sensual slide, he'd stood up, too. He'd surprised her with his anger. She had been confused, had even felt backward with him. She didn't know what he'd been feeling.

That day weeks ago at the brewery, they had connected. When he'd handed her the ledger, and explained its contents with such empathy, she had trusted him completely. But he was also quixotic. One moment he seemed sensitive; the next, he appeared perfectly able to cut Kim out of his life.

Lordy, she had to stop thinking about him so much!

"Granny," she said, swiveling from the window, "how do you think Kim's doing?"

"Why, you know I think she's doing fine." At last, the flow of floss through Granny Maple's fingers stopped. She studied Amber. "What are you saying, honey?"

"I don't know exactly. I keep thinking she's doing fine, too. And then I wonder if she isn't too perfect."

Granny Maple chuckled. "Too perfect? That's a new one. A girl of thirteen being too perfect?" She returned to her work. Still, when she spoke she was serious. "There's no such thing as too perfect. Just give the child some time."

"It's more that... Well, she doesn't seem to have any friends her own age. In her spare time, she's always around Etta Fay and Mick and me. And you. She never brings anyone home from school."

"And what about that group she's met? The ones who also play the cello?"

"Yeah, well, she's friendly with her string group. But most of those kids are already in college. And then, she only sees them on Saturdays and Wednesdays when she's at the university. What I'm talking about are kids her own age. I mean, I never hear a word of slang, or see a stubborn look. She's absolutely programmed about doing her homework. Those hours she spends practicing every day are positively abnormal. Oh, I realize she gets a lot from her music. She never says she doesn't want to do it. She never avoids her lessons, or... Oh, I don't know. She's just too perfect."

Amber sank into the chair across from Granny Maple's. She leaned toward her, watching the even stitches merging, one by one into a lovely, intricate spider web. "I know Kim used to play with the children down here. I mean, she was with you regularly, and it seemed that whenever I picked her up, even when I started helping Francie with her, Kim had someone tagging along."

"Well, it's been cold. The children aren't out as much when it's cold. And then, like you say, Kim's gotten serious about her music. And finally, you have to remember she's had all these adjustments to make. Her experience has matured her. On top of everything else, she's outgrowing her old life.''

She paused a minute, as if to be sure of her thoughts, then went on. "But, no, sweetie pie. I've told you before, for all she's been through, Kimmy's doing just fine. What's more, you're doing fine. And now, Nate will do fine, too. Just watch and see. It's only a question of time.''

Amber had never known anyone whose opinions she respected more, but in this case she thought Granny Maple had to be wrong. After all, the woman could only judge by what she saw of them. Of course, she saw Kim often and Amber regularly. But she hadn't seen Nate since he'd been nineteen. She had to be wrong about Nate.

Thinking about Nate yet again made Amber check her watch. "I'd better go. It's nearly dinnertime, and if I'm late again Etta Fay will have my head on a plate.''

BY THE TIME Amber entered the friendly, brightly lit kitchen, she expected a lecture on punctuality. But Etta Fay was in such a good mood that nothing could burst her balloon. No fewer than three old, lead-glass vases lined the tiled countertop, each one filled with gloriously fresh tulips.

"Look!" Kim exclaimed. "From my dad! Aren't they wonderful?''

Yes, the shell-pink tulips, resembling Easter eggs on graceful green stems, did look wonderful. "So many,'' Amber murmured.

Etta Fay swept an open box of chocolates under Amber's nose. "I got candy. But you can't have any. Not until after supper, which you just about missed again, missy."

Etta Fay dredged up "missy" from Amber's past only when Amber walked a thin line with her.

"Well, I—"

"And *you*—" Kim said, dragging Amber by the hand, on through the passageway to the entry.

"Five minutes!" Etta Fay called, as Mick entered by the rear door.

"*You,* —" Kim repeated, with a broad sweep of the hand not holding Amber's "—got *this.*"

This was another old treasure, originally from Germany Amber was sure. It was a glass ball, full of water, containing white flakes which, when shaken, made a whirling snow scene inside the ball. Tucked against a small mountain and even smaller trees, a tiny chalet endured a howling snowstorm.

"Isn't it wonderful?" Kim asked, apparently stuck on that word.

"Wonderful," Amber admitted, stuck on it, too.

Shaking the ball again, the pair watched the snow resettle. Amber didn't know what to say. Luckily, Etta Fay rapped orders from the kitchen.

Over dinner, Kim described Nate's visit in a stream of ongoing babble. She recounted her meeting with her "dad" verbatim, as if she had it memorized minute by minute. Etta Fay punctuated what the girl said with more accolades, "wonderful" among them.

Mick and Amber ate quietly while Amber puzzled over Nate Fields. One side said, here was more proof of his capacity for belonging. The other recognized him for the loner he'd been since childhood, the man who'd readily taken offense on the night before in the tack room.

By ten o'clock, Allswell was quiet. Kim was in bed, her room decorated with pink tulips, listening to the bittersweet strains that could only be pulled from a cello. She was playing the CD her "dad," yes, her "dad," had brought. Since Kim used the term freely, Amber adjusted herself to using it.

In silky pajamas and a wrapper, Amber closed herself into the sitting room she now used as a private office.

She sat down at her desk by a window that was actually a pair of doors opening onto a little balcony. Within a couple of weeks, there would be flowers in the boxes topping the balustrade. Geraniums. But for now, nothing obscured the view to the west, out over the stables and paddocks. It ended at the woods, falling away as the bluffs descended abruptly to bottomland.

All evening, she'd been thinking she ought to call Nate. She needed to thank him for the glass ball he'd left for her. The ball sat in the middle of the desk. She picked it up and shook it. As soon as the snowstorm inside subsided, she examined the scene and shook it again.

Before she lost her nerve she dialed the number he'd given her, scribbled on the paper beneath the now-dying storm.

He picked up, almost on the first ring. His brusque hello put her off. Wary of his mood, she did not speak right away.

"Hello?" he repeated, even more impatient.

"Hi, Nate, this is Amber. Is this a bad time?"

He paused, and apparently collected himself, because he sounded better when he spoke again. "Uh, I'm sorry, I've been busy. But I was just about to call you."

"Oh?"

"Yeah, uh, how's Kim?"

Amber wondered at the question. "Kim's fine."

"Oh."

When he went quiet, Amber couldn't figure why. She chose to be up-front. "What makes you think she's not okay?"

"I don't know. Not exactly. It's just that when I left, I was worried I'd upset her."

"Upset her? But she's been bubbling over!"

"You're kidding!"

"No, but...what happened?"

Again a pause—as if he swept long fingers through his midnight-black hair. "Oh God, I don't know. I think I said something wrong. We were talking, and she seemed fine, and then she mentioned something about hanging out at bluffs by the Big Bend in the river, and I told her she'd better never go there. I knew, even as I said it, that my approach was all wrong. It was just that, all of a sudden, I was terrified of anything happening to her. Especially down there. It scared the hell out of me, and I think I scared her."

Amber sank back in her chair. "Nate, I think you've misinterpreted Kim's reaction. She's been happy since I got home and surely before that. The tulips you brought are wonderful—" that word again "—and she put on the CD you bought her the minute she finished her homework. Maybe you're just not used to talking to her yet. I know she can seem a little mercurial sometimes. Frankly, girls her age are. But as far as I can see, there's nothing to worry about.''

"Thank God," she heard him mutter.

Now that Nate was reassured, Amber felt it was a good time to change the subject. "I want to thank you for the glass ball with the snowstorm inside. It's obvious why you thought I'd like it."

"Oh, yeah, I bought it on a trip to Germany. I've had it for years, but I brought it down from Chicago on impulse. I'm glad you like it."

Amber's smile softened her voice. "A chalet has to make me happy, whatever its size."

"You're welcome to it. Listen, I'm wondering if I should still come on River Day. Kim's doing so well that I'd hate to throw her off track again."

"Nate, I don't think you threw her off track. You simply stated your opinion about playing beneath the bluffs, along that stretch of river. I've drawn my lines, too. But surely you remember how the kids around here are about that place. We..."

Good Lord, she'd almost mentioned the cave by name! "Anyway," she said, blushing so furiously she was glad he couldn't see her, "parents have rights, too. We have the right and the responsibility to warn our children of danger. If we didn't, it would be neglect."

"Yeah, I see what you mean." He sounded somewhat more confident. "I guess I'll come, then."

"You'd better. I think, if you didn't, she'd be terribly disappointed."

"I guess you're right."

When Nate's next pause stretched out, Amber thought the conversation had reached its end. She was on the verge of saying goodbye when he spoke again, his voice low and husky this time.

"Do you remember, Amber?"

She knew what he was talking about. That day in the cave. She didn't trust her own voice to reply. And sure enough, her voice also dropped. "Yes, I remember." She cleared her throat. "That day when I... when I swam the river and you saved my life and my horse. I—I'm sorry that I never thanked you."

"I'm not asking you to thank me, Amber. I'm asking if you remember."

"Yes, I... Goodbye, Nate."

"Good night, Amber."

Shakily, Amber let the phone drop in its cradle. Of course she remembered. She remembered his heat. And hers. She felt it again. But she straightened her shoulders, redirected her thoughts. She couldn't afford to remember. Not with Nate.

Amber forced her mind to the most encouraging part of their conversation. Nate had revealed that he was worried about Kim. Amber saw this as a good sign, another indication that he might make an excellent parent for Kim. He was definitely good about carrying out his promises. And once a problem cropped up, he dealt with it right away. She admired that. That kind of steadiness and prioritizing counted with children.

THE NEXT MORNING, Amber decided to ask Kim if Nate's warning about the cave had upset her. And while Kim still walked on air, Amber took an opportunity at the breakfast table to broach the subject.

"I talked to Nate last night," she said.

Just as she expected, the girl's eyes lit up. "Oh! What did he say?"

"I thanked him for the glass ball, and he said he—well, he said he was a little worried."

"Worried? What about?"

"He said you discussed the cave below the cliffs. When you admitted that you and your friends sometimes sneak off there when you get a chance, he thought he might have come down too hard on you."

"Oh."

When Kim set aside her cereal spoon, Amber felt a twinge of uncertainty. Kim was so sensitive that Amber avoided intruding where she shouldn't.

"Yeah, it's true," Kim said. "I have gone to the cave."

"As I told Nate, and as he himself knows, kids find it hard to resist the place. But his worry isn't only that you go there. He thinks he might have been too firm when he didn't need to be. Do you understand what I mean?"

Kim usually gazed at Amber levelly. When she dropped her eyes, her retreat indicated more confusion than Amber had expected. "Kim?" she coaxed. "What is it?"

"Well, it's not that I go there so much as..."

"Yes?"

"I don't see my old friends down in the village very much anymore, and sometimes..."

"It's funny that you say that. Granny Maple and I were just discussing the fact that you see your old friends less. Granny Maple says it's because you're so busy. And then, it's been cold, and you're growing older. Are we right? Or is there something else?''

Kim hiked a shoulder. Amber thought she might not go on. But then those green eyes met Amber's again, if with a disturbing shimmer. Kim was on the verge of tears.

''What is it, honey?''

''It's— The kids down there don't talk to me. They say I live at the big house now. They say I'm snooty because I play the cello, and because I don't have time for them. Even when I go to Granny Maple's and I try to talk to them, they don't say much. It feels awful. Even my two best friends from when I was little—you know, Tracy and Letty Jo—they say I'm different.''

Amber kneeled by Kim's chair. She put her arm around the girl and hugged her, not really knowing what to say. She realized she'd picked a bad time. At any minute, the bus would arrive.

''Maybe,'' Amber suggested, ''I should drive you to school so we can talk some more about this.''

''No.'' Kim got to her feet, wiping the tears she hadn't allowed to fall with the sleeve of her shirt. ''I'm doing fine. I really am. I don't want to worry you.''

Amber stood up, surprised. ''Me? This isn't about me, Kim. I want to know what's going on in your life. Inside of you. If you don't feel comfortable talking about something, just tell me. But for goodness' sake, don't protect me.'' The fact that Amber had always protected her brother flitted through her mind. ''Let me drive you to school so we can talk.''

"No." Kim plucked up her books, tugged on her jacket. "I'm just fine. I have new friends. I have my music now. I don't need Tracy and Letty Jo."

Amber had no choice but to let Kim peck her cheek and leave. What's more, she wasn't sure she'd bring up the subject again. As an emerging young woman, Kim had to deal with her friends on her own.

The situation unsettled Amber. She hated to see Kim hurting again. And the idea that Kim might be protecting her, as she herself had habitually protected Dolph, was a new complication. But she supposed her biggest worry was, why would Kim *need* to protect her? Surely she wasn't feeling insecure anymore. Did insecure girls overcompensate by trying for...perfection?

CHAPTER ELEVEN

NATE WALKED through the trees along the river, toward the groups of people lining the bank. The afternoon was perfect for a picnic, and the community was out in full force.

Last night, when he'd called Kim, she'd sounded as bright as the day. She told him that she and her Uncle Dolph were entered in the river-float contest. In parade form, the hand-decorated floats would drift down from a point a few miles upstream. They'd finish at the new park, where they would be judged from the bank.

The prizewinners, she'd told him, would pull into the dock by the new pavilion. The rest would be taken out farther downstream. If Kim and Dolph didn't win, Nate was supposed to meet her at the second landing. If they did, she'd insisted, she wanted him to be there. She wanted him to see them tie up their raft at the dock.

This was all new to Nate, though he'd heard from Beaver about the recent community efforts. For several years, the residents had been working on the park, the fishing dock and the pavilion. The project had pulled the already close-knit community together even more. The park symbolized the blossoming of an area that had suffered a lot of hardship. No one who lived along the river was rich, but they'd strengthened their neighborhood, and he sensed their pride in it. He felt a little of it, too.

He scanned the noisy people cheering the arrival of the first floats. He did indeed recognize most of them, though he didn't remember every name. As Beaver had also told him, there were new residents on the river. No longer a home merely for those who barely scraped by, the community was becoming an attractive place to retire, to have a weekend house or even to raise a family.

Nate felt happy for his one-time neighbors. Most of them had been good to him, and he was determined to give a little back. Now that they were openly, if also belatedly, acknowledging him as Kim's father, he especially wanted to keep an eye on things. Familiar with the residents in general, he was sure they'd continue to give his child the chance she deserved.

He spotted Amber. She was standing beside a tall, thin woman with ash blond hair and long, pale features. Unlike her companion, who was wearing a skirt, Amber wore buff-colored slacks and a tidy white top that was cropped to reveal quick glimpses of her midriff when she moved. Talking animatedly to her friend, she looked sweet and approachable—really happy. Nate had chosen right in wearing khaki slacks and a black polo shirt.

Walking toward Amber, Nate took in the floats beyond her. Most of them were inflatable rafts of varied shapes and sizes and colors. Crepe paper and bobbing balloons added to the bright confusion. And while the river seemed to be cooperating as much as the weather, it was swift enough and high enough from recent rains to call for precautions.

Everyone on the water wore life belts or jackets. Canoes sliced by, while the intrepid drifted in inner tubes, either singly or in groups roped together. It was a happy scene.

Nate spotted Beaver standing on the wooden fishing dock. As Nate could have expected, his mentor was right in the middle of the action, obviously the host for the day. Beaver's attention was riveted on the floats. With his paunch bulging over his shorts, he laughed and joked in his ready way, calling out with a megaphone.

Whatever Beaver said escaped Nate. As he came up beside Amber, she noticed him.

"Nate, I'm glad you came! Have you met Lillian Hewlett?"

Dragging his eyes from Amber's beaming face, Nate accepted introductions to Lillian Hewlett. He had heard of her. She was one of *the* Hewletts who had been close to Amber's family. Squelching his automatic resistance, he chatted amiably with the woman. She seemed friendly enough. Then their attention was drawn back to the happenings on the river.

Most of the floats were paddling around, holding themselves stationary against the current as the judges made their final choices. Beaver's voice boomed through the megaphone. When he announced the third-place winner, the crowd broke into applause and shouts and whistles.

"Do you see Kim?" Amber asked, nudging him with a forearm and pointing across the water. "She's with Dolph. They decorated their raft—the red inflatable—with red-and-white checked tablecloths. Those black spots are actually large ants Kim cut out of black construction paper. There's a picnic basket so..."

Nate nodded, smiling. "I get the point."

"Only the floats with themes will be judged," Lillian remarked.

Again Nate nodded, feeling somewhat excluded from the general enthusiasm. He couldn't recall having been to a picnic. Except for a couple in grade school perhaps.

"And now for the second prize!" Beaver announced. The crowd hushed. "It's called Picnic Fare, and it's sailed by Dolph Brandenberger and Kimmy Gibbons."

"I named it," Lillian said, with a controlled bounce.

Nate and Amber also cheered. But it was when he saw Kim's face that Nate felt the full impact of her victory. His daughter—yeah, his daughter—was delighted.

Kim and Dolph paddled toward the dock, and before Nate could think about it, he stepped forward to meet them, helping to secure the raft. After tying it down, he reached a hand to Dolph, shaking it. "You two looked good out there," he said to Kim.

The girl was so excited she flung herself into Nate's arms. Not expecting such an enthusiastic greeting, he hardly had time to return her squeeze before she scurried away to hug Amber and Lillian.

Both awkward and pleased, Nate turned to Dolph who stood next to him, grinning. Nate hadn't seen him since the brewery sale, but the young man didn't seem to be holding a grudge.

"It's great of you to be here, Nate," Dolph said, confirming Nate's evaluation. "Kimmy's a little trouper, huh?"

When Lillian stepped up to give Dolph a hug, Nate's eyes met Amber's. She'd been watching him. She smiled softly, just for him. He felt as if he'd won a prize, too.

At Beaver's announcement of the first-place winner, everyone turned to the river, cheering the float as it approached. A yellow raft, sporting the head and neck of Big Bird, was filled with younger kids and their parents, all dressed in yellow. Even Kim and Dolph conceded that their float wasn't quite as good. In any case, and in lieu of the lost prize for first place, which was a family pass to Six Flags Over Mid-America, Dolph promised Kim a day at the amusement park, too.

Gradually, the gathering broke up, and a pair of girls, who had to be Kim's age, rushed over to congratulate her. While Kim seemed pleased, she stuck to Nate's side like glue. Still, when her friends insisted she come with them to the turtle races, Nate joined Amber in coaxing Kim to join them.

Just then, Beaver rapped Nate on the shoulder. Beside him, Mabel-honey, the buxom blonde who manned Beaver's checkout at the store, matched Beaver's smile.

"Hey, Nate!" Beaver said. "So good to see you here. Whatcha think about Kimmy's second-place finish? Great little float, huh?"

"Great," Nate said. "I see you're the main man today."

Beaver laughed. "Hell, I don't know what they'd do without me. Came down this morning and started the bar-be-cue pits. You're gonna stay for bar-be-cue, ain't you? Shouldn't be too long until lunch. Brats and wieners and stuff like that. Tonight, we'll have chicken and ribs and a big spread. I hope you're gonna make a day of it."

"I'm not sure, I—"

Beaver slapped Nate on the back. "Yeah, yeah, it's so good you're here!"

Nate greeted Mabel-honey, who then excused herself and moved toward the tables. "I gotta help set up lunch."

"Yeah, honey," Beaver said. "You go on. I'll be there in a minute."

Nate noted that everyone had moved back from the river to stand beneath the canopy of spring leaves.

"Uh, Nate," Beaver said. "I'm glad you're here. You remember that house I told you about? The one I said might go up for sale?"

"Yeah."

"Well, it looks like the guy wants to get rid of it real quick. His parents died, his dad just lately, and he has to get it off his hands. Now, you remember I told you this one's a little bigger. I mean, it only has two bedrooms, but it's got a long porch on the back. More like a Florida room, really, with jalousie windows facing the river. It needs some work, but it's pretty nice as these places down here go. You said something, one time, about buying a place like this for your dad, and I, er—"

"Yeah, thanks," Nate said. "It sounds good. But the truth is, I haven't thought about it lately. I've been busy. I, uh, haven't looked him up yet."

"I hear what you're saying, old buddy. I just thought I'd mention the house again. Since we'd talked about it before. It's not too often one as nice as this goes on the market."

"I get the picture. If I'm going to do something, I have to move on it."

Beaver nodded. "Exactly. Well, old buddy, I gotta go. They need me," he added with a big grin. "Liable to get all messed up if I'm not there to organize things."

Nate chuckled. "If you weren't here, the whole place would probably slide into the river!"

Beaver guffawed. "You know it, you know it! See ya later!"

In watching Beaver walk away, Nate refocused on the buzz of activity in the park. The river had been forgotten. Groups of men collected at the horseshoe pits. Families and friends played badminton, and tossed around balls and frisbees with their dogs. The elderly relaxed in lawn chairs, talking, while women watched over the tables and tables of food. Everywhere Nate looked there was food.

He was searching for Amber. He spotted her getting hot dogs with her brother and Lillian and another couple of gals he recognized from his high school days.

Nate couldn't help thinking about how Amber's short top revealed the tawny color of her midriff. Surely, the shirt kept her cool. But the flashes of bare flesh teased him. Absorbed, he was surprised when another familiar face from the past materialized in front of him. In spite of its familiarity, however, the face of his best friend from his earliest days along the river looked different.

"Hey, Eddie! Where'd you get that bush on your face?"

Eddie Conyers smoothed his full beard and mustache. "What do you think of it, Nate?"

"I think it looks like trouble."

Eddie laughed. "It is, but I've always wanted one, and my wife—I don't know if you heard I married Peggy Havencroft?"

"I heard."

"Yeah, Beaver says you keep in touch. Anyway, Peggy said since I always wanted a beard, I should try one."

When Eddie sobered, even clapped Nate on the back, Nate got the feeling that his friend had not approached merely for casual conversation. Last year, Nate had covered some of the expenses for Eddie's son's operation, anonymously, of course. But Nate suspected that Beaver had told Eddie where the money had come from, probably on condition that he not reveal to Nate that he knew, even to thank him.

Nate suspected that Eddie wanted to raise the subject, but Nate resisted and redirected the conversation. Once they were back on neutral territory, he felt much more comfortable. In fact, it was good to talk with Eddie again. The pair stood for almost an hour, catching up.

Nate grew more relaxed. It struck him, again, that his life along the river hadn't been all bad—certainly not as bad as it had seemed at the time. He had had good supportive friends, and he and Eddie had been really close. The worst part about it had been his embarrassment about always being on the receiving end of their charity, with no hope of giving back. It had hurt his pride and soured him. It had made him desperate to get out.

He learned Eddie had done all right for himself. He hadn't achieved what Nate had, but then, in the scheme of things, few people did. No, in sticking it out at the river community and marrying a girl from the same background, Eddie had found his own happiness and Nate was happy for him. Maybe someday his own past wouldn't haunt him so much. Maybe it would stop driving him.

He finally went for a hot dog. Beaver saw to it that he had a full plate, and then reintroduced him around. Another couple, Beaver's friends and contemporaries, welcomed Nate warmly. Nate could tell that Beaver bragged about him the way he would have a son. But the couple, the Johnstons, seemed glad to hear every word.

The afternoon settled into visiting and games. Nate passed through the crowd, keeping an eye on Kim's activities. She played almost every game. Nate also talked with Amber and Dolph and Lillian, making a fourth in their threesome. It was pleasant.

Finally, Nate joined Granny Maple where she sat with some of her friends. The elderly group laughed and talked. Granny Maple wore a straw hat decorated with plastic daisies that Kim had won for her at a ring-toss game.

"Nate," she said, welcoming him, grasping his hand in both her worn brown ones. He took the vacated chair next to hers.

"I've been watching you," she said. "I've been waiting for you to come and say hello."

"I'm sorry I didn't get here sooner."

"You don't need to excuse yourself to me, sweetheart. I've seen the royal welcome you're getting today. Lots of people are happy to see you, Nate."

When their eyes locked, Nate felt as if he'd never been away. That gaze had always been there for him, loyal and steady. Whatever else had been going on in his life—no matter how scary it had grown, especially in the early days when his dad had abandoned him—this woman had been his anchor.

"You know," he admitted, "I've been in town for a couple of months, now. I don't want you to think I've been avoiding you, but—"

"But—" she said for him, her smile charming, "—you were afraid you'd visit me and run across Kimmy. What do you think about her, Nate? Isn't our Kimmy wonderful?"

The emotion that had been building in Nate all afternoon, the unaccustomed feelings, clouded his throat. "She's great. I only hope..."

"I know what you're hoping. You'll do fine. It's gonna get better and better. Just wait and see."

Yes, Nate thought. He'd been wrong in judging this place so harshly.

The afternoon wore on, warm and lazy. Nate was commandeered by Kim into a softball game with a mix of adults and children.

Dolph, who seemed to spring to life when playing games, pitched while Nate caught. Nate thought the pair of them took it seriously enough to challenge the St. Louis Cardinals. Still, it was a soft game, played on a soft afternoon. And no one suited the ambience better than their soft, chuckling shortstop—Amber.

Kim was so radiantly happy that Nate thought his heart might break. He'd never felt such a flux of emotions. And to think that he'd almost decided not to come! He might have missed out on the time of his life. He felt accepted, a part of something he'd left behind only to rediscover when he was finally on track enough to appreciate it. It was, in short, an amazing afternoon.

AMBER THOUGHT the evening would be as enjoyable as the afternoon had been. Certainly, the third annual May Day River Day had proven the most successful yet. And, as evening approached, the colors of the waning sun in the west, the advancing purples and blues in the east, the music promised by the band setting up in the pavilion, contributed to a satisfied mood.

During the lull, Amber sat with Dolph at a picnic table, watching her brother try to eat a hot marshmallow Kim had skewered and roasted for him. Nibbling gingerly at the toasted brown on the outside, he was trying to keep the gooey inside from dripping onto his clean clothes.

The mood of the event was changing. Since late afternoon, people had been coming and going, putting children down for the night, getting cleaned up for the dancing at the pavilion. Amber had gone home and showered. She'd changed into a military-style outfit, green slacks and a shirt with dull gold buttons.

Kim and Dolph had also showered and changed. Nate had freshened up at Beaver's. Since he hadn't expected to stay for the day, much less for the evening, he borrowed a baggy brown shirt from Beaver and some snugly fitting jeans from Eddie Conyers.

But even in the ill-fitting clothes, he looked spectacular. And not just to Amber. All day Amber had noticed how other women had watched him. And while he seemed oblivious, focused on Kim and Dolph and herself, Amber knew he must be aware of his sensual appeal. Especially when women did everything from greeting him with pointed glances to striking up conversations with him with bold grins. Amber wavered between resentment and laughter at some of the stuff that had gone on right under her nose.

Still, Nate seemed not to notice. He joked with Kim and her two friends, Tracy and Letty Jo. They suspended marshmallows above the coals of a dying fire, the latter two girls flirting with him as only budding teens could.

In this natural setting, father and daughter made a stunning pair. Amber was sure that was part of Nate's attraction. What female could resist the gentleness with which Nate treated his daughter? The pair weren't completely comfortable together yet, but Kim's pride at being with him simply melted the heart of anyone who knew their story.

Everyone, Amber thought, except for Dolph. Looking back at her brother, she wondered if *any-thing* ever registered with him. Downing the last of his sticky marshmallow with a drag of cola, he looked over at Amber across the picnic table.

"Yuck," she said. "Everything you've eaten for the last twenty minutes was nothing but sugar."

He shrugged. "It's that kind of day."

She chuckled. "Its been a good day, huh?"

"Mmm-hmm."

So what had she expected? Enthusiasm? He'd get excited again only if he had the softball and glove back in his hands.

"When's Lillian supposed to get back?"

He glanced at his wrist, which was bare. "I'm not sure. She said Warner would drive her back out."

The news took Amber by surprise. "Warner? I didn't know he was even in town again."

"Yeah, been back a week or so. Didn't I tell you? He wants to see you, so he said he'd drive Lillian out after she got cleaned up."

"*Dolph,*" Amber said in disgust. "Why didn't you tell me?"

Dolph had the grace to look somewhat abashed. "Sorry. Thought I did. It won't be awkward, though. You and Warner don't make people feel awkward."

Amber decided to go ahead and ask the question she'd been wanting to ask all day, just to see *him* squirm. "Did you ever call Hargrove Kandel?"

Dolph looked puzzled. "Didn't I tell you?"

"*Tell me what?*"

"That I've gotten my first project from him."

"Dolph!"

"Yeah, yeah." Suddenly as animated as when he'd had his ball and glove on, he was immune to her barely contained exasperation. "It's a great project! I was telling Nate about it earlier. He thinks it's interesting, too. You see, the Surgeon General wants some ways of encouraging pregnant women not to drink during their pregnancy. What's needed is a psychological profile on women drinkers, then a campaign on abstinence. I've got this study to do, an outline of. . ."

Delighted as she was to hear her brother's enthusiasm, Amber's impulse was to reach across the table and wring his neck. Why hadn't he told her of this sooner? As always, he'd let her sweat it out, and now he expected her to listen when she had other things on her mind.

"Dolph," she said as he wound down.

He peered at her uncertainly.

"Lordy, Dolph! Once and awhile, it would be nice if you'd let me in on things. Especially things that concern me. Like Warner coming here, for instance."

Again, he looked sheepish, and Amber's annoyance dissolved. She considered asking how he and Lillian were faring, and decided against it. From the way they'd behaved today, everything seemed to be fine. Besides, Dolph might misread her friendly interest as a desire to become involved, which she would never do. Ever.

In any case, Nate interrupted them. "Are you sure you don't want a marshmallow, Amber?"

"No thanks. Too sweet for me."

Amber caught her breath, squinting at him. He looked great in the last, slanting golden rays of the sun shimmering through the trees. What a spectacular, finale to the day. Even the river flowed like molten gold.

"And what about you, Dolph?" Nate asked. "Just one more marshmallow?"

"Well..." Dolph considered. "Okay, but I'll get it."

Dolph went to the pit where Kim and her buddies giggled a welcome to him. The ensuing horseplay was Dolph's style, and Amber watched, enjoying it. When she turned back to Nate, she took advantage of their moment alone. He sat next to her on the picnic-table bench, also observing Dolph and Kim and the other girls.

"I've been thinking about that day a couple of weeks ago when you drove to Allswell and talked to Kim about the Big Bend."

"Yeah, I've been thinking about that, too. Kim and I have talked about it some. Here, today. I apologized for coming down too hard, and then explained that I was only concerned about her safety. She said that during our conversation she'd been thinking about losing her friends, and that's what had upset her, not what I was saying. It seems it was more a misunderstanding than anything."

Nate appeared so relieved Amber smiled. "I'm glad the two of you can talk. That's what it's all about, you know. And then, you have to realize that thirteen-year-old girls—well, to put it as nicely as I can," she added with a wry smile, "they chug along on emotion."

"It's pretty complicated for me. I'm afraid I'll inflict some permanent damage without knowing it."

Amber tried to match Nate's crooked smile. She knew he was making light of his fear, but he also meant what he said. "We just need time."

He looked as if he might disagree with that statement, but their attention was diverted by Lillian's arrival. She appeared cool and fresh in a conservative but expensive dress and low heels.

The man who walked behind her was of greater interest. Amber felt Nate stiffen. How would he know Warner?

Since Dolph had fallen in with the new arrivals, he introduced Amber's ex-husband to Nate. Nate rose from the picnic bench to shake Warner's hand.

Fortunately Kim interrupted the proceedings then.

"Granny Maple wants to go home," she said. "Is it all right if I walk her back?"

"Sure," Amber said.

Then her brother turned to Lillian. "What do you say, Lillian? You want to walk along, too? I just ate more dessert than I should have, and I could stretch my legs."

Amber felt ready to shake Dolph. Could he be so oblivious? Was he really going to leave her here alone with Warner and Nate Fields?

Yes, he was. Blissfully ignorant, Dolph strolled off with Lillian and Kim toward Granny Maple, who waved good-night to Amber and Nate.

"Well," Amber said, looking from one of her companions to the other. "Would you like something to drink, Warner?"

Warner's expression was shrewdly charming. He looked pleased and he certainly picked up on Nate's stiff reaction to him. Amber's ex smiled deeply into her eyes, then glanced back at Nate. "Nothing to drink, Kitten. I'm only staying long enough to say hello. I drove Lillian out so she and Dolph wouldn't have two cars."

"Yes, well," she said, forcing a smile, and also glancing at Nate.

Talk about a stone face. Knowing Warner, Amber wondered if he might chuckle out loud. He had a sense of the ridiculous that was as sophisticated as everything else about him. Who but Warner would show up at a country picnic in a blue blazer and white slacks—yachting dress? Even for only staying a few minutes to say hello.

"So," she said, scrambling for a subject, any subject. "Have you been to see your granny lately? The last I heard, you were joining her in Deauville."

Warner smoothed a hand along his perfectly arranged gray hair. His eyes continued to shine—softly, gently mocking Amber's discomfort.

"Since I saw you last, two and a half months ago, I've spent a few weeks in Paris, a few in Deauville. I warned you I'd translate your poetry into French, and I think I've found a publisher over there. Now, it's a matter of the translating. I hope I have the touch for it, Kitten. I wouldn't want to either ruin your work, or make a fool of myself."

Both of them knew that translating poetry into French was as natural to him as breathing. Warner's gaze slid over to meet Nate's hard stare. "I'm sure you must know what I mean, Mr. Fields. May I call you Nate?"

Nate shifted his weight. "I didn't know Amber wrote poetry and, yes, you may call me Nate."

"Good, good. And you must call me Warner. I can see you're friends and I still care about Amber. Unlike some divorced couples, we're still friends. Isn't that so, Kitten?"

Amber nodded warily, unsure where this conversation was leading. Warner seemed to be enjoying himself. He liked to toy with people sometimes, especially when they resisted his native elegance and charm. Warner's ease contrasted all the more sharply with the stiffness of Nate's large body and hard, black gaze. Nothing about Nate was the least bit charming.

Amber's two lives, past and present, had never been juxtaposed like this. She prayed to heaven Warner would leave. She knew he wouldn't intentionally hurt her. But he obviously sensed something in Nate, something that was disturbing him.

"So, Nate," he said, "if you haven't read any of Amber's poetry, you have a treat in store for you. In fact, I happen to have extra copies of her books in the car. If you'd like—"

"Oh heavens, Warner," Amber said, embarrassed and irritated. "Just because we were married doesn't mean you have to promote me."

His gaze again engaged hers, warmly. "It's not promotion, Kitten. I think Nate has an interest, and I'd like to show him how talented you are."

"Actually," Nate said, surprising Amber even more, "I appreciate the offer."

Warner beamed. He'd accomplished some purpose of his own. After he dropped a peck on Amber's cheek, saying that he'd keep in touch, she had the exasperated pleasure of watching the unlikely pair walk away from her in the direction of the parking lot.

"Save me a place," Nate called back over a shoulder to Amber. "I'll be right back."

Amber glanced at the scattering of late picnickers, at the growing activity around the pavilion.

"Save you a place?" she muttered. "What are you talking about?"

Too aggravated to watch the two men any longer, she went to the pavilion. She joined a group who were cleaning up after the last of the supper crowd. As always, there was plenty to do, and she was busy until the crowd collected again. Lillian and Dolph and Kim found her, as did Nate, who had been gone close to an hour. From his attitude, she suspected Warner had won him over.

She wouldn't have been surprised. If he set his mind to it, Warner could win anyone. But Nate wasn't carrying the books of her poetry that Warner had supposedly given him. Tired of the whole business, she threw herself into the evening's entertainment.

In a charmingly haphazard fashion, colored lights had been strung around the pavilion and the bingo tables. The band swung into action, and that meant the square dancing that was popular at their picnics. Gals in long full, flounced skirts and cowboy hats paired off with guys decked out in cowboy-style shirts and shiny boots that had nothing to do with cows and horses.

Amber plunged into the ceaseless swirl of dancing, absorbing the fun and music. The caller was a local man, so he knew all the favorites, the calls everyone liked best. Amber felt the air growing cooler, but the activity kept everyone warm. Looking around, she saw faces flushed with pleasure and exertion.

From the corner of her eye, she noticed Nate watching her progress from partner to partner. He refused to dance himself, even with Kim, claiming he'd never gotten the hang of it. As he used to do a long time ago, Nate Fields simply observed her with black, sometimes haunting, eyes.

CHAPTER TWELVE

THE SQUAWK of the microphone wrenched everyone's attention to the stage. Beaver was standing there with the band, taking in stride the calls from the roomful of disgruntled dancers.

"I know, I know. Sorry about that, folks," he said of the ear-piercing sound. "Now, I know some of you guys out there will say this is only the shank of the evening. But others wanna go home. Of course, the band's paid up for another hour or so, but I have to say something while the party poopers are still here. I mean, what the hell? I've been up since dawn, and I'm still going strong! And I ain't no spring chicken!"

Along with the renewed rush of remarks and whistles and applause, Beaver laughed before continuing.

"Friends," he said, turning both sentimental and serious, "this has been such a good day, and there are so many people to thank. So many people have made this possible that I can't mention them all. So, I'll just call on some of those you might not know about."

Amber stood with Eddie Conyers and his wife, Peggy, frozen in the square that had just finished before Beaver had started speaking. She shifted uncomfortably, her eyes again catching Nate's stare.

He was standing at the edge of the floor with Dolph and Lillian. Kim also remained among the dancers with her partner, Ozzie Johnston. At least four times Kim's age, Ozzie mopped his brow with a handkerchief, also winking at his wife, Joan, who had another partner.

Despite her enjoyment of the evening, despite her sense of beginning to belong, Amber would be embarrassed if Beaver did what she dreaded he might do.

He plowed on. "There's no particular order here now, folks. I'll just start where the spirit leads me, and if I miss anybody, holler. First, there's Slim and Zondra Perkins. Slim got the paper products at a discount from his company Container Co. Thanks, Slim."

Everyone applauded, and Beaver continued, grinning, speaking through the complaining microphone.

"And then there's Amber. Honey, where are you?"

Amber blushed, unable to escape. Eddie pointed her out.

"There she is," Beaver called in acknowledgment. "Everybody knows Amber, Amber Reinhart. I wanna mention that she tells me the old tower from the gravel operation should be completely gone in about a month. Thanks, Amber honey," he said, holding up a hand to halt the renewed appreciation. "But there's one more thanks to Amber. She donated the meat we cooked here today, and believe me, it was one helluva lot. I should know—I cooked it!"

With a nod and the hope that Beaver would move on, Amber recognized the applause.

"Next," Beaver said, his gaze moving in an unexpected direction. "I gotta mention Nate Fields." When the assembly fell into a surprised hush, all eyes turned to Nate. Amber looked at him too. He didn't flinch.

He merely looked back at Beaver, obviously not expecting this, either.

"Now, Nate," Beaver said with a big grin, "I know you don't want me to tell, but it's high time you quit bein' so modest. Folks—" he turned back to his listeners "—Nate wrote me out a check to finish paying off the pavilion and the dock!"

When another cheer went up, Beaver lifted his hand. "What's even better, while he was writing out his check, Dolph Brandenberger wandered into the business and got hooked into donating the same amount that Nate's saving us. Since we'd decided that our next goal down here's to do some landscaping, that'll now be paid for, too, by Dolph."

Amid cheers of approval, Beaver grinned broadly. "So, folks, thanks to these people, we find ourselves at a place we've never been before. What with the money we took in tonight, for the bar-be-cue and all, we're actually ahead. Would you believe it? And that means," he said, "that we have money to spend! Now, what I'm trying to say, I guess, is that we're open to suggestions, folks. We wanna know how you want to spend this money, so show up at the next town meeting and we'll talk about it. There's lots of places it can go, so be there."

Finally, the noise overwhelmed him, and Beaver set down the mike with a wave. The musicians picked up again, but rather than accept a turn on the floor, Amber shook her head and smiled. "Sorry, Eddie. I have to sit this one out."

Eddie was good enough to oblige, and even escorted her through the press that thanked her while the squares moved back into action. Amber headed for

Dolph, who was standing by Lillian and Nate. Kim rushed up, excited about Beaver's announcements, which none of the three involved wanted to discuss.

"Don't you think it's time you danced with Amber?" the usually shy teen asked Nate.

Although he smiled, he also shook his head. "I told you I don't dance." When his daughter seemed disappointed, her father chucked her chin. "I will, however, ask her to join me in a stroll outside. Just until she cools off," he added, his gaze again on Amber's face.

"And I," Dolph chimed in, "will—if Miss Lillian will be so kind as to excuse us—ask you, Miss Second-Place Float Winner, for a final turn before Miss Lillian and I throw in the towel."

"Good idea," Amber agreed, noting that Kim was, despite her high spirits, wilting around the edges. "I'm just about ready to call it a day, too."

Looking as if she would resist, like any self-respecting kid would, Kim hesitated, then relented. "All right, Mr. Second-Place Float Winner, I'll dance with you once more. But you'll also let me watch while you dance your last dance with Miss Lillian."

Kim grinned and Lillian nodded. "Nicely settled, Miss Second-Place Float Winner," Lillian said.

Since Kim spent time with Dolph and Lillian, Amber knew the girl liked the woman who might someday, she hoped, be her aunt.

"Then," Dolph said, sweeping Kim away, "it's a done deal!"

Amber was left to smile at Lillian and Nate, their smiles fading as Nate took Amber's hand and excused them.

"Let's go outside," he said to Amber.

On moving back through the gathering, Amber and Nate encountered numerous smiles. Her blush returned. She felt the heat in her cheeks. As if the effects of Beaver's announcement hadn't been enough, the look of Nate's muscular body in Eddie Conyers's way-too-tight jeans and Beaver's stretched-out shirt drew all kinds of attention, including hers.

Outside the brightly lit pavilion, the cooler night felt good. Colored Christmas bulbs threaded the woods as if a drunken sailor had tacked them up. Nearby tables of bingo players matched the liveliness of the dancers. Nate guided Amber across the grass toward the wooden dock. There, a couple of torches burned in the night, their reflected flames licking the surface of the water. When Amber turned to Nate, she could see the pinpoints of raw gold deep in his dark eyes.

"They're just setting up Dolph's dance with Kim," she said.

He nodded.

"After he dances with Lillian, Kim'll have to go. She's already tired."

Again he nodded, and Amber crossed her arms over her chest, staring past the river to the trees on the opposite bank. The night that surrounded their gaily lit spot was dark and starlit.

"Is it too chilly out here?" he asked, standing next to her. He kept his eyes on the flow of now-black water below.

"After the heat, this feels good."

A moment elapsed before he spoke again. "I didn't know you write poetry."

She squirmed at the subject. "I don't anymore."

"If Warner hadn't told me, would you have?"

"I don't know. Probably not. It's not part of my life now."

"Warner says you're good."

"Warner always *wanted* me to be good."

"Then you aren't?"

"I don't know. Like I say, it's not something I feel the urge to do anymore."

"So writing poetry is an urge, then?"

"I guess it is for me."

The pair stared at the velvety black water. Now that her eyes had adjusted, Amber could discern the rusting edges of the enveloping woods where they met the night sky. She picked out the song, if it could be called a song, of a nearby tree frog. Actually, she corrected herself, the frog and the rest of the river critters were damned noisy. And she was damned uncomfortable. Especially when Nate pursued the topic she wanted to drop.

"I was surprised that Warner's such a nice guy."

She had to chuckle at that. "As one of his victims, I'll verify that Warner can win over anyone he wants to win over. Welcome to the club."

Nate stiffened, and she regretted the cynicism in her voice. "Never mind, I'm sorry I said that. Warner is, as you've discovered, a genuinely nice person. It's just that he's also charming and that he can win over anyone he chooses."

"Would you like to walk a little? The path along the river has an occasional torch."

Amber nodded. She needed to move. She plunged her fists into the pockets of her slacks.

Stepping onto the path, with Nate closing in behind her, she spoke over her shoulder. "I'm sorry if I sounded harsh. About Warner, I mean. I'm not bitter about what happened to us. He's been good to me—in a way, better than anyone. Although he's not exactly old enough to be my father, he's always had that aura of the older, more sophisticated man."

She smiled, a soft, wry smile. "I can remember thinking of him as an uncle. He'd swoop down on my boarding school and take me out to lunch. He listened to me, and since I seldom saw my parents, and didn't get much from them when I did, I hung onto what I had with Warner. Later, I guess my feelings developed into a crush. My girlfriends always oohed and ahhed over his 'gentlemanly' attentions. He seemed very dashing and romantic."

"And so you married him."

That Nate listened so carefully caused Amber's fists to uncurl in her pockets. It was good to share her past with a sympathetic ear. And while she wondered if she should, she still considered Nate the person she instinctively trusted.

"I didn't marry him right away. After college, he got me a job in New York, at a gallery selling art. And while it was considered a glamorous job and I learned something of selling, which has been good for selling horses, I wasn't fulfilled by the art scene. Not like I thought I'd be. Instead, I was out every night with Warner."

Pausing, she scuffed a sandal along the dirt path. She knew Nate would listen. "We had everything in common—background, an appreciation for the arts, and of course, all the plays and concerts we attended, all the books we read. Finally, one day at lunch I told him I was too tired to do anything that night. He laughed and said we'd get married. He said I'd quit my job and we'd explore the world together. When he showed up at dinner with an engagement ring I laughed. I thought he was kidding. But he wasn't. By the time my parents and his family, the Hewletts, got wind of it, I couldn't have backed out without causing a mess."

"Anyway, you didn't want to back out," Nate said, his voice somewhat muffled.

As they traced the river path, from the dappled light of one torch to the next, his upper arm brushed softly against her shoulder. They met only one other couple, teenagers rushing toward them, giggling. Passing the pair, Amber continued her story.

"Who knows whether or not I wanted to get out of the engagement? I was always so eager to please others that I hardly made any decisions to please myself. I simply went with the flow, and the flow was strongly in favor of me marrying Warner. Still, I have no one but myself to blame. All the guys my own age seemed immature and pale by comparison, and for the most part, I was happy to be with Warner. We were friends."

"I remember seeing your wedding written up in the papers."

"What? All the way in Chicago?"

"No, Beaver sent me articles from the St. Louis papers."

"You've kept in touch with Beaver all along, haven't you?"

He nodded. "But we were talking about you."

"Oh yeah, interesting me. Well, anyway, there's not much more to tell. We were on the Continent, living it up, for almost two years. There was the theater in London, entertaining in Paris and winter in Rome. We were always together, and Warner has lots of friends over there, so we were constantly busy. Still, he encouraged me to write poetry." She sighed, then came to the turning point of her tale.

"One day, I simply woke up. I couldn't imagine myself living that way for the rest of my life. I came home. My mother was unwell, and after she died my father got sick and passed away. Somewhere along the line, Warner and I finalized our amicable divorce. He didn't put up any resistance, and I was already in knee-deep at Allswell. And that's that," she said, glad she'd told him and cleared it away finally.

They'd reached a large overhanging tree. Stopping, Amber turned to look at Nate. "And you? What were you doing while I was eating up the Continent with a teaspoon rather than a knife and fork? Were you carving up Chicago with a butcher knife?"

"Now, that sounds like poetry. But it wasn't anything so glamorous."

"Still, you must have been happy. You were doing what you wanted to do, and making it big."

Beneath Beaver's old shirt, Nate shrugged a large shoulder. "I met a guy in college, Tad Coldsdon. We hit it off, and when we graduated, his dad asked me to join the business with him and Tad. Since they already did what I'd decided I wanted to do, I felt as if I'd gotten my lucky break. I was determined to make the best of it."

"And now?"

"And now I'm thinking about leaving Coldsdon and Fields."

"Leaving? But I thought you loved your work."

"I do. But they're moving into bigger jobs, and I prefer smaller projects I can handle on my own. I'm sure the parting will be friendly. It's just a matter of having the guts to make the move."

"If anyone has the guts to go out and get what he wants, it's you. You've already done that. You have a lot to be proud of."

Amber realized, then, that Nate had crowded her back a few steps, close to the big tree behind them. Beneath its foliage, dark shadows swallowed them up. A thick branch hit her at the middle of her spine, then stretched, rustling, to the river that flowed a few feet away. She leaned into the branch, trying to get her bearings.

"I'd say you have a lot to be proud of, too," he whispered, encircling her to lean on the branch. The tree didn't budge. Amber couldn't. Her eyes, her thoughts, were fixed on Nate.

Through the dimness, his face close to hers, his voice sounded soft. "You've had to hustle every bit as much as I have. Getting Allswell back on its feet can't have been easy."

"Well ... I love it."

Nate nuzzled at her lips with his. Softly. His words stayed soft, too. "Warner says the marriage didn't work because he couldn't be a husband to you."

Shock coursed through Amber, bringing her up short.

"Wh ... what do you mean?"

He nibbled again. She pressed at his chest, but he leaned closer to her. "You know what I mean. He couldn't make love to you."

"He told you that?"

"In his own gentlemanly fashion. He had me feeling sorry for him." Nate sipped at her lips. "And for you."

"I...why, I can't imagine." Suddenly, resistance came easily. "Warner just met you!"

Nate's voice was as shadowy, as suggestive as the puddled darkness within the tree's embrace. "He thinks there's something going on between us. And, frankly, I think so, too."

Amber was stunned. Before he could nuzzle her again, she pushed firmly at Nate's chest, and turned her face away from him. "How much did he tell you?"

Nate straightened. "Enough. He said you'd never tell me because you're too loyal. So he told me himself."

"But why?"

"He says I'm the first person you've been interested in. He wanted me to understand that you're not the, uh..."

"That I'm not what?"

"Look, as far as I'm concerned, I'm glad I know. Otherwise..."

Amber bristled. "Don't do me any favors!"

She stepped away from the tree. She was mortified, frustrated, with both Warner and this know-everything who followed her back onto the path. It was all she could do not to explode. "How do you think I feel, knowing that the pair of you talked about me as if . . . ?''

"We didn't talk about you. We said nothing that was meant to hurt you. In fact, we—and that goes for Warner, too—intended to make things easier for you."

"Things? Make things easier for me? In what way?''

When he stood beside her, looking simultaneously confused and oh-so-knowing, she turned and paced furiously down the path. Nate tracked her so closely so that she didn't have to embarrass herself further by shouting.

"Don't think, Nate Fields, that the old guard has passed its instructions on to the new guard, because that's not the way it is with me anymore. You and Warner may have made a 'gentlemanly' agreement that something's going on between you and me, but you and Warner are all wet."

For someone who was considered non-assertive, Amber felt damned assertive. First, she'd laid out Ray Cox—who hadn't called her since—and now Nate Fields. Wondering why she didn't feel prouder of herself, she re-entered the picnic grounds with Nate on her heels beneath the zany Christmas lights.

As they entered the pavilion, Amber realized she and Nate had returned in time to hear the last strains of "Good Night, Sweetheart." The music, sentimental and sweet, was just the opposite of how she felt. She struggled to control herself.

"Look, Amber," Nate said, reaching for her arm.

She tugged away. Besides, the party was breaking up. Kim, along with Dolph and Lillian, caught up with them.

"Guess what?" Kim asked, still smiling, still excited.

"What?" Amber said, mustering her own smile.

"Lillian wants me to spend the night at her mother and father's house. In the morning we can sleep late, and then all of us will meet Dolph for brunch at the Cheshire Inn. Won't it be wonderful? Can't I go?"

Lillian had spent time with Kim before, shopping and lunching and that sort of thing. Amber wanted the pair to be friends. "Well," she heard herself say, "the only thing—"

"I know, practice time. Lillian says I'll be home by two in the afternoon."

Amber glanced around her. The crowd from the pavilion and bingo tables noisily shifted into the parking lot and nearby streets. Lillian and Dolph, and even Nate, waited for her reply. "We'll have to drop by home and get you some stuff."

"Oh, Lillian says she has an extra toothbrush and plenty of pj's. I've changed, and she says I'll be fine for brunch tomorrow. Oh, please, can't I?"

Sensing the strain she'd felt on the pathway with Nate diminishing, Amber smiled. "Sounds like fun to me."

Kim, and then Lillian, gave her a hug. Dolph was already meandering in the direction of the parking lot.

"Just to be safe, we'll see you home," Lillian said, turning to tell Dolph to hold up.

"No." Amber sent her friend a cryptic smile. "If my brother's not concerned, why should anyone be?"

When Lillian chuckled, still looking as if she'd call Dolph, Nate interjected.

"I'll see Amber home."

That was all it took, and Lillian hurried to catch up with her two companions. Amber collected herself and glared at Nate. "I'm leaving," she said, "and no one's following me home."

"Somebody said Mick and Etta Fay are at their lake house. That means—"

"That means I'll be on my own. But I've told you before, I'm on my own a lot and you're not following me home. Good night."

With that, she headed for the parking lot. Headlights and red rear lights swam dizzily through the darkness. Amber kept up her pace until she heard someone calling her name. Turning back, she saw Beaver. Naturally, Nate, who was nearby, stopped, too.

"Here you are, Amber honey." The elderly man was still full of energy. "I, uh," he added, glancing at Nate, then focusing on her. "I hope I didn't embarrass you tonight. You neither, Nate. I just thought it was time people down here know how much you help out. Surely, there's nothin' wrong in that."

Amber smiled. She liked Beaver. No one worked harder for his community than he did. He'd embarrassed her, but that hadn't been his intent. "No," she said, giving him a reassuring hug. "You didn't embarrass me too bad."

He laughed, turning to Nate. "I hope you forgive me too, old buddy."

When Nate nodded, Beaver pushed a foil-covered plate into Amber's hands. "I think you oughta escort this little lady of ours home, Nate."

But Amber shot a warning glance at Nate and he backed off. "No, she says she'll be fine. It was a great time," he added, moving in the direction of the other cars and pickups. "Anytime you cook, Beaver, call me."

Beaver laughed, standing with Amber for a moment, staring after Nate until he disappeared. They talked and by the time she got away from Beaver and the few others who wanted a last word, the lot was nearly empty.

The truth was, Amber didn't mind being on her own. She needed a respite. She needed time to consider her conversation with Nate about his incredible talk with Warner. Now, *that* had been embarrassing. To think of Warner discussing her with Nate Fields the way he had was mortifying.

On her way up the back road to Allswell, Amber concluded their talk couldn't have been easy for Warner, either. Those times hadn't been easy for Warner. Rolling down her window, she let in the rush of cool air. She allowed it to soothe her raw feelings and nerves. What had happened between her and Warner hadn't been merely frustrating for his wife. It had been sad.

In recent years, Amber had recognized that it could have gotten even sadder, even worse. In the time she'd been away from Warner—after he had gone completely out of her life—she'd grown to believe the situation had worked out for the best. She hadn't loved Warner, not as she should have, and their breakup, her determined escape from the life she'd lived with him, had been inevitable. Who knew how unhappy they would have made each other had they stayed together?

No, they were both better off. And while she wished she hadn't wasted the years she had, that couldn't be changed. That, too, was something she'd grown to accept and to live with. Now she hoped she would continue to make up for those lost years.

Everything looked as it should as she pulled into the cobbled square at the rear of the house. Lights glared from the garage, which she opened with her car remote control. Behind her the porch light shone. The single difference was the black Porsche, waiting in the spotlights with its own interior lights on.

Nate sat inside, obviously reading one of her books of poetry. He did not glance up when she drove into the garage.

Only when she walked toward him and the house did he look up. She matched his nonchalance. The chilly drive from the bottomland had cooled her temper. Warner and Nate hadn't meant to hurt her. Just the audacity, the sense of invasion of her privacy, still rankled.

She neared the porch. Nate uncurled himself from his black car, tossed the slim volume on the seat and closed the door. He approached her, still wearing Beaver's shirt and those damned jeans.

He'd cooled off, too. "Look, I'm sorry. I didn't mean to hurt you or to get you upset."

Amber smiled cryptically. She walked up the steps and went on to unlock the kitchen door. It took her only a moment to find her key and insert it in the lock. "I accept your apology. As far as I'm concerned, the past is behind me."

Glancing over a shoulder, she caught an old familiar mental image of Nate, just outside the screened-in porch. She struggled with wither or not to ask him in.

He spoke first. "Where's the, uh, Gnaw?"

"He's fishing with Etta Fay and Mick."

"If you're going to have such a big dog, he could at least be a guard dog or a watchdog."

Wavering between renewed exasperation with Nate messing in her life and amusement at the idea of Gnaw serving any useful purpose, she chuckled. "Didn't you know? Anyone who sets foot on this property is treated as a long-lost friend."

"But this place is simply too big for you to be here alone!"

Sighing, Amber pushed the door open and flipped on the kitchen lights. Bright, white light spilled through the door and the nearby windows. On the verge of firmly stating good night, Amber's gaze engaged Nate's black stare. The scene was so reminiscent of the boy who'd watched her years ago that she felt herself softening.

"Would you like some coffee?"

Nodding, he mounted the porch. They entered the kitchen. He locked the door behind them. She laid her purse, with Beaver's foil-covered plate, on the black and white countertop.

"You know I only fix instant," she said, "and that's decaff."

In response he covered the few feet between them and took her, almost roughly, into his arms.

His voice, too, was rough. "I don't want coffee. I want you. I've wanted you ever since I can remember."

CHAPTER THIRTEEN

AMBER HAD EXPERIENCED Nate's kisses before. Years ago in the cave. That night in the old tack room down at the stables. But those kisses had hesitated just within the bounds. Even when he'd kissed her an hour or so previously along the riverside pathway, he'd been restrained, surveying her response while communicating his desire. But Nate's rush of kisses now, in the kitchen, where he pushed her up against the countertop and held her tightly, were a different story.

She surrendered herself. She'd just recalled the boy he had been, the one who had always watched her. He had said he'd wanted her for as long as he remembered. Dormant emotions awakened, all the more intense for their years of sleep.

To be in his arms was amazing. Nate, in himself, was amazing. He ensnared her, his mouth hungrily at hers, then moved over her face, possessing himself of every inch and feature.

He plunged wantonly ahead, taking her with him. Along the length of hers, his hard body implied mystery and magic. His warmth, his scent, overpowered precaution.

His mouth moved back to her lips, pressuring her. His voice sounded raspy and needy. Like she felt. "Do you remember when we first saw each other? I mean, when we really first looked at each other?''

Amber couldn't remember two minutes ago.

''You were around seven and I was about nine.''

His breath was on her face. Although she groped for what he tried to coax from her, she couldn't remember anything.

''I was sweeping the stoop at Beaver's, and you came in with your father. You stared at me, and when I made a face at you, you stuck out your tongue.''

Amber's memory remained blank. He thrust his tongue into her mouth. There was a little revenge in the act, a lot of possession. Then, as if reconsidering, he gentled his thrusts. He used his tongue to rouse hers, to awaken her, to entice a response.

When Amber replied with a tentative lick to his, he moaned, and kissed her deeply again. He'd read her signal. He loosened his embrace, lightened his kisses.

He smoothed a hand up between them. His fingers slid over her breast. He claimed it. Again, he moaned, pleasuring her as much as himself. She slumped into the countertop, leaned into the firm, tender touch at her nipple.

Pulling his lips from hers, he paused to search her eyes with a provocative stare. ''Whenever I see you, you're all buttoned up.'' He thumbed the dull gold button at the top of her shirt. ''You still are.''

Amber snuggled her face into his shoulder. He gentled his advance. ''It's all right, babe. You don't have to be afraid with me. I've been tuned into you since day one.''

Touching her again, warming her breast through the fabric with his breath, he nudged her back into the enchantment. Kissing her, he undid button after button, the fingers of his other hand persistent around the cup of her bra.

Amber joined him, encouraged him to surmount the last barrier. She wanted him to touch her there. She yearned for it so precisely that when he slid his long fingers between her flesh and the fabric, she felt a great relief. She arched into his hand.

His response soothed and aroused simultaneously. She anticipated the next step. She wanted it. Pushing down the cup, plumping her tender flesh, he lowered his mouth to the circle of her nipple.

Sweetly he suckled her, then looked up at her, his eyes sultry in the bright kitchen light. He cuddled her against his shirted chest. With his forehead pressed to hers, curling his hand around her neck so she couldn't inch away, he rolled his head against hers.

"Oh, Amber. You gotta let it happen." He was so close, his eyes blurred before hers. "Say you want it, too. It has to be."

Along with everything else, Amber had forgotten the word "no." Knowing it, Nate swept her up in his arms, took her to the light switch.

"Turn it off," he said.

"But it'll be so dark—"

"Turn it off."

The switch clicked. He carried her, surely, back through the kitchen to the corridor leading to the entry.

"Be careful."

"My God, Amber," he murmured against her ear, "this place is imprinted on my brain."

But when they reached the staircase, he let her legs slide along him to the floor. With the next switch, she illuminated the core of the house. Taking her hand, Nate quickly mounted the stairs with her, his eyes searching out the spaces, and evidently his memory, too.

"Do you remember when you brought me up here that one time?"

Now *that* Amber recalled. That had been the day he'd fallen off his father's tractor. Her heart had wrenched for him.

"Is your room still pink?"

"No, I—"

"The switch," he coaxed. "Where's the next switch, babe? Turn it off."

They'd reached the balcony, and Amber cast them back into darkness. Now she felt the house, too. She sensed Nate sensing her, then felt his hands on her body. When she touched him, her nerve endings exploded. He'd removed his shirt and dropped it to the floor. His wide warm chest was hers to explore. He encouraged her. He tugged her out of her shirt and bra and let them, too, fall away.

Twisting against her, he rubbed the hardness of his chest into her soft breasts. He fit his belly into her abdomen, his groin into hers. Amber thought she might collapse right there on the floor.

Again he lifted and carried her, along the wide balcony. He was sure of his direction. At the door of her bedroom he paused, and as she reached for the light switch he stepped in. Here, the lights from the stables streaked through the windows. Silver lay in shafts across the carpet, shimmered over the wide, old-fashioned four-poster bed.

With assured steps, Nate moved toward the bed. Yes, the house was in his brain, and perhaps, under his dusky skin.

After he stripped back the jade and cream spread, Amber found herself on cool, apricot sheets. With a firm hand, he reached for the lamp, then changed his mind. "Shall I build a fire?"

"No," she whispered.

As if sensing her unease and her anticipation, he bent over her, kissing her and peeling off her slacks, her lacy briefs, her sandals. When he stood beside the bed, Amber knew he watched her. Because his eyes were deep-set, she couldn't see them in the dark, but she knew he watched her. Just like always.

"You're so beautiful," he said simply. Then he moved to work himself out of his clothes. He stretched to tuck something he retrieved from a pocket beneath the pillow. "You're so warm against me in the silver light. What color is it in here now?"

"Apricot, mostly."

He grunted his satisfaction, sliding over the sheets. Like the lush room itself, Amber welcomed him into her waiting arms. Her dusky lover with shadowed eyes ground out a note of deep pleasure. "You're so sweet," he whispered. "Everybody likes you."

She spread her hands through his thick black hair. "Do you like me, Nate?"

His eyes, were deep, unreadable jet. His silence was his answer.

He grasped her hand, drabbing his tongue along the calluses between her fingers and her palm. "I used to stand outside this house, resenting you and what went on in here. Your lights shone pink at night. I've always known you were elegant." He rubbed his fingers along the hard spots. "But I've been wrong about you, too. You're soft and sweet and hardworking and determined and..."

He stretched out beside where she lay flat and open to him. But he separated himself enough to take her hand, to rub it, purposely abrading the slight roughness in her palm along the round of his hip. "That day in the cave." His whisper enchanted her. "Do you remember, Amber?"

She nodded, her movement silky against the pillows.

His voice echoed the sound. "That day, in the cave, when I stroked myself with your hand, you set me on fire. I've been on fire ever since. I think you're the only person who can give me any peace."

Amber waited, going still. He insinuated their hands into the crease of his groin. But just as she drew in a shuddering, wanting breath, he rolled over onto her.

With his chest and his belly and his one leg, he tucked her into his warmth. He tongued her mouth open and explored it over and over. An unfamiliar urgency began to ride Amber. She wanted to rush at something and grab it. This was her chance.

But Nate wanted to go slowly. She recognized his desire, as desperate as hers. She could feel it in his restrained movements, in the way he'd draw back. He'd allow himself to go so far, then he'd ease them with gentler kisses. She felt patience and affection as tangibly as she felt heat. His concern for her flowed out and over her, warm and embracing.

Then she sensed him letting go, and she followed suit. She tugged at him, persuaded him to rock with her. She pulled his knee up onto her belly, stroking his thigh with her hand.

His kisses grew blunt and blatant. He hadn't unleashed himself completely, but he was oh, so close.

He even voiced it. "Are you sure?"

She grasped him behind his knee, moving his other leg between her legs as well. It was a bold invitation, and he accepted it.

Straightening above her, he found a packet he'd pushed under the pillow and opened it. Head bent, he looked away from her just long enough to put on the condom. When he finished, he looked down at her. He was a shadowy, wide-shouldered lover, hovering above her, as velvety as the night. His voice filtered to her, dusky and deep.

"This is a dream come true for me, babe. I want it to be for you, too."

Reaching up, she smoothed a hand over his breastbone, then moved it down over his firm chest, along the ribbon of dark hair to where it flared into a triangle.

Catching his breath, he adjusted her legs around him, and slowly eased into her. Then out. Through the silvery light, his gaze met hers. She pleaded with her hips. She needed him to soothe the ache. She thrust her pelvis into him.

The invitation was again accepted. Finally, at last, he let go. She didn't want to be handled with kid gloves. She wanted the gloves off. What she needed was so deeply embedded within her and in her past that it would only be satisfied by this total possession by Nate Fields.

The sharing was good. And the tenderness was good. But she needed this intensity to build, needed to strive for something she'd never known. Then, suddenly, she found it. Surely, like someone stumbling on a gold mine, or unearthing diamonds. She shuddered, gasped, arched into Nate, her body begging him to press against her, and it did.

He knew what she needed. He helped her make it last. Then, just afterwards, she took him into her arms, smiling and hugging him, coaxing him against her, cajoling him toward his own deep dark treasure. He was more than ready to accept. He, too, gasped. He shoved, buried her in the mattress. Still and silent and sated, he collapsed onto her in accommodating inches. She welcomed him with another embrace. She hoped he'd never move away from her. Never.

Nate was as patient and sweet as he was dark and troubled and haunting. She knew it at last. She was in love with him. Her love had lain dormant in her for a long, long time. Nothing with Warner, nothing with anyone else, would have ever worked.

It was funny that she'd never known. It was funny that, for her, it was a blinding irrevocable truth, while for Nate, the moment was merely another dream he'd forced into fruition.

NATE WOKE to soft apricot light shading his skin, spilling over Amber's lighter, more golden hue. He'd slept so deeply and felt so truly at peace that it unsettled him. Looking at her where she snuggled into the curve of him, he confronted two choices. But, no, he had only one. He had to make himself get up.

Both of the condoms he had brought were spent. If he didn't get out of her bed, away from the cozy temptation and apricot light, he'd make love to her again. And he never, never initiated lovemaking without protecting himself and his partner. When he'd asked Francie if the child she'd carried has been his, she'd lied to him. Even then the possibility had scared him so badly he'd never forgotten. He hadn't made love without a condom since.

God, he'd really done it, he thought. He was really here. He thrust a hand through his hair, trying to tamp down the ready renewal of desire before he gave in. Sweeping up Eddie's jeans from the carpet, he headed, naked, for the bathroom.

Nate knew the layout. It was just that the suite of rooms was now that of a woman, not of the girl he remembered. That girl was fast fading from his mind, replaced by the woman she'd become. Although scary in many ways, the real Amber of the present far outweighed the dream he'd harbored for years.

In the bathroom, Nate faced two more choices. He should go home and he knew it. But he couldn't leave her. Not until he saw her smile, felt she was okay. In their second round of loving, he'd been a bit too unrestrained. He'd let himself get a bit out of hand. He knew he hadn't hurt her. That wasn't in him to do. But she'd been inexperienced, and he wasn't used to that.

If he stayed, and if he didn't remove the scent of her from his body, he'd end up back in bed. He switched on the shower and stepped into the warm spray. Because it felt good, he soaped up twice and rinsed off.

When he got out and toweled off, he discovered Amber still hadn't budged. He was hungry, but could hardly go down to the kitchen and find something to eat. Not that he wasn't familiar with the kitchen.... Nor would he prowl around the house, tempting though the idea was.

Pulling on Eddie's too-tight jeans over his damp body proved a challenge, but he managed. Leaving the fly open made it bearable. Rather than chance another look at Amber, he stepped, barefoot, into her study.

He didn't intend to nose around in her things. But the sight of the glass ball he'd given her, the one with the snow scene trapped inside, lured him to her desk where he plucked it up and shook it. Catching sight of her two volumes of poetry, he decided that that was how he'd pass the time until she woke up. Last night, before she'd pulled into the drive outside, he'd glanced through the books in his car. Now, he was free to study her poems at length.

Easing his large body onto the chair behind the desk, he took a moment to scan the view through the glass doors behind it. On the balcony, a long wooden box filled with geraniums and trailing ivy interrupted a view to the stables. It had to be summer. The flower boxes at Allswell always overflowed with geraniums and ivy throughout the summer.

He forced himself not to think about the stable beyond, and remember the way the stable lights shone into both this room and the adjoining one at night. He looked down at the desk.

His eyes rested briefly on the weekly planner. He noted the neatly listed entries for the next week. A lot of her time was spent calling clients. Occasionally she would meet them at the airport and roll out the red carpet. He could imagine her list of clients. She sold her fine western-style pleasure horses to people who could afford the best.

Determining again to mind his own business, Nate plucked up the first book. *Skipping Stones and Remembering*. He could appreciate the quality of the printing job, but beyond that...well, what did he know about poetry? About as much as he did about classical music.

Still, he remained as he was, reading through the second volume, *Remnants of Memory*. Most of Amber's poems had been written when she'd been in Europe with Warner. And, frankly, he thought it showed. He knew diddly-squat about putting words together in an artistic way. But yearning and homesickness he did understand. In picking up the clues between the lines alluding to place, he sensed her need for Allswell.

Poetic or not, Nate felt he did know Amber now. He also knew Allswell and the river below. In Europe, Amber had been on the outside. He sympathized with that kind of isolation completely. Not for the first time, he realized how fully his former beliefs about her contrasted with who she really was.

Nate didn't realize how engrossed he'd become until she opened the door to the office. She stood against the jamb, one bare foot on top of the other, fresh from a shower, tying a silky wrapper at her waist. With her wet hair and freshly scrubbed face, a memory of the little girl flitted through Nate's mind. He felt tied up in knots. He wanted to make love to her.

"Hi," she murmured, toweling her hair. "I saw the clothes and couldn't figure if you'd left."

Nate glanced at the clock. A couple of hours had passed since he'd sat down. "I can't believe it's almost eleven," he said inanely.

"Are you hungry?"

He'd forgotten his hunger, too. "I could be."

"I'll dress and make some instant coffee. I hope Etta Fay left something in the fridge. Do you cook?"

Nate got up from the chair. He watched her take in his state of undress, his yawning jeans. Walking toward her, he gathered her in his arms. He couldn't help himself.

"Are you all right?" he asked softly, kissing the rose in her cheek.

Thank God, she smiled at him. She remained the same, sweet Amber, just somewhat more knowing. She hugged him.

"I'm great," she said, openly pleased that he had approached.

Her enthusiasm delighted him. Feeling better and better, he kissed her again. She responded again. From above her, Nate absorbed what their closeness revealed of her from breast to belly. He pressed her against him, whispering in her ear. "You don't happen to have a condom, do you?"

She curved back in his arms, looking up at him. "Uh, no. I've never needed anything. I mean, even with Warner's, er, problem, I always wanted children."

The awkwardness they both felt might have wedged between them. But it didn't. She smiled at him. "I've been wanting to show you something for a long time," she said.

All he could think about was making love. "What is it?"

"Come on." She rotated gracefully away from him, still smiling. Her happiness was contagious. "This you're gonna like. This you haven't seen."

With his hand captured in hers, Nate followed her. Passing their shirts where they lay crumpled on the balcony floor didn't ease his libido, either. His mind seemed set on one track and one track alone. He doubted anything she had to show him could be engrossing enough to derail him.

She wove them through a heavily draped bedroom and sitting room. They had entered the master suite at Allswell.

"Someday I want to redo the rooms," Amber explained, just ahead of him. "But I don't have the money for it now. Nor the need. As you can see by the dust, this part of the house is closed. It's too much for Etta Fay, and besides it's never used. But here—" she said, swinging a door wide open "—is what you'll like."

Indeed, the door revealed a small room that was a treasure from the past, preserved in mint condition.

"When Mother and Father had the suite redone, my father insisted this be left for posterity. Mother thought he was joking. She wanted yet another walk-in closet. Thank goodness he didn't give in!"

Stepping into the masculine room, Nate looked around, absorbed. It was lined from floor to ceiling in cupboards and doors, executed in cherrywood, according to the finest cabinetmaker's art.

"It was my grandfather's bath. Of course, he had a valet at the time."

Nate's eyes traveled over the marble floor, the brass appointments, the single, narrow window that admitted the scant light. A strop hung from the marble console.

Standing inside, Amber motioned to a porcelain shaving mug, with a sable shaving brush. "It's exactly as it was. Even some of the soaps he bought in London," she added, opening a cupboard door, "are here."

But Nate's attention stopped at the barber chair. It sat center-stage, facing the marble countertop and sink with the beveled mirror above. The chair was elaborate, wrought of old-fashioned metals and porcelain and burled wood. Soft dark leather padded the seat, the oval back and the headrest.

"Everyone's always interested in the shower," Amber said brightly. "It was one of the first to be installed in the area, and has dozens of showerheads and a bench."

She opened it, but he didn't really notice. He was drawn to the window overlooking the expanse of smooth lawns, the drive leading to the iron gates. Here was the very heart of the Brandenberger lair. Nate wanted to hate it. But he didn't; not anymore. In fact, his feelings were just the opposite. His pleasure in old spaces had never been so intense.

Turning back to Amber, he tried to swallow the emotions that were threatening to overwhelm him. They were just too much for him to handle. That's why he'd never belong to anyone. Not even to someone as special as Amber, or as much a part of him as Kim.

"I like the chair," he managed, smoothing the cool curve of its back with one hand.

Amber looked bewildered. "I thought if anyone would like it, it would—"

"Come here," he said, opening his arms to her.

She responded as she had the night before, immediately stepping into his embrace. She smelled so good. She felt so good. So trusting. He gave up fighting the feelings that she and the exquisite little room evoked. For once, he couldn't bury his emotions. Not yet. He needed to indulge them, to wallow in their warmth. For just a bit. He longed to absorb the pure beauty of the moment, the pure gold of this woman.

Catching sight of himself holding Amber in the old beveled mirror above the barber chair, Nate experienced the swift surge of desire he'd been suppressing all morning. This time, he knew he was already lost.

Kissing her and coaxing her, he ended up in the large chair with her on his lap, eager and soft in his arms. Glimpses in the mirror doubled the intensity of his passion. He urged her to also look. She blushed. He knew he was already too far gone, that it had to happen again. Only the knowledge that they had nothing to keep Amber safe from pregnancy, lent him any sort of anchor.

Desire ripped through him. And through her as well. He could feel it as tangibly as he did her soft skin and her wet, eager mouth. Sliding his hand down, into the spread of her silken wrapper, he whispered in her ear. "No more buttons."

She smiled at him, kissed him, goaded him to the edge.

"It's gotta be a little different this morning."

She nodded her understanding, and he lost himself in the rich coffee color of her eyes.

Oh God, he couldn't resist the subtleness of her beauty, the mirrored image of her elegant profile set against his own mustard-brown shoulder. With caressing fingers, he loved her again in the old barber chair. Then, he showed her how to sate his need. In his heart, he knew it would be something he'd never forget, something he'd never come close to again. Amber would remain the ideal guiding force in his life. His unattainable North Star.

CHAPTER FOURTEEN

NATE'S WEEKEND with Amber and Kim left him feeling agitated on Monday morning. By early afternoon, he was in his car, on his way to Flat River. From Beaver, he'd gotten his father's last known work address. Nate didn't have a home address for him. Nor would he have expected one. Gerald hung his hat wherever he found cheap quarters.

Driving through Missouri farm country south of St. Louis, Nate avoided thinking about Amber. That relationship felt shaky. On the other hand, Kim was now an integral part of him. He felt almost as if he carried his daughter in his pocket, and that he always would. Just as he now carried her photo.

He admitted to himself that he was afraid to face his own father. Afraid, and, more than anything, angry.

At the farming community town, it didn't take Nate long to locate the garage and gas station where his dad worked as a mechanic. The run-down look of the place didn't surprise him. That was his dad's style. His dad lived one day at a time, eking out what existence he could. That meant frequent moves from one town to the next. A drifter, he'd find some favorite bar to haunt at night, some woman or another to flirt with while he drank. Gerald lived with no attachments, no money, no desire other than the will to survive.

As for Nate's mother, Nate knew only her name and that she had been Irish. He had never seen a picture of her. The few times he had mustered the courage to inquire about her, his dad had said she didn't matter. If Nate ever wanted to look for her, he wouldn't have known where to begin. Certainly, not with his father.

Parking his car beyond the gas pumps, Nate felt the anger. He felt other things, too, emotions he wouldn't explore. He hadn't changed out of his expensive suit, nor did he remove his sunglasses, even when he entered the dark interior of the garage. The contrast of the bright May day outside made the garage even gloomier.

Coated with the unique grit and grease combination they attract, the service bays resembled the inside of a junk pile. When a man, apparently the owner, approached him, Nate said simply, "Gerald Fields."

"Back there." The guy hitched a shoulder toward the rear of the garage where a car sat with its hood up.

The large back door of the garage was open, and once again, Nate was struck by the contrast of light and dark. A tall, large-boned silhouette of a man moved against the backdrop of light. Still Nate didn't remove his dark glasses. Not even when he reached the car.

Then Gerald Fields raised his head, his hair silvered black, and Nate knew he recognized him. If he was surprised, he didn't show it. Gerald never showed emotion. Nate wondered if he'd ever felt any.

"Nate," the man pronounced, leaning back against the car.

His son nodded.

The moment spun out. He said nothing. His father turned and resumed his work on the motor. Nate noted the familiar work-hardened hands, the mechanic's towel draping the dirty overalls pocket.

He could remember when he'd seen his father last. It was definitely before Nate left the river community at nineteen. He saw again the proud carriage, the evidence of Osage Indian blood stronger in his father's profile and features than in Nate's own. The fact that that same blood now could be discerned in Kim suddenly took on a new meaning for Nate.

The possibility of family.

Watching his father work, Nate reconsidered the man who had abandoned him years ago. The man was not all bad. No matter how transitory his jobs had been, Gerald had worked hard at them and Nate admired that. Years of heavy labor etched the older man's hands and face. And when Gerald Fields did make friends, his loyalty was without question. At least, for as long as he stayed in town.

He'd just never made friends with Nate. From the beginning, he and Nate had been as different as night and day. Nate had been a dreamer. He had wanted more than Gerald wanted. Furthermore, Nate had been willing to pursue his dreams with discipline and single-minded determination.

It all flooded back. The old truths, the old frictions, the old resentments. However, those were tempered by what he saw now. His father was growing old. Older than his years. And though Nate had been sending him money for a long time, the years of hard labor were taking their toll.

Nate didn't expect or want gratitude. His father had never asked him for the money. If it stopped coming, Nate doubted he'd miss it. But the man lived on the edge of financial disaster. A month or two out of work, and Gerald Fields would be hurting. He blew what extra money he had on backroom gambling and cards, on rough but shared male companionship. He always had.

Irritated that his father wouldn't look at him, that he treated his only son negligently even more, Nate stood his ground. Stubbornness was something they both understood. Still, if they were to speak to each other, he would have to initiate it. The problem was, he couldn't explain why he'd come.

"How's the job going?" Nate finally asked.

"Okay."

"How long do you plan to work here?"

"As long as the work lasts, I guess."

"Aren't you getting tired of working?"

His father's laugh was a hard, choking sound. "Dammit, boy, working is what I do."

Nate wished to hell the man would pull himself out from under the car's hood and talk to him. But that would be too much to ask. Neither one of them had ever learned to communicate. This shared inability had grown into an I-don't-give-a-damn attitude that defined their time together. Nate had often wondered why his father had bothered to keep him. Certainly, at some point, Gerald had had to decide to take him off his mother's hands. He wondered, again, when that had been and how it had been sorted out. He wondered if the man had somehow cared.

At last, Gerald pulled himself upright, wiping his greasy hands on the dirty mechanic's towel. Nate stripped off his sunglasses. The picture of Kim in his breast pocket burned in his mind. But his father spoke first.

"So, boy, what brings you to Flat River?"

Nate felt the rebuff. *You do, you ass,* he wanted to say. He took a breath. "I'm working in St. Louis for a couple of months."

"So Beaver tells me."

"There's a house up for sale. Along the river. I thought you might like to retire. Do some fishing. As I recall, you like to fish, and—"

"Retire?" Gerald Fields peered at Nate as if he thought he was nuts. "Hell, boy, didn't I just tell you that what I do is work?"

Nate ignored the retort. He saw Gerald's haughty judgment of his own clothes and confident stance. The man had to be proud of what Nate had accomplished. But Gerald would never reveal his pride in his son. Nate slipped his glasses back on. With a terse goodbye, he walked away.

To think that Gerald Fields would call him back, or even offer so much as a minute over a cup of coffee or a muttered goodbye, was out of the question. When Nate glanced back from the doorway separating the gloomy garage from the bright light, Gerald had already ducked his head back under the hood.

Any hope Nate might have cherished of a renewed relationship with his father vanished like the wishful thinking he'd done as a kid. Nothing between him and Gerald Fields had changed. Nothing ever would. From before Nate could remember, they'd been frozen into their roles. Likewise, the future he'd begun to glimpse with Amber and Kim over the last couple of days was as much a dream as all the dreams he'd abandoned a long time ago. Dreams equaled pain. Work was the ready, familiar refuge.

BY THE TIME Nate pulled into the gates at Allswell that evening, he felt raw but determined. He didn't know what in hell had possessed him to visit his father. On their own, they each managed well enough. Together, they were a disaster. But more to the point, he couldn't figure out how he'd even considered a future that included Amber and Kim. Even the mere idea scared him.

Now he was back on track. His encounter with his father, such as it was, had set him straight. He'd already accomplished what he originally set out to do. He and Amber had agreed that Kim should get to know him. The weekend had seen to that. Now, it was time to extricate himself from Kim's life, allow her her brighter and very different life. Seeing his father had proven that his original understanding with Amber was for the best. He didn't know how he had strayed from the idea, but he wouldn't stray again.

Of course, as Nate entered the gates at Allswell he encountered the galloping hound who charged the Porsche. Nate's aggravation increased. The overgrown puppy could get hurt chasing cars. Then where would Kim be with another loss to deal with?

As Nate eased into the drive in front of the house, Kim ran out to greet him. Apparently, she'd been walking with Gnaw. When she reached the car, she grabbed Gnaw's collar and tugged the straining galoot to the veranda and into the house. Relieved, Nate crawled out of his Porsche.

Kim came back with a big smile on her face. She'd become at ease with him since their hours at the picnic—had it been just the day before yesterday? The differences between today and Saturday shook Nate to the core. Saturday had been pleasure and sunlight and hope. . . .

He remained determined. Even though Kim looked especially vulnerable, with her long black hair twisted into a single braid down her back, with her shorts and T-shirt that advertised the high school football team in green and gold, he promised himself to hold firm. He was the adult, and she'd been hurt too much already.

"Hi," Kim said breathlessly.

"How are you?" he asked. He examined the heartrendingly familiar features, the intelligent green eyes.

She shrugged. "I'm fine," she said, still smiling. "Would you like to walk?"

"Sorry, I haven't much time. I came to. . ." Why had he come?

"I had a great day Saturday," Kim said. Her eyes were enormous and trusting.

"I did, too."

The pause wasn't too awkward, but Kim's next words took him by surprise. Her smile grew more forced.

"Guess what?"

"What?"

"A while ago, Amber told me there's a woman coming to the university. She wants to hear me play."

"Well, that's good news, isn't it?"

"Yeah, really good news! It's nothing official yet. She's just a friend of my cello teacher, but she knows other people at The Juilliard School in New York. If she thinks I'm good, then Amber says I might end up going to school there. I'd board."

Nate didn't know what to say. Despite the smile, something felt wrong. "So," he said, "when will this friend of your teacher hear you play?"

"Oh, it's still up in the air. I have to prepare a few pieces. There's lots of hard work. But maybe she'll come this summer. I could go away next winter. Or, if they think I'm really good, this fall."

"That sounds good to me."

He felt the pressure of what he had come to tell her. He opened his mouth but suddenly found his arms full. Kim snuggled into his chest, squeezing him tight.

"Oh," she said, "I'm going to miss you when you go!"

God, this wasn't what he needed. He couldn't handle it. And yet he knew he had to think of her first. He had to figure out what *she* was feeling. But before any of that would come clear, she was talking into his chest, not crying, but maybe not wanting to look at him.

"May I— May I call you Dad?"

Relieved, Nate stroked the top of her shiny black head. "Of course you can. That's why I've been hanging around these last few days. We'll always be in touch, you know. We'll write and call. You'll always have my number."

God, how awful that sounded, he told himself, even as she looked up at him and smiled. She understood what was happening. He'd be in her life, but only in a secondary role. They were saying goodbye. She was bravely accepting that, and Nate thought he might choke up.

He didn't have time to consider beyond that. Kim tugged herself away from him, still smiling softly. *Amber.* Thank God, Amber was riding across the lawn in their direction.

Again in English riding boots and jeans, only this time with a tomato-red halter top, she rode the big red gelding toward them. With her own hair in a braid, she looked as young as Kim. Nate found himself torn again, between his yearning to belong and the impossibility of it all.

"Hi, you two!" Amber called, like Kim, smiling a welcome to him. "We've been looking for you."

"For me?"

Pulling to a smart halt, she jumped down from the snorting creature. Still smiling. *She's remembering the weekend,* Nate thought. After all, what did he expect? They could count themselves lovers. He must have been out of his mind, letting go the way he had.

"Beaver's been looking for you today," Amber said. "He says there's a house for sale along the river, and that—"

"Yeah, I know."

"Well, he's worried the guy might sell it before you get back to him. Someone's looking at it, and he seems really interested."

Nate felt a renewed wash of anger. With his father. With himself for having thought he could settle his father comfortably. Evidently, Kim sensed his turmoil, because she waved a little goodbye.

"I need to practice," she said, smiling at them both in turn. "See you guys later."

Nate surprised them all—especially himself—by tugging Kim to him and dropping a kiss on her forehead. She was a brave girl.

Evidently sensing his mood as well and wanting to give him some space, Amber tied Jazzer to a carved hitching post. Kim disappeared into the house.

"I don't want to keep you," Nate said, indicating the still-twitching animal with a nudge of his chin.

"No, this'll be good for him. Teach him some patience. Come on, we'll get something to drink."

"No, I don't have time."

"Well then, why don't we sit on the veranda steps for a minute?"

He nodded, following her toward the house. *The house.* It looked its best, decked out in geranium-filled flower boxes. Chicago seemed a dream away.

"So, what do you want to do about the house?"

He didn't know what to say for a moment. "The house? Oh, yeah. Well."

The pause lasted so long that Amber spoke. "What's wrong, Nate?"

He couldn't seem to tell her. Or, even put his finger on anything for himself.

"Is it Kim?" she asked.

"No, I think we're doing pretty well."

Amber waited patiently. Perched on the steps of the house she had made into a home for herself and Kim, she looked beautiful, even glowing.

"This morning," he said finally, "I told Tad, my business partner and friend, that I'm going out on my own. Relocating. It looks as if it'll really happen, now, and the split should be amicable."

"Well, that's good."

"I've been considering some place nearby, where I can be close to Kim."

"I hope you will." Indeed, hope burned in her gentle brown eyes, in her lovely face, and Nate knew he had to stamp it out.

"About that house. I'd thought I'd buy the house for—"

"I know, for your dad. Beaver told me. It's wonderful of you to help him retire, Nate."

Nate swung himself away from her. After the softly shadowed veranda with its soft occupant, he confronted the glare of May sunlight blinking. He cleared his throat. "Yeah, well, he won't retire, so I'm not going to buy the house."

Only now, in his own voice, did he hear the extent of his own disappointment.

"Look," she urged. "Beaver gave me the key. Since I already have it, why don't we just go see the house."

He turned on her. He felt so damned angry, so frustrated. "There's no sense in seeing it."

"Why not? Maybe, if you see it, if you talk to your dad again—"

"Don't you understand? I'm not handling any of this right."

"What do you mean?"

"Oh, hell, I don't know what I mean! Everything. Kim. I'm hurting her. My father and I have never done anything *but* hurt each other."

You, he wanted to add. *And now I'll hurt you, too. You're not made for weekend flings, for short-term affairs.*

But he couldn't say that. He couldn't make that break just yet. Besides, even aside from her inexperience with men, Amber was surely savvy enough to know he had nothing to offer her. After all, her inexperience was merely sexual, and even there she was catching up fast.

"Let's see the house," she said again. She was on her feet. "I'll ride Jazzer to the stables, and you follow. We'll drive down together from there."

THE SHORT RIDE to the house along the river was too brief for Amber to collect herself. Nate had changed from the attentive new father and the approachable lover he'd been on the weekend. He was floundering and she didn't know why.

She had her own purposes now. She'd seen enough of the vulnerable Nate—of the man Granny Maple described as soft as butter—to feel she could win him to a settled life with Kim and herself. She knew enough to see it would be difficult. But she was determined to give it her best shot.

Except for the long porch along the back of the house on the side facing the river, the place differed little from the other small residences perched in the woods across the road from the bottomland. Nate and Amber moved through its small rooms quickly, then paused on the porch. They stared down from the second-story windows to the wide muddy ribbon of water.

Nate's examination of the house had been swift and silent. Amber stood beside him, waiting on his thoughts. It was evident that he remained troubled. He absently thumbed his lower lip, a gesture that reminded her of him in other, more sensual contexts. But that sensual side was closed to her now.

"It needs a little work," he finally muttered, "but it can be fixed. It's too bad."

"Your father won't retire, then?"

Nate's smile was pure cynicism. "He'd rather work himself into some hole somewhere and die than have anything to do with me."

"Are you sure that's it?"

He swung away, propped himself in the bank of jalousie windows and looked back at the river. "Hell," he said, more softly. "I don't know what to do with him any more than I do with Kim. I'm just no good with any of this."

Amber thought "this" must include her and the loving they'd shared, since he showed no affection toward her now. In fact he kept moving away from her, even when she tried to get close to him. The idea that their night together had been a one-night stand was shattering.

Still, for the moment, Amber appreciated the importance of focusing on Nate and Kim and their needs. Anything between her and Nate couldn't happen until he sorted out his feelings. Returning to St. Louis had become more than an upheaval in his life. It was obviously a turning point. Over the next weeks, or even days, he'd be making the important decisions that would either give or deny her love a chance.

"But you're doing great with Kim," Amber managed, carefully watching his chiseled profile.

He continued to keep his eyes from hers. "If I'm doing great with Kim, then why is she unhappy?"

"But she isn't unhappy."

"Yes, she is. I can feel it."

Amber saw that he didn't grasp the finer points of dealing with a thirteen-year-old. How could he?

"While I admit that Kim has been concerned about something lately," she said, "and I haven't put my finger on exactly what it is yet, she's still the happiest I've ever seen her. We just heard there's a possibility of her being accepted at—"

"Yeah, she told me. At that music school in New York."

"Surely you're proud of her? Of her talent and hard work. I mean, this interview is a really big deal for someone her age."

"Of course, I'm proud of her. And I know you'll handle it all just right."

"Now, wait a minute."

Amber didn't know exactly what side she was arguing, but she felt she had to defend herself with Nate.

"You have to know it's not as if I want her to go away," she said. "On the contrary. But, now that I'm acting as her mother—"

"Now, that you *are* her mother—"

"Well, anyway, I don't want her to go either, but I have to encourage her to do what's best for her. And this excellent music school has to be good for her."

"I'm not arguing with you on any of that. I know you'll handle everything the best way possible."

Still, Amber persisted. "She's making new friends now. At the university."

"She seems to have a pair of nice friends from the river. I met them at the picnic."

"Well, they're sort of on-again-off-again friends. Frankly, I think they were more interested in hanging around you than in being with Kim." Amber's smile twisted wryly.

His smile was brief. "I still don't see what you're talking about."

"At thirteen, Kim's has her ups and downs with her peers."

"Like what?"

"Well, she's different from most of the children her age. She has this special talent that sets her apart, both intellectually and in the way she spends her time. Also, she's always been sensitive about how tall she is. She's inches taller than most of the kids in her class. And then . . . Well, you have to know that she's . . ."

"What are you saying? Is it her being part Osage Indian?"

"At this age, any little difference seems like a mountain. Kids want to be like everybody else, and Kim's background, the recent death of her mother— it's only natural she feels different. And while she struggles with all of these issues very bravely, it hurts me to see her struggle. Lately, I think she's trying to be Miss Perfect. Sometimes, I wonder if she's protecting me from something. I don't know. Granny Maple says it's just her age, but I guess I'm still trying to figure Kim out."

Amber sensed a sudden shift in Nate's emotions. And in his demeanor. He'd been watching her mouth as she talked. Now, his gaze dropped to the scanty cover of her red halter top. Everything inside her swung topsy-turvy with need and hope. But he pulled his eyes back up to her face. And while he stretched out a hand to cup her chin, she could tell he'd purposely fortified himself against anything sensual happening between them.

Amber wanted to hold onto reason, too. For all of their sakes. Neither she nor he needed this additional roller-coaster ride of beginning and ending a love affair. Still, Nate's simple act of tenderness was impossible to resist.

Obviously arriving at the same impossible conclusion, Nate dropped his hand from her face. "I'll talk to her again," he said. "Hell, I don't know what good I can do," he added, with another smile, "but maybe a little more input could help you."

Yanking himself from where he'd propped himself in a window frame, he headed toward the rear door of the house. "I'll get the key back to Beaver."

"And what about your father?"

"I guess I owe it to him to see him one more time. I didn't tell him about Kim, and I think I should have."

Nate drove Amber to Allswell in silence. She knew he was fighting with himself about many issues. She felt for him, but she knew better than to push or cajole. She had settled on what she wanted. Now he needed to do the same. She'd give him time. She'd have to. For now, at least, she'd wait.

CHAPTER FIFTEEN

NATE DIDN'T GET AWAY from the brewery until Thursday. Then, on another fine spring afternoon, he drove down to Flat River. When he arrived at the garage, his father wasn't there. The garage owner told Nate it was Gerald's day off, and gave Nate an address where he could find him.

The boarding house was typical of so many Gerald had inhabited over the years. It wasn't so much squalid as shabby. Nate was directed to the front bedroom on the second floor. As he climbed the stairs of the old house, the cooking odors from the kitchen, the dingy paint and the creaking staircase swept over him, pulling him back to the days when he had lived with his father in similar lodgings.

At the first door on the right, Nate knocked. Gerald called out that the door was open, and Nate let himself in. His father sat in a used, overstuffed chair, watching a baseball game on television. The breeze that blew in through the single window was the only thing that was fresh.

"Nate," Gerald said, showing the same lack of surprise he'd shown at his son's unexpected arrival before. "Have a seat. At least today I'm not busy," he added so as not to give too much.

"Thanks," said Nate, removing his sunglasses. "I appreciate it."

What Nate wanted to say was, "Don't do me any favors." But he also wanted a good start. He had to sacrifice what he could of the past in hopes of building a future. A future that would include Amber and Kim. Over the last few days, ever since he'd last seen Amber and his daughter, Nate had thought of little but that possibility. If he could only make peace with his dad, he could then take the next step in creating a new life for himself. And even if he only managed to convince his dad to settle in the house along the Meramec, at least he would know how Gerald fared as he grew older.

Without betraying what was at stake, Nate withdrew the picture of Kim that he carried in his breast pocket. He leaned forward and held it out to Gerald, who remained seated.

At first, Gerald barely dragged his eyes from the ball game. Then he accepted it and took a second, longer look, squinting. "She's yours?" he finally asked.

"Yes. Mine."

"She looks pretty old. How long...?"

"She's thirteen, but I've only known about her for the last few months."

Gerald handed the picture back. Nate wondered if he realized the implications. Gerald had a granddaughter—a lovely granddaughter who resembled him a great deal. "Her name is Kim," Nate said. "Aside from being a very special girl, she plays the cello."

"The what?"

Nate sank back on the hard wooden kitchen chair. "She's a wonderful girl, Dad," he said softly.

Gerald turned his attention back to the game. "Yeah, well, I don't know much about girls."

Nor about boys, Nate wanted to add. But he didn't. He clung to the image that had inspired this visit, that of himself, Kim, his father and Amber becoming some sort of family. If he gave in to his habitual pride, he would never accomplish his goal.

"I know Kim would like to meet you," Nate said.

Gerald looked at him, a little surprised. "Meet me?"

"Well, after all, you are her grandfather."

Gerald looked completely taken aback. "Yeah, I guess."

"The other day at the garage," Nate hedged, "I wanted to tell you about a house. It's up along the Meramec. It would be a great place to retire, to do some fishing. It's also close to Kim."

The television was forgotten. Gerald's eyes drifted to the open window. "I suppose you're offering to pay for all this luxury."

Nate felt a reluctant smile seeping across his face. "It won't be luxury exactly. But it'll be as secure as I can make it. Also, it won't be so different from what you're used to. It's private, quiet . . ."

"I dunno."

"Why don't you at least come see the house?" Nate leaned forward. His hopes flowed stronger than even he would have dared to imagine.

"I dunno," Gerald repeated, but not as stubbornly as his son could have expected.

Nate wondered if Gerald was feeling his years.

Feeling closer to his father than he'd ever felt in his life, Nate tumbled into a subject he'd always tried to broach with him. Without caution, he again spoke softly. "Dad, do you remember much about my mother?"

Incredibly, Gerald didn't stiffen and rebuke him, as he had at the same question in the past. "She was a pretty thing," he admitted, his gaze at the open window. The breeze fluttered the cheap gauze curtains. "She wasn't at all dark like you and me. She was Irish, you know."

"Yes, that much I recall. Well, not actually recall. It's just that you've told me that before."

"Yeah, well, she had a temper to go with her pretty Irish ways. I don't remember much, but I do recall that temper."

"And me?" Nate asked, afraid that his father might refuse to go on. "Was I with her at all?"

Gerald shrugged. "We were all together for the first few months after you were born. Hell, we even talked about getting married. But then. Oh, I dunno…"

"You don't remember?"

"No, I don't know what happened exactly. We fought a lot, and she left. I mean, there I was with diapers and a squallin' kid, and…"

Nate carefully settled back on the chair.

Abruptly closing himself off, Gerald turned back at the television. "I paid someone to keep you until you could go to school. Then you followed me around for awhile. When you were big enough, I…" He shifted in his seat. "Hell, I did what I could."

Wanting to explode with all the long-buried anger but knowing it would do no good, Nate watched his father turn back to the ball game. Nate's anger was futile. Gerald simply hadn't known how to do better than he did. And now Nate knew that feeling from firsthand experience.

Realizing he would never understand his childhood any better than he did now, Nate stood up. Oddly enough, his turmoil had abated somewhat. The pain of his past and his crippling relationship with his father didn't seem to have quite the same razor-sharp edge. Nate inhaled a cleansing breath.

"So," he said, drawing his father's eyes to him again. "Will you see the house I've just told you about?"

Nate watched the man waver, and he realized that he would accept his father's decision peacefully, whatever it was. Nate relaxed, pleased that his anxiety over the matter had abated. The decision was his father's and his father's alone.

"Well," said Gerald, "I guess there's no harm in seeing the place."

"And in meeting Kim?" Nate pressed.

"Yeah, I guess."

AFTER MEETING with his father, Nate felt better than he had in a long time. On impulse, he stopped by a roadside pay phone. Getting out of the Porsche, he felt the sunlight on the shoulders of his suit jacket and heard the traffic whizzing by. He called Amber and asked her what she and Kim were doing that evening.

"I have a client to meet," she told him. "I'm taking him out to dinner. But Kim will be with Granny Maple after school. I'll probably come in late, so she'll spend the night there. Did you want to see her, Nate?"

With a smile she couldn't see, Nate responded to the hope he could hear in Amber's voice. "Yeah, I thought I'd take you both out to dinner. I know it's short notice, but..."

"Well, I don't mind short notice. It's just that I can't get out of this business dinner."

He listened, entranced by her sigh, by the possibilities it implied. "Don't worry. There'll be other times. It's just that I visited my father today. I told him about Kim."

"Oh, Nate, how did it go?"

Again he felt his own smile, slow and sneaky. "Well, it's still too soon to break out the party hats and horns, but he's agreed to seeing the house and to meeting Kim."

"I'm so happy for you!"

"Well, like I say, I'm not counting on anything. And I don't think we should encourage Kim to, either. My father is unpredictable, to say the least."

"I understand."

At the rush of a trailer truck whooshing by, Nate plugged his one ear with a finger. "Look, I've gotta go. But since Kim will be with Granny Maple, do you think I could see her there?"

"Of course, you can! They'll both love it."

"I've got something to pick up at the office, and then I'll drive out."

"Sounds fine."

They both let a pause draw out. There wasn't much more to say, yet there was so much.

"I'm sorry I won't see you," he said.

"Well, like you say, there'll be other times."

He grinned. "You can count on it."

NATE EASED HIS PORSCHE to a stop outside Granny Maple's little stilt house along the river. He hadn't seen the place in a long time. And while it looked pretty much the same, he remembered Kim and Amber telling him that it needed repairs. He'd also heard that they hadn't been done because Granny Maple couldn't afford them while she stubbornly refused financial help. According to Beaver, not only had his own more anonymous offers been declined, but so had Amber's.

Kim was standing at the top of the rickety staircase in the open doorway, smiling at him, waiting. He had phoned Beaver, asking him to relay the message to Kim and Granny Maple that he'd be visiting them. Now, he saw Kim's anticipation like light in her face. He felt anticipation, too, and something new. Confidence, maybe. Confidence in himself and in the future.

Climbing the stairs with a a soft hello, Nate dropped a kiss on the girl's cheek. She beamed, and then, as he entered her home, Granny Maple beamed, too. He realized some things never changed. Some people never changed. He remembered what this place and this person had meant to him when, as a frightened boy, he'd first arrived at the river community with his father. He'd come a long way since, and Granny Maple knew that better than most.

"Honey, you look so fine," she said.

"You look pretty good yourself."

Her smile cut through her dark face, charming and dimpled. "I look fine for an old lady, you mean."

Hugging her, he whispered, "You'll never be old."

He hadn't had many hugs as a kid, except from this woman. But somehow, Kim had gotten him started in the habit. It felt good.

"So," he said, taking the chair across from Granny Maple, "I hope you don't mind me interrupting your afternoon together."

"You know you aren't. Kimmy's spending the night. Amber says she'll drop by this evening, before taking her client out to dinner." The old woman patted Kim's hand where the girl perched on the arm of her chair.

No, Nate thought, things here didn't change. Granny Maple's chair looked like a lumpy, familiar teddy bear a child wouldn't discard. Damp patches from years of rain stained her ceiling.

"I'm just sorry to trouble Beaver with running my messages," the woman was saying.

"I can fix that, you know. I can have a phone installed within the week."

She grinned again. "You're such a big man now! I bet you have even the phone company at your beck and call."

Nate chuckled, relaxing. "Yeah, all sorts of people kowtow to me."

"Oh, why don't you get a phone?" Kim asked enthusiastically.

Granny Maple patted her hand again. "No, honey lump. I don't want a phone."

Even though they each knew that was that, Nate took the opportunity to make another offer. "Actually, I'd like a couple of guys from my work crew to come out and repair the roof and shore up those steps outside. And maybe you'd like a new sofa. Remember, in my business, I can lay my hands on all kinds of furniture. Anything you want, really.''

''No, no.'' While Granny Maple smiled softly, she remained firm in her pride. River pride. Nate recalled this very woman saying that the river bred pride like it did mosquitoes, stubborn and pesky.

''Well,'' he said, backing off, ''if you change your mind, get in touch with me.''

''I sure will. But you know,'' she added, a twinkle back in her eye, ''some of us down here have figured out who's playing fairy godfather.''

Nate felt uneasy, especially with Kim drinking in every word. He was grateful when Granny Maple changed the subject. ''And now, why don't you two take a little stroll along the river while I make us something to drink? How about some fresh-squeezed lemonade?''

Nate thought Kim's eyes couldn't have glowed any brighter. ''All right!'' she said, getting up.

''I notice the river's high,'' Nate commented. ''Higher than it was at May Day River Day.''

''Heavens,'' said Granny Maple, ''you know how it is down here. It can rain and flood almost any time of the year except summer.''

''Granny Maple says she's seen Christmas lights reflected in flood water,'' Kim added.

''I sure have, sugar pie. But you two go on now, and I'll have the lemonade ready when you get back.''

Nate and Kim sauntered along the riverbank, discussing the high water. He had a lot he wanted to say to her, but he didn't know how to begin. An envelope and a tiny box were burning a hole in his pocket.

"Can we walk to the park and back?" Kim asked. "If we go along the river, it's not far. We can sit for a minute in the pavilion, if you want."

"That sounds fine."

Indeed, any one of the numerous, narrow dirt paths crisscrossing the area would serve Nate's purposes well. As they walked, Nate recognized sycamore, cottonwood, willow and white oak. As he recalled, this particular path wound past a number of houses, viewed from below and behind. Then it continued on through the park and into the woods where Amber exercised her horses. Beyond that, it threaded its way to the front of the cave, becoming abruptly gravelly and treacherous as it petered out at the Big Bend beneath the bluffs.

Everything came back to him, and in such detail, that it amazed him. Even the warm, musty scents swam in his head as if he'd never left. He watched Kim, walking ahead of him on the narrow path, and remembered what he had to say to her. He was on the verge of speaking to her when she turned around to smile at him, her black hair swinging. He could see the hero worship in her gaze.

That made him uncertain again, and he decided that maybe he'd better start the conversation with something more familiar. "How do you feel about playing for this woman who's coming to hear you?" he asked.

"I'm nervous," she admitted, sobering somewhat.

Those great green eyes flashed and changed course like her moods. "Well, anyone would be nervous. But how do you feel about this important step?"

"Amber says it's a great opportunity. And my cello teacher is really excited. I don't mind the work. I like to play."

Knowing he hadn't quite elicited the information he wanted, Nate tried his next topic. "I'm happy about the family you have with Amber. I like Dolph. That day at the picnic, we had a good time together."

She chuckled. "I love Uncle Dolph. He's so good to me. I'm spending next weekend with him and Lillian. We're going out to Six Flags like he promised."

"You know, Kim." Nate cleared his throat. "My dad lives not too far from here. In Flat River."

Kim rotated on the dirt path and peered at him. The sun remained bright. Light spilled into the trees, dappling the low underbrush and Kim's shiny black hair. "Your dad?"

"Yes, he's considering a move here, to live along the river. I thought you two should meet each other."

Again, Kim's emotions were written all over her face. Tentative and excited, she listened for more. "I've heard about him from Granny Maple. His name is Gerald."

"That's right. But he's not used to children. Don't expect him to be as comfortable with you as Dolph is."

"Oh, I hope he'll move here! I'd be so glad if he was close by."

"Yeah, but you have to remember he's not what you're used to, so—"

"I think I know what you mean. My mom was gone a lot, too. Just like your dad, Gerald."

Ah, the experience in those green eyes! Too much experience for such tender years.

"Anyway," she said, again cheerfully, "I have a great family. I have lots of people who care about me, and now I have you, too."

"Yes, and I want you to remember that."

"I will."

Nate went on. "You know, your grandfather, Gerald, is half Osage Indian."

"Amber says that means I'm part Indian, too."

"The Osage were a tribe who lived here in Missouri long before the explorers came. As a people, they've pretty much disappeared. But I've looked into the Osage a little, at the library. I think you should know some of the things I've read about them. Early explorers, and even Audubon, the famous naturalist, said they were a tall people, over six feet. That's probably why we're so tall. You and my father and I."

Nate waited for Kim's reaction, and when she seemed pleased, even eager to hear more, he went on. "They weren't merely warriors, but a noble people, a people that were respected by other tribes of the Sioux nation. They considered themselves a people who came from the stars. They sought an order among themselves that was as peaceful as the order they saw in the night skies."

Since she seemed really taken with the story of her Osage Indian ancestors, he went on. "There's a lot to learn about them, a lot to admire. In fact, I've got something for you." He placed the box and envelope into Kim's hands. "I want you to wait to open these later. Inside the envelope is some information on the Osage that I copied at the library. Inside the box is a surprise."

Her gaze glowed into his. She nodded, and he saw again a maturity that wrenched at his heart.

"I understand," she said, stuffing the box and envelope into the pocket of her shorts.

"Good."

They walked on, entering the cleared area of the park. With a sense of satisfied companionship, they sat in the pavilion, watching the river course by.

Nate was feeling more and more a part of the world, more and more a part of the life of the girl who resembled him and his father and their indigenous ancestors. "The Osage," he murmured, "called the willow 'the tree that never dies.'" He repeated the words he wanted her never to forget. "They believed they came from the stars."

They spent some time skipping stones across the swift water. It was a skill every kid along the river honed. Then they moved on.

"I've been wondering," Kim said, winding a blade of grass around her slim finger, "what you think of Amber."

"Here," he said, "give me that." Taking the broad, coarse blade, Nate held it taut between his thumbs and blew through his cupped hands. The whistle made her smile. He smiled back. "Can you do that?"

She tried, giggling, when after several attempts she got a growling whisper from it. Yes, Nate thought, they were both a product of this singular place. And it wasn't a bad place anymore. Maybe it never had been.

"So," Kim said, glancing at him. "What do you think of Amber?"

He had hoped to avoid that question. *Smart*. His kid was as bright as a penny.

He kept his eyes to the path. "Amber? I've told you I'm happy you have her. She's told me how you and your mom and she were friends. Nobody'll know you better than Amber. Nobody'll love you more."

"I know that," Kim said, sneaking another look at him. "But what do *you* think about her?"

Ah, yes, budding teenage girls. They picked up the vibes.

"I, uh." Here he'd been thinking they were doing so well. And he really did want an open flow of communication between them. But on the subject of Amber, he felt his emotions tangle up. When he looked at Kim again, she was smiling at him. A Mona Lisa smile.

"I think you like her," she said. "I think you like her a lot."

"And you're right. I admire her. She's done a lot of good stuff for a lot of people. And for herself, too."

Kim shot another sideways look at him—a green glance over the blade of green, green river grass. He knew she was reading him like a book. All the hope, all the inadequacies—all the love burning inside him. His daughter read it all.

WHEN AMBER pulled into the gravelled patch outside Granny Maple's stilt house, she was surprised to see Nate backing out. Evidently, he'd spent most of the afternoon there, and her curiosity was piqued. Still, he only paused and wished her good luck with her client before driving off. She was decked out in a neat black and white polka-dot dress and pumps, and she had hoped he would notice. And maybe he did. But still, he just drove away.

She found Kim and Granny Maple inside, grinning like satisfied cats.

"Well, I see you two had a nice afternoon," she said, grinning back at them.

"We did!" Kim exclaimed, throwing herself into Amber's embrace. "I wish you could have been here! My dad and I had a long walk along the river, and then Granny Maple made us lemonade."

"I even shared the rest of the sugar cookies you brought this morning." The old woman nodded at Amber, radiating a know-it-all look. Obviously, Nate's visit had been very successful.

"Do you have to go soon?" Kim piped.

"Pretty soon." Amber didn't like entertaining clients in the evening, but usually she couldn't help it. She was glad Kim had Granny Maple and Dolph.

"Can you stay just long enough to watch me open my present?" Kim held up a small box wrapped in rosebud paper, enthusiasm shining in her face. "From my dad. Can you watch me open it?"

"I suppose I have enough time for that," Amber said, laughing.

Of course, Kim already had the paper off, and the lid open. Inside, a tiny silver star gleamed at them.

"Oh my," Granny Maple said admiringly.

Since Kim didn't speak, Amber watched the girl attach the fine silver chain around her neck, adjusting the star just at the base of her throat. Next, Kim opened the envelope, almost with reverence.

"I know why my dad got me this," she said, unfolding the papers inside. "Listen," she added, "it's about *us*."

Kim settled on the arm of Granny Maple's chair. "It's from a book by Joseph Matthews. 'They were pure and clean and noble because they had just come from the stars—from among the stars, say the holy men. They were all Sky People, but when they descended to earth, the Sacred One, they found her divided into land and water, over which the Great Mysteries chose to send the wind howling like wolves...'"

As Kim read on, Amber's eyes met the reflected mistiness in Granny Maple's wise old stare. Yes, Nate was doing well by his daughter. She only hoped he could see that for himself.

CHAPTER SIXTEEN

AMBER FELT HAPPINESS like a sweet possibility she might just grasp. For the past two weeks and then some, Nate had been at Allswell regularly. Getting his father's agreement to visit the empty house along the Meramec had lifted Nate's spirits immensely. Amber felt the changes in Nate with a subtle, growing pleasure.

But she was also aware of Nate's lingering uncertainty. His father clearly meant a lot to him. And, apparently, to see his father settled in a real home would help to cement the life Nate seemed to be making for himself. Nate's plans for his new business, which he had decided to set up in St. Louis, were also going well.

Optimistic as she was by nature, Amber knew enough not to let her dreams run away with her. For one thing, Nate was only just finding his feet, only just laying the groundwork for his future. For another, he hadn't made love to her again, or even approached her on her own. And finally, though Gerald had agreed to think about relocating along the river, he still hadn't made a move to see the house for himself.

With all this in mind, Amber kept her attention on practical matters as much as she could. She allowed Nate and Kim their time alone together. To see the confidence Nate was gaining with his daughter also buoyed Amber's spirits. But, but, but . . . Amber cautioned herself continually. She and Nate hadn't talked and they didn't talk. Not intimately. He needed time and space, and she did her best to understand that.

"So here you are," Nate said.

Amber looked up from where she was pouring orange juice into three glasses. The sour sounds of Kim tuning her cello floated into the kitchen from the family room.

"I thought I'd fix something to drink," she said. "We've been listening to Kim play for over an hour."

May pressed its increasing heat and humidity against the kitchen windows. Inside, air-conditioning kept the house comfortable. Even Gnaw lazed around more. Amber had left the dog cooling his tummy on the hearthstones in the family room where she, Nate and Kim had been sitting.

It was another lovely afternoon in a regular string of them. With Nate's involvement, weekends had become particularly special. Amber could barely contain her happiness. In worn jeans and a T-shirt, comfortable and approachable, he looked as if he belonged with her and Kim and Gnaw at Allswell on a Saturday afternoon.

Perhaps he sensed a little of what she was thinking. Leaning toward her, he took her into his arms. Because he'd been steering clear of intimacy of any kind, Amber let herself revel in the embrace. When he kissed her, she hugged him close and tight. He responded with a deep secretive mingling of his tongue with hers.

When he pulled back, he smiled down at her and whispered, "Teenage girls make very effective chaperones."

Amber also grinned. "But teenage girls are so great they're almost worth it."

"Almost," he whispered, kissing her again.

Still, they knew better than to go too far, and they separated. When Amber picked up two glasses of orange juice, Nate grasped his as if to follow her back into the family room. But before doing so he had a piece of news to impart.

"My dad's coming to see the house next weekend. I thought I'd pick him up at Flat River, and then meet you and Kim there. Would you mind?"

At the kitchen door, Amber paused. "No, I wouldn't mind."

"I think it would be good for Kim if you were there. I have no idea how this will go."

"But are you sure? I mean, I'm not family."

He sobered. "Hell, Amber, old Gerald and I are hardly family either. But most of all, I want you there for Kim. Just in case."

Amber couldn't imagine what could go so very wrong, but she knew that if Nate wanted her there she'd be there.

AFTER ANOTHER on-again-off-again rainy week, the first Saturday of June rolled around with clearing skies. It was warm and felt like spring. In the heavy humidity, many trees and flowers remained in bloom, and the grass was a lush tropical green.

In cotton-print summer dresses and sandals, Amber took Kim to meet Nate and his father in the empty house along the river. Given Nate's apprehension and the importance of the meeting to him, Amber was concerned for him. She also watched him closely to gauge her reactions. Strained introductions were made, and the foursome made a quick tour of the small rooms. Little was said beyond a few more awkward comments.

Then Gerald announced that he wanted to step outside. Kim tagged hopefully along. Amber and Nate remained on the porch that ran the back of the hollow-sounding house, watching them pick their way to the bank below. The river beyond was nearly full. Gushing and twisting along, it looked unfriendly.

"The ground is saturated," Nate murmured, picking up on Amber's thoughts without glancing at her. They stood silent, side by side, gazing down the treed and weedy slope.

They'd been so at ease with each other over the past few weeks that Nate's new reserve hurt her. She knew his relationship with his father couldn't be good. Nate had to be feeling the strain, and she tried to be understanding.

Amber had come to her own conclusions about Gerald Fields. He was very much like his son, tall and dark and self-contained. Gerald's resemblance to Kim was breathtaking. For the first time, Amber realized why Nate was so knotted up inside. For the first time in weeks, she faced the possibility that Nate would grow old like his father had, never capable of relating to others, even to those he loved.

She could see that the two men loved each other, and that made everything worse. The implications made her sad for Kim and for herself. Worse, she could be sure that Nate's stony expression reflected the fact that he was arriving at the same conclusions.

Wanting desperately to make contact with him, but not knowing how, she stated the obvious. "You look so much alike."

He stiffened, startling her. "He eludes me."

Her heart swelled with his pain. And with hers. "My parents eluded me, too. They were emotional vagrants. For all I wanted to, I never really communicated with them."

His glance was quick and cutting.

Amber couldn't help her retort. "Yes, Nate, even rich little girls living on the hill can have parents who neglect them. A close relationship with one's parents isn't something that money can buy."

His shoulders slumped. When he finally met her eyes, she felt his regret. "I'm sorry. I know I haven't cornered the market on difficult childhoods."

She relented, too. "Sometimes our own pain blinds us to the pain in others.

After a pause, he seemed to force himself to speak. His voice was quiet, fraught with mixed emotions. "I just don't think I can be a parent. No more than he could. I mean, I've never seen it done, and I don't know how to even begin."

"But Nate, you're already doing it. These past few weeks have been wonderful for Kim. And besides, you've had other lasting relationships in your life. Look at your friendship with Granny Maple."

He grunted. "She's a saint. She gets along with anyone."

"But you've lasted with Beaver, too. And then there's Tad Coldsdon and his father, and that lawyer friend of yours—what's his name?—Bernie—?"

"Bernie Hirsh. But you're talking about other men. Yes, I have friends. I've had some women friends, too. But we're discussing a whole different level here. With you...well, with Kim," he said, correcting himself. "The truth is that the man you see out there, the one who can't express himself with more than a few barely polite words, is the man I'm afraid I'm destined to become."

Amber couldn't stand it. She wanted to point out the caring he'd demonstrated just these past weeks. Day by day, Kim was growing to love him. And with Amber, just that once, he'd been a tender, if also fierce, lover. And then there were the ways he had helped the river community.

But she knew Nate wouldn't believe anything she had to say. He simply couldn't see his own capacity for love.

So Amber stayed next to him, silently watching his daughter and his father climb back up the hill in the direction of the house. When Nate thumbed his lower lip in that now-familiar, contemplative way, Amber turned aside. She wanted to hug him, to press her lips to the fullness of his lower one. She yearned to tell him he could do it. But the knowledge had to come from within. She just had to wait and watch and hope.

Kim and Gerald entered the rear porch door. Kim slipped off her sandals and hurried over to Amber and Nate with them dangling from one hand. Her eyes sparkled with excitement.

"Boy, is it muddy out there!" she said.

Standing just inside the door, Gerald looked dark and barely approachable.

"So what do you think of the house, Dad?" Nate asked.

"I think it's nice. Real nice. Could probably do some good fishing out there once in awhile. Could get me a boat, I guess."

"Oh, everyone down here has boats," Kim chirped. "Even Granny Maple fishes."

"Uh-huh," Gerald said, finally looking directly at Kim. "I recall Granny Maple. Still lives down here, does she?"

Kim nodded. Amber noted the silver star glinting at her throat, almost as shiny as her eyes. "I spend lots of time down here. Mostly with her."

"I see." Gerald did not point out that if he moved, Kim could visit with him, too.

"Do you think it will flood this month?" Amber said, hoping to redirect the conversation away from anything that might hurt him. "Everyone claims we've been lucky so far. But Granny Maple says not to rest just because summer's around the corner."

"I can remember it flooding," Kim said. "At least, I think I do. I was little the last time there was a really bad one. Granny Maple says everybody's talking about the forecasts and the river stages."

Amber put an arm around Kim's shoulders. "It's nothing to worry about, honey. If it floods, everybody down here knows what to do."

"Yeah," Nate said, joining in. "The National Weather Service issues warnings. There's always enough time to pack up and go to a motel or to a friend's house until the water rises and falls."

"Oh yeah?" Gerald pressed doubtfully. "Well, I remember it a little different." He didn't realize that Kim needed reassurance, not raw truth.

"There are always the diehards," he said. "Going out to get their groceries and moving their cars and trucks to higher ground, and then staying on. If they need to, they can get out in their boats. But most of 'em just stay in their homes, hoping the water won't get too high and wash 'em out."

"Wash people out?" Kim asked.

Finally, Gerald noticed the look on Kim's face. Her green eyes were enormous.

"Naw now," he said hastily. "It's nothin' to worry about. People hardly ever get washed out down here anymore. Besides, from what I can tell, the old neighborhood is in better shape than when I lived here. Everything's built good and sturdy now."

"Kim," Amber said, to change the subject yet again, "have you told your dad the good news?"

"Oh, gosh, I almost forgot!" Kim beamed at her father. "Uncle Dolph is going to marry Lillian, and I can call her 'Aunt' Lillian now."

Nate smiled. "Well, that's good news!"

"They told me at dinner last night. Well, actually, they told Lillian's parents, and I was there, too. Anyway, Aunt Lillian says she'll only marry Uncle Dolph if he brings her a ring this time and does it right. So later, after diner, Uncle Dolph made me promise to remind him so we can go shopping for a diamond. He's afraid he'll forget."

Nate chuckled. "Thank goodness he has you to remind him, or poor Aunt Lillian could end up waiting for her ring for a very long time." Then he sobered a bit. "And what about your audition for Juilliard? Have you heard anything more?"

"Oh, yeah," Kim said, her eyes briefly lowering to her hand. "Lillian took me to the university yesterday and and we picked my pieces. The woman's coming in six weeks."

Nate's eyes met Amber's. "Is that enough time to prepare?"

"It'll be a lot of work," she admitted. "But Kim only needs two pieces, so we think she can do it. In fact," she added, jostling Kim affectionately, "we know she can do it!"

"She can do it all right," Nate said, smiling.

When Nate looked up, Amber also noticed his father hovering by the door, obviously uncomfortable. She again felt the tragedy of the two men. Nate tried to bring Gerald into the conversation by talking about other aspects of the granddaughter's life, which didn't help. Finally, Nate said he'd drive his father back to Flat River. With curt jerks of his head toward Amber and Kim, Gerald said goodbye.

On their way to Allswell, Kim was a bit glum. But Amber didn't feel up to trying to explain Gerald Fields's behavior to the girl. Nate would have to do that. Besides, the subject of bottled-up men had suddenly become too frightening to face again.

AFTER THAT DAY there was a definite change in Nate. He began avoiding Allswell. He claimed he'd gotten busy at the brewery, but Amber wondered if that wasn't just an excuse. He was floundering again, and it was almost more than she could bear.

Hoping to keep her spirits, and Kim's, from sinking until Nate steadied himself once more, Amber tried hard to distract herself. Even so, Nate was never far from her thoughts.

One night, when she was really tired and really aching, she wandered over to her desk. She hadn't written a poem since she could remember. But one flowed from her, short and sweet and perfect. It was unlike anything she'd ever composed before, so sensual it was almost erotic. Quickly, she slipped it into her top desk drawer, not wanting to examine the frustration, the plaguing memories, that had inspired the words.

NATE WAS STRUGGLING, and when he struggled he tended to close himself off. As much as he hated to retreat from Amber and Kim, especially after things had started to look up, he was afraid to reach out to them in his pain.

Finally, after a hellish week at the brewery, he forced himself to spend a Saturday afternoon with Kim, despising himself all the while for avoiding Amber. The visit did nothing to improve his state of mind. To watch the joy, the expectation, the hero worship shining in his daughter's big green eyes was bad enough. To see her calm acceptance of his possible withdrawal from her life almost broke his heart.

When he dropped her off at Granny Maple's, other worries compounded his turmoil. Over the last few weeks there had been a number of flash-flood warnings and flood watches. So far the expected floods hadn't materialized, and the postings had been canceled.

Today, the river again swelled to capacity, and the probability of more rain over the next twenty-four hours was high. While he'd experienced a couple of floods as a kid and knew everyone was basically safe as long as they took certain precautions, he didn't like the idea of Kim and Granny Maple remaining at the old woman's stilt house.

He knew the condition of the place. He decided not to worry Kim and the old woman unnecessarily.

As he was pulling away from Granny Maple's, however, the clouds that had been threatening to burst all afternoon did so with a blinding flash of lightning. Hail battered his car. Winds buffeted the nearby trees.

Switching on his windshield wipers, he veered up the old back road to Allswell. He didn't want to think about why he did so. His worries about the possibility of flooding, about Kim and Granny Maple in that rickety house, his concern for Amber who was afraid of storms... He just wanted to be with Amber. After the phone call from his father that morning he *needed* to be with her... for at least one last time.

He drove straight for the house, got out of the car and slammed the door shut behind him. Mounting the veranda, he ducked his head under the onslaught of the pelting hailstones.

He knocked at the door and waited. Storms were fiercer on the hilltop than anywhere else. Since no one answered, he supposed Etta Fay and Mick were away. He tested the knob. Inside, the house was hushed. Nate wondered where Gnaw was, shaking his head over the uselessness of the dog, the unlocked door. Amber's refusal to worry about the isolation of the old house really worried him.

The old house. It rested, a quiet haven from the rising storm outside. He called out a few times into echoing space. He wondered if Amber were in the house and simply didn't hear him. He decided to find out. Mounting the staircase two steps at a time, he strode directly to her rooms.

She had to be in her study. She wouldn't hear him in there.

Ignoring the bedroom and the memories it evoked, he opened the study door. Here, the hail rattled at the windows beyond the desk like scattering shot. Another flash of lightning emphasized the seriousness of the storm. It had grown abruptly darker.

Where was she? Was she afraid?

What was he doing here?

"I'm leaving a note, that's what."

Because the desktop was clean except for the glass ball he'd given her and the desktop planner, he shoved open the top drawer in search of a paper and pen. "Or even a pencil," he muttered, his hands grasping a sheet.

Since the paper he had pulled out was already written on, he decided to use the space at the bottom. But his attention was caught by the oddly measured lines. Poetry. Amber had written a poem and stuck it in the drawer.

Helplessly, he scanned the lines, and what he read shocked him to the core. Desire, additionally intense because he'd lived with it since his one beautiful night with her, shot through him like an electrical flash. He began at the first sentence again—

"Are you looking for me?" Amber said, standing in the doorway. She wore the tomato-red halter top, jeans and her English riding boots, all soaked through. Her hair was disheveled.

"Are you all right?" he asked.

"I just ran up the back way from the stables."

Her gaze dropped to the page he held in his trembling fingers. "I—" He couldn't think. "I wanted to leave a note. I'm worried about Kim and Granny Maple in that damned little crackerbox on legs."

"Yes." She was always easy, always ready to listen. *His Amber.* "I know what you mean. But you can't hover over them every time there's a storm. We've had several warnings these past few weeks alone."

The intensity of their being alone chewed at Nate. Gruffly, he changed course.

"Why can't you lock up here? And where's that damned dog?"

Amber actually smiled at him, shrugged a bare shoulder. "He's under the back porch. He hates the rain, too."

"And what's this?" he inquired, holding up the paper he still clutched.

She stared him down. "I'm sure you've already guessed."

She was elegant. Even in a tomato-red halter and jeans. Even without makeup and in a mess, Amber was the salve to his soul.

And now there was the poem as well. It thrilled him to know that Amber, too, could be blatantly desirous.

Letting the paper slide from his hand, Nate stepped around the desk. He knew he shouldn't. He'd promised himself he wouldn't. But he couldn't help himself. She was waiting for him to come to her.

He was the raging storm, and she the hushed, patient house.

"If you're going to say no," he said, "you'd better say it now."

She looked unwaveringly into his dark eyes. "I'm not going to say no."

Sweeping her into his arms, he whispered some of her own words to her. He carried her into the storm-darkened bedroom. The apricot hue was burnt with umber, then penetrated with pale blue light. As he lowered her to the bed and kneeled at its edge to remove her boots, her socks and her jeans, the hail stopped suddenly, leaving only the steady downpour of rain.

Knowing Amber watched, Nate stripped out of his polo shirt and slacks, shucked off his loafers and removed his socks. He reached for the packets in his wallet. Joining her in the bed, he eased her out of the halter top and disposed of their briefs.

By then, raindrops pattered on the sills, dripped from the gingerbread carvings, the windowboxes, the balconies. Late afternoon shone with the luster of hushed silver. He whispered lines from her poem to her. He coaxed her with more hot words of his own. Together, they built their own storm.

Jade, apricot and Amber. Always Amber. Those words were his.

"It's always you, babe," he whispered, leaning back and tugging her, fulfilled and willing, into his body.

"It always has been you. It always will be you, no matter what."

Her warmth eased him toward a restful sleep. A steady drip somewhere regulated the world. Colors and words, dusky dark to tawny light, shaded his satisfaction. He couldn't help his surrender. He gave into it all—the shadowed colors, the words, the peace of Allswell.

CHAPTER SEVENTEEN

AMBER WOKE UP. Feeling the heat of Nate's body, the hard, possessive press of it, she gently disengaged herself and got up. It was nine o'clock in the evening. The weather had settled, but she felt disoriented. She went into her office and called Beaver, who allayed her concerns about the rising river. The earlier afternoon storm had been violent but brief, and there was no danger of flooding. He told her that everything was fine.

With one more look at Nate, who slept like the proverbial log, she padded down to the kitchen. She let in Gnaw and fixed them something to eat.

She thought she should waken Nate. She wanted to talk with him. On the other hand he clearly needed the sleep.

She smiled to herself. Even though he had never mentioned love or marriage she had more hope than ever. He might triumph over his past. He might let her assist in the victory.

Finally, she returned to the bed. He cuddled against her, and, without a word, pleasurably, sleepily, made love to her again. Then she, too, fell asleep.

As soon as she woke again the next morning, she knew she and Nate were back to square one. When she smiled at him across the pillow she got only a shuttered black stare in return. Her heart sank. He looked away. Their intimacy hadn't gotten them anywhere. When he tossed back the jade and apricot sheets and stood up, she felt forlorn, but was determined not to let it show. She got up, too.

Halfheartedly, they tried to recapture yesterday's mood. Amicable words got them through showers and finding the extra toothbrush. Nate's little kisses eased them into the kitchen. But Amber knew he was withdrawing from her again.

Finally, she couldn't take any more of it. Finishing the dishes, she dried her hands on a black-and-white-check towel and turned to him. With her arms squared across her chest, she considered herself ready to hear the worst.

"What is it, Nate?"

In a tender gesture, he stroked her cheek. "It's nothing to do with last night, babe."

"That's not enough."

He leaned into the countertop, looking at his loafers. Amber waited.

Finally, he spoke. "It's my dad. He's not going to take the house."

He paused, then continued. "It's not that I resent him for doing what he wants. God knows, he's never done anything except what he wants. He's a drifter and he always will be. It's just the way he did it."

Amber said nothing.

He plunged ahead, his pain more and move evident in his chiseled features and dark eyes. "He didn't even have the courtesy to call me and tell me himself. He phoned Beaver. He told him to let me know, and that's supposed to be that. I told Beaver to tell the guy to sell the house.''

When Nate gazed into her eyes, all his earlier restraint vanished.

''Oh God, Amber, you know that I love you, don't you? You know that I love Kim, and, God help me, even this damned house. But Amber, I'm exactly like him. I'm just an updated version, with all the old hang-ups.''

Amber met Nate's stare calmly. She knew he was not at all like Gerald Fields. Visit after visit, he'd proven that with Kim. And with her, too. But the hour had come. She couldn't convince Nate of something he didn't recognize himself. Not with a million words, not with a lifetime of effort, not with the patience of Job.

''Okay,'' she said softly. ''I understand. But we have to think of Kim. You can't keep riding in here like a knight on a white horse, and then riding off again. I know you've given her as much as you can, and she's accepted that. Now I will, too.'' She started for the kitchen door, the one that would take her away from him, deep into the house. ''Just do me one favor, will you?'' she said, turning back.

He didn't reply. He stood as he was, leaning into the countertop, frozen in misery.

''Don't come back too soon, will you? Wait a while. Call her and write to her, but don't come back until she's on her feet. Until I'm on my feet.''

He seemed unable to respond. Still, she knew he understood. From now on *she* would set the limits.

NATE WAS STUNNED. To see Amber—patient, sweet Amber—walk away from him was something he'd never expected to happen. His plan had been to sacrifice himself in leaving her, not for her to give up on him. He'd felt abandonment before. Time and again. But Amber's leaving so floored him that he couldn't seem to think, couldn't move from the jog in the countertop.

A honking horn in the rear courtyard startled him out of his paralysis. Turning to the window, he saw Beaver's battered pickup. Nate walked out to meet his friend. It had begun to rain again.

"Hate to bother you, Nate," Beaver said from his open truck window. If he was surprised at finding Nate at Amber's late on a Sunday morning, he didn't show it. But Nate's head had cleared enough to read the concern in Beaver's familiar features.

"What is it?" he asked in raspy tones.

"Well, it's probably nothing to worry about."

Nate's heart began to race. "What is it?"

"Now, don't look like that. It's just that Granny Maple got word to me that Kimmy went for a walk a little while ago. Now, don't worry. You gotta know we ain't had much rain, but the word's out that central Missouri got a real blast last night. The water's headed this way, and we just thought—"

"I'll get Amber." Nate was already running back into the house. He bounded through it, calling Amber's name, rousing even Gnaw to scramble up the stairs with him.

Emerging from her room, Amber met him on the balcony. She'd changed into a run-down pair of cowboy boots. *Probably on her way to clean a stall,* he thought.

"Now, don't worry," he said, borrowing Beaver's phrase.

Nate felt compelled to remain calm for her. He loved her. He adored her. He wouldn't see her hurt for anything. That's all that mattered.

"Please, Nate."

"It's just that the water's getting a little high. I thought you'd want to drive down with me to get Kim and Granny Maple. You'll do better with Granny. She'll probably be stubborn."

"But that's not all of it."

"Come on, babe. We'll talk in the car. We'll take the old Mercedes. I'll drive."

Amber went silent. Outside, Beaver's pickup waited. She waved at him. While she waited for Nate to get the old car from the garage, she studied the sky, chafing her upper arms.

Finally, they were on their way, following Beaver's truck down the road. Nate explained about Kim's walk, the unexpected high water.

God, he did love them. All he could feel was his fear, his love. It was like a double blow to his gut.

Kim. He couldn't imagine anything happening to her and him surviving it. For all the pounding fear, it was as if his mind had cleared. Surely he didn't have to lose what he loved because he was too late.

Reaching across the console, Nate took Amber's hand. It felt cool. He squeezed it, and when she glanced at him, trying to smile, he couldn't hold back any longer.

"Amber, I love you. I love you and Kim so much. I can see now that, like my father, I've been a coward. I've been avoiding my problems. I'm not good at talking things out, but I promise, babe, that I'll work at doing better. If I can't be with you and Kim I'll be lost. God knows that I pray nothing happens today. But if you'll have me, if you'll hang in there with me..."

He couldn't finish. Tears blurred his eyes, and he had to blink rapidly to see through the exhaust from Beaver's rattletrap truck.

Thank God, she returned the squeeze. That was enough for now. They'd reached the road along the bottomland. He had to drive. He had to think.

The fields on the one side of the road stretched below the bluffs, nearly covered in shallow water that he knew was only a couple of inches deep. For weeks, the ground had been soaked, and the fields had drained as much as the fall of the land would allow. They'd either stay that way now, until the sun dried them, or they'd begin to fill up as the water rose from the river to steal across the road.

As Beaver had said, it hadn't rained enough last night to threaten the populated side of the river. Within its course the usually placid river tore at its banks now. It roiled along, the color of mud, churning up crests of dirty foam.

As Amber stretched forward for a better view, Nate again squeezed her hand. Then he guided the car into the gravel patch outside Granny Maple's. Or rather, what had to be the gravel patch beneath a few inches of the water.

Before the car completely stopped, Amber jumped out. Inwardly, Nate cursed the tottery stairs. He should have insisted on repairing them before. He followed Amber up, into the door at the top.

Inside, the woman who normally possessed the wisdom of the world was distraught. Although Granny Maple stood firm, tears welled in her black eyes. Rain dripped, even streamed, into an odd assortment of pots and plastic containers.

"Oh, God forgive me," she said, letting Amber hold her. "I've been such an old fool."

"I can't imagine that," Amber said, while Nate looked on.

"When either of you, or even Beaver, insisted I install a phone, I was always too proud to agree. Well, now I pray that someone else doesn't pay for my pride."

"Where is she?" Nate asked.

"That's just it. She said she was going to take a little walk, only where I could see her from my window. You know how deep water fascinates the children down here. I turned away for long enough to fix some tea, and when I looked back she was gone. She must have walked on down toward the bluffs."

Nate's heart began to pound in his ears. "I'm going. Don't worry, I'll bring her back."

Amber's eyes locked with his, transmitting a thousand messages. She wanted him to be safe. She loved him. She wanted Kim to be safe. She wanted to go with him, desperately, but she couldn't.

"I'll stay here," she said, still holding on to the older woman.

Granny Maple bridled. "Don't you dare stay with me. You want to go. You need to go, and I'll feel worse if you stay on my account. I've learned my lesson. I'll have the phone and those hospital tests. I'll be as grateful for your help as I should have been all along. Now, you go with Nate. You find our Kimmy."

Giving her a quick hug, Nate and Amber went back down the old staircase. He didn't want Amber to come, but the only person who could have stopped her hadn't. Orienting himself at the bottom of the stairs, he saw conditions had already worsened. The first, low tide, only an inch or so deep, was ominously washing over the standing water. Soon, the washes would deepen and then one speedily moving layer after another would flow in, deeper and deeper and faster and faster.

He and Amber turned toward the river. Only Beaver's old truck pulling up alongside them distracted them.

"I've been cruising the road," Beaver said, "seeing if I could spot her. No luck. But Slim Perkins says he's already walked the other direction. Granny Maple hollered for him to call me, and him and his boy have been out lookin' since. Kimmy has to have gone in the direction of the bluffs."

Nate nodded. "That's where we're heading." He didn't want to say what he had to in front of Amber. "You better call rescue."

Beaver nodded.

"Find someone to get Granny Maple up to the big house."

Ready to pull off, Beaver leaned out his window as another truck joined them. Ozzie Johnston's equally ancient pickup nudged between, hugging the higher road.

"Heard you was out looking for Kimmy," Ozzie said, also draping himself over his open cab window. "We're going with you," he said, and his wife, Joan, sitting beside him, nodded.

Nate wouldn't refuse any help he could get. And sure enough, more and more people appeared, most on foot, a few in vehicles they lined up along the road. Nobody drove in moving water. They shouldn't even have been walking in it.

Even old Murray and his sons, the men who farmed Amber's bottomland, picked their way toward them in floppy galoshes.

Yeah, Nate thought, taking Amber's elbow. *No one could come from any place better than this.*

Eddie Conyers, his sodden, bearded face making him look like a dressed-up bear, ran toward the gathering, shouting.

"Some of the leftover stuff from the tower's got loose! The debris's ripping along the riverbanks! Toward the Big Bend!"

AMBER KEPT TELLING herself that, yes, everything should look and feel strange. Unlike those who walked with her, testing their footsteps as they moved through the steady rain, she had never experienced a flood. Following her companions' example, she concentrated on where to put each foot, on keeping the rain out of her eyes.

The normally solid ground had become a rippling, confusing flow stretching in all directions. She used landmarks, like trees and houses and even bushes and rocks, to orient herself. Strangest of all was the river. Only once had she ever tasted its treachery—that day when she'd tried to swim Sovereign across and Nate had rescued her.

This was so different. Now, the river rose and churned, roaring a warning as savage and primitive as nature itself. And today, more than the usual debris tossed in the deluge. Like everyone else, she glimpsed the occasional piece of junk that had torn loose from where the last of the rusted tower was being razed. Menacing, unidentifiable chunks raced along, snagging at the banks, then plunging madly ahead.

That Kim could be trapped somewhere, or worse, Amber refused to contemplate. Like the dozen or so others who walked with her and Nate, all of them aiming for the bluffs that loomed ahead, she focused on just getting there and finding Kim.

No one talked much. Each person helped the other when someone stumbled. And stumbling was inevitable. All of them had been cast into a wacky fun house, only there was nothing funny about it.

Naturally, they resembled a pack of drowned rats. Amber kept unsticking her T-shirt where it clung to her body. At least she'd changed into her cowboy boots. Nate wore loafers and slacks. His black hair plastered his scalp, accentuating his strong facial features.

Beside Amber, Mabel-honey looked especially curvaceous in her wet T-shirt. Amber exchanged an "aren't we glamorous?" smile with her, then they returned to their task. After what seemed like hours, the group came to a halt. They'd reached the bluffs. Now they were faced with a frightening decision. The terrifying possibilities that no one had voiced could no longer be ignored.

Could Kim have gone on down the path? Could she be trapped in the cave? Or could something worse have happened to her? Could worse be happening to her now somewhere else?

Everyone seemed so sure Kim had to be in the cave that the discussion was brief. Someone had to go look for her in the cave.

Swiping away the clump of brown hair that kept washing into her eyes, Amber met Nate's gaze.

"I'll go," he said above the noise. "There's no sense in more than one of us going. I can holler back if I need help."

Amber wanted to shout "No!" She wanted to go, too. But that would upset him. Besides, it was too late. He squeezed her forearm, accepting first a flashlight someone produced from a pocket, and then the life vest Ozzie Johnston had brought from his truck. Finally, one end of the coil of thick rope that Eddie Conyers had been carrying on his shoulder was tied around Nate's waist.

Gazing down at the sheer wall of the cliff to the dark mouth of the cave ahead, Amber appreciated the precautions. Already, the river lapped into the cave. There was every reason to believe the path running just along the bluff had washed out. Either way, it couldn't be seen.

Because the river continued to rise, growing angrier and angrier as it pushed its burden of refuse along, the would-be rescuers didn't have much time. Kim simply had to be in the cave.

Everybody except Amber grasped the rope as if playing tug-of-war. After a last look for her, Nate tested it at his waist. Then he began to pick his way through the turgid water where it buffeted into the bluff, where it began its long sweep into the Big Bend.

Amber was almost numb with fright. Positioning herself as far down the rock wall as her companions would allow, she watched Nate ease himself along. She'd be the one to relay any messages between the two parties. Steadying himself with his hands against the sheer rise of the cliff, he moved farther and farther away from her.

A movie scenario had come to life. Glancing at the faces behind her, Amber saw the varied expressions, the concentration, the white-knuckled grips on the rope stringing past her. Nate could easily lose his balance. They might not be able to retrieve him.

Finally, Nate edged around the mouth of the cave and disappeared. They knew that, for now, the rocky substructure of the path remained. At any minute, though, it could wash out.

They waited. It couldn't have lasted more than minutes, but the tension was unbearable.

"I've got her!" they heard faintly above the sounds of the wind and rushing water.

Everyone buzzed with relief. Then Nate appeared with Kim. She wore the life vest, and had the rope secured around her waist. Nate edged her back to where they waited. Amber could hear nothing over the roar of the water. The little figures below were frustratingly silent as she watched them. She thought Kim was very brave. She wanted to tan her hide, as the old-timers would have recommended. But she wouldn't do any such thing. All she wanted was to have her and Nate safe.

The long climb back seemed endless. At last, Amber could grasp the sodden girl in her arms. Nate joined their hug. Amber choked up, then surprised herself by laughing. She heard the others congratulating them, passing mutual congratulations among themselves. Yet the sense of urgency to get back overrode the little group's joy.

When Nate's hold loosened, Amber let Kim move slightly away. But not far. Through her tears and the rivulets of rain, she grinned into Nate's face, savoring the simple, uniting truth: they were a family. He grinned, and she wondered if he were crying, too.

"Oh, Amber," Kim said, gasping.

"Come on, honey." Amber urged the girl to walk between her and Nate. "We can talk later."

"Oh, but...?" Kim stumbled, talking anyway. "I'm sorry. I don't know what I... No, I knew I wasn't supposed to go there. Not today for sure. But I..."

"It's okay, honey. We'll talk later. Just watch where you're going."

As the crowd continued to move off, Kim stopped. Amber and Nate stopped with her.

"I can't," Kim insisted.

Amber tried to understand. "You can't what, honey?"

"I don't want to go," Kim said.

Amber couldn't seem to grasp anything. "You don't want to go home?"

"No, I *do* want to go home. But I *don't* want to go to New York."

The mulish set in Kim's features was so typical of any thirteen-year-old girl that Amber had to laugh. Kim was no longer trying to be "perfect."

"Is that what this is all about?"

Kim nodded, looking at Nate, then back to Amber. "I want to do what you want me to. I've tried so hard to be good, but I just wanted to run. I just wanted to do something to make somebody see. I love you. I don't want to go. And I love you, too," she added, looking at Nate.

Rain streamed down their faces. Their clothes clung to them like second skins. Friends from the river community moved ahead, leaving them behind with questioning glances. But Nate evidently knew what Amber knew. Even in the rising water, they had to take one minute more. Kim needed the minute now.

To Amber's surprise, Nate spoke, and not in the least bit hesitantly. "It's okay, honey. We love you, too. Sometimes we all want to run, but the most important thing is that we don't run. We gotta stay. We gotta hang in there. We gotta talk. We gotta listen. We gotta try. I'm staying. And so are you. Until you're ready to leave."

Kim looked at Nate, then at Amber. She was trying to absorb his words. "You mean, you're staying at Allswell?"

Nate chuckled, and grinned at Amber. "If Amber will have me."

A huge smile split Kim's face. "I knew it! I knew it! I knew something was going on with you two! This is so amazing! This is too cool! This is awesome!"

"Yeah, well, *awesome* or not," Nate said, "we'd better move our butts. But just one thing," he added as they started to walk again, still clinging to each other. "You and I and Gnaw are enrolling in obedience school. There's no way I'm coming home every night and having that dog chase my car up the drive and pounce on me when I get out."

"Awwwesome!" Kim shouted to the rain, even to the nearby river. To her new life.

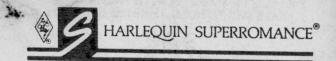

HARLEQUIN SUPERROMANCE®

COMING NEXT MONTH

#542 WORTH THE WAIT • Risa Kirk
Jack Stanton's dream was to buy the Gallagher family ranch and make
Margaret Gallagher his wife. But Margaret had her own plans . . . and
they didn't include Jack or a life on a Kentucky horse farm. She
belonged in New York. So why was she having such difficulty leaving
the farm?

#543 BUILT TO LAST • Leigh Roberts
Mary Ellen Saunderson had put her romance with Ramsey MacIver
behind her until her eccentric aunt decided it was time for them to
rekindle the flame. What Aunt Alma didn't realize was that her
scheme had put her niece's life in danger. Ramsey had enemies who
would stop at nothing to harm him——even if it meant hurting
Mary Ellen.

#544 JOE'S MIRACLE • Helen Conrad
Though Carly Stevens had just returned home to California to take a
breather and make some decisions, for Joe Matthews, Carly's arrival
was a miracle. His kids were crazy about her, and so was he. But then
she began asking questions about her family's past, and Joe knew he
had to keep her from learning the truth . . . for all their sakes.

#545 SNAP JUDGEMENT • Sandra Canfield
Women Who Dare, Book 4
There was no way Kelly Cooper was going to be a willing hostage.
Will Stone would rue the day he had broken into her apartment to
enlist her aid in clearing his name. He said she owed him——her
photograph had implicated him. Deep down Kelly was sure Will was
innocent, so maybe she'd help him. But not before she taught him
some manners.

AVAILABLE NOW:

HARLEQUIN PRESENTS®

A Year
DOWN UNDER

In 1993, Harlequin Presents celebrates the land down
under. In April, let us take you to Queensland, Australia,
in A DANGEROUS LOVER by Lindsay Armstrong,
Harlequin Presents #1546.

Verity Wood usually manages her temperamental boss,
Brad Morris, with a fair amount of success. At least she
had until Brad decides to change the rules of their
relationship. But Verity's a widow with a small child—the
last thing she needs, or wants, is a dangerous lover!

Share the adventure—and the romance—
of A Year Down Under!

Available this month in
A YEAR DOWN UNDER

THE GOLDEN MASK
by Robyn Donald
Harlequin Presents #1537
Wherever Harlequin books are sold.

YDU-M

Where do you find hot Texas nights, smooth Texas charm and dangerously sexy cowboys?

COWBOYS AND CABERNET

Raise a glass—Texas style!

Tyler McKinney is out to prove a Texas ranch is the perfect place for a vineyard. Vintner Ruth Holden thinks Tyler is too stubborn, too impatient, too... Texas. And far too difficult to resist!

CRYSTAL CREEK reverberates with the exciting rhythm of Texas. Each story features the rugged individuals who live and love in the Lone Star State. And each one ends with the same invitation...

Y'ALL COME BACK... REAL SOON!

Don't miss *COWBOYS AND CABERNET* by Margot Dalton. Available in April wherever Harlequin books are sold.
